I'm Engaged to Mothman

I'm Engaged to Mothman

Mothman in Love Book 2

PAIGE LAVOIE

4 Horsemen
Publications, Inc.

For anyone who has read a fairytale and
thought, "Yeah, I'd kiss the monster."

Table of Contents

1.

TOP FIVE THINGS THAT CAUGHT ME off guard when I uprooted my #influencer-life and moved to a cabin in the middle of the woods:

You can't escape the sound of angry tweets even if you log offline because birds and squirrels are way louder than anyone tells you.

Literal actual Mothman falling on my roof during a storm.

Falling in love with said Mothman, whose human form is unspeakably good-looking (though, I've grown pretty fond of how he looks as a monster too).

A monster-obsessed hunter using me as bait to lure Moth out of hiding.

And lastly, becoming mortally wounded and permanently transformed into an immortal moth-creature...

Yeah, I'm still *kinda* processing that last one.

Not exactly the calm #cottagecore life I was looking for, huh? My life in the woods had a rocky start, but honestly, ours is a classic love story. Girl meets cryptid, nurses him back to health, and they fall madly in love—all the drama surrounding our story is not what I need to be focusing on.

Despite all the wild rumors posted online and sightings of Moth in the woods and me at the nearest Trader Joe's, we've managed to create a pretty cozy little life in the mountains together. I've been capturing it one snapshot a day; the photos are just for me, and once in a while, for my social platforms. I don't feel pressured to share anything I don't want to, not anymore.

This morning is typical—for us, at least. It started with sweet moments cuddled in the cabin, records spinning and our limbs intertwined. Now, we're out stretching our legs and wings before a brunch date with Rosie and Clara. They'll be over in a few hours, and honestly, I had to get Moth out of the house before he devoured all the treats I made. The legendary cryptid from Point Pleasant has my heart and one hell of a sweet tooth.

We walk through the forest together, birdsong filling our ears while leaves crinkle at our feet. After everything that happened last year, you'd think I'd be terrified to be out here in the middle of nowhere, but Moth is never far away. It's easy to relax when he's at my side. When we're alone in the woods, I try to get used to my new form. The glistening green wings are gorgeous, but I bump into everything—and I mean *everything*.

There isn't a knickknack or picture frame that the tips of my wings hasn't toppled over in our cabin. I don't know how Moth does it, but he's been spreading his wings in the more metaphorical sense lately. He's still not a social butterfly, but he's working on it, and I'm proud of him for that.

As intimidating as he can be, he's a goofy gentle soul, and I'm glad more people are getting to see that.

I take his hand, swinging our arms as we walk. He grins, his pointed teeth gleam in sun, and my mind wanders to images of his fangs digging into the exposed skin of my shoulders. I'm about to pull him into a kiss when something odd and prismatic catches my eye.

"Hey, do you see that?" I move forward, feeling Moth catch the tip of my wing to try to slow me.

I rush toward the source. The hollow of a tree ripples and gleams gold for a moment before something flies through the center. Moth catches a piece of ancient-looking parchment in his claws. His handsome face creases in a frown as his eyes flick over the page, a golden glow the shade of sunrise beginning to encircle his body. It starts at his wrists like a puff of smoke then flows between us like a heavy cloud.

"What? What is it?" I ask. Until this point, I've been working under the assumption that the strangest thing in the forest is standing right next to me.

"We have been summoned." Moth draws me close until his chin rests upon my head, and his arms wrap tightly around me. Shielding my body, he attempts to lunge out of the golden light, but it keeps hold of us like a force field. The world around us is tinted in yellow and carries a faint scent of flowers as it continues to build and glow around us.

No, no, no, no–

Oh my god, whatever this is—whatever is happening— it's something even he can't stop.

"My flame..." he says desperately. For a moment, I'm unsure if he's going to try to push me away—to do this alone. I hold tight around his waist and am glad when he doesn't let go. Swallowing my nerves, I melt into him.

Whatever happens, I'm just glad that we'll be in this together.

"Where are we going?" I ask as the light turns to liquid gold. I tightly close my eyes, tucking my head so it rests on his firm chest.

"Home." His voice ripples as the world twists and turns like a tide during a lightning storm.

Home...

How can that be true when that's where we already are?

So, like, when Moth revealed he was some kind of royalty banished to the mortal realm, I figured it was kind of a done deal. They sent him to my world as a punishment— no way they would try to bring him back, *right*? Apparently, I was wrong because waiting to greet us when we zap into Moth's old world are a dozen winged guards who look just about as confused as I am. They wordlessly shuffle the two of us inside a castle that looks like something out of a fantasy novel while I shout a million questions that go unanswered. Moth remains calm and silent at my side.

"Where are you taking us?"

"What do you want?"

"Where are we?"

Hah! Whatever their orders are, talking to us isn't one of them. I puff up. Moth has always been the strong, silent type, but couldn't he at least say something? I glance at the row of guards and feel a lump form in my throat. I assumed there were more creatures like him wherever he was from, but seeing this many pairs of wings is still surreal. They march with stern looks on their partially obscured faces, their full armor shining in spotless silver. I shrink closer to Moth, finding a small comfort in his strong arm encircling me as we we're led forward.

He could take the guards out with a snap of his claws. Why is he still in human form anyway? Why is he just letting them lead us to our doom? With every step, anxiety takes my heart in its hand and squeezes.

I wonder if he's worried that transforming will give them a reason to attack. *Ugh.*

As far as Sundays go, this is a pretty bad turn of events. I mean, not only could we get murdered, but worse, I have homemade gluten-free cinnamon rolls cooling on the counter. They are going to get stale if they're left out.

Why did we have to get pulled through a portal *today*?

I know Moth did something terrible to get banished, but damn, it's clear that his reputation is way worse than I realized. Twelve armed guards in full armor seems like a lot for two people.

We're led through a flower-filled hallway with high arched columns. Everything is light and floral with high ceilings bleeding into the natural elements outside. The walls are sculpted in what looks like shining white marble. It's hard to believe that my dark, brooding cryptid came from a place so ... pastel.

"I will not let harm come to you." Moth's deep rumble is a warm blanket pulled over my ears. I shouldn't be worried. I know how powerful Moth is. In the mortal realm, with him at full strength, we'd have nothing to worry about. But we're not in the mortal realm, and I have no idea what could be waiting for us here. I tightly clutch his elegant, clawed fingers to keep from trembling.

Our friendship with Rosie and Clara may have helped him brush up on his people skills, but if there was any time to go "full monster" and knock these guards down like a stack of playing cards, it would probably be now, *right?*

Oh my god. They're going to make us prisoners and feed us stale bread and water for the rest of our lives, and I can't even eat bread! I'll wither away and be horribly bloated for the rest of our dark and damned days in the castle's dungeons.

"My flame," Moth whispers, squeezing my hand. "No harm will come to you." His complete disregard for himself makes my shoulders puff up. I refuse to step into this afraid, not when there might be some way I can help.

"So we're just letting them take us to ... whoever is in charge?"

"Yes."

"And you have a plan?" I whisper from the side of my mouth, hoping the guards don't have supersonic hearing.

"Yes."

"And you're going to tell *me* said plan?"

His red eyes shift to the guards. *Right.* That makes sense. I'm not the quietest of whisperers. That's evident from the glances we're getting from the guards. *Ugh.*

At least one of us knows what they're doing. Though, it would have been nice to have a little time to strategize before the enemy captured us. I straighten, shaking off the panic that—let's be honest—is still gripping my heart. This, unfortunately, isn't my first time being kidnapped; the whole thing has my skin crawling with memories. This time feels much more dignified than being tied up and pulled from my cabin in the middle of the night, which gives me time to think and look around for any possible exit plan.

The guards are big, but Moth is bigger. They have numbers, but I'm sure he's handled himself in worse situations. If negotiations are the solution, I once talked a trendy designer brand into letting me wear an unreleased sample at a red carpet in my heyday.

Together, we can handle anything.

We're led to a giant door with intricate carvings at the end of the hallway. I'm prepared for either bloodshed or the verbal battle of a lifetime. Instead, the impossibly large door is pushed open to reveal a woman—pale with dark Old Hollywood curls and deep mauve lips—standing as stiffly as a mannequin in a window display. She's on what looks like a stage at the end of the room with a series of thrones behind her.

Sunlight streams through a massive skylight, making it look like part throne room, part greenhouse. The scent of flowers tickles the back of my throat, threatening to drive a sneeze from my nose—which would be one way to break the ice.

"It really is you," the woman gasps. If this realm has a queen, it's got to be her. Her brow pinches at the center as she regards Moth and me, squinting as if trying to clear her vision. The heartbreak on her face suggests whatever Moth did to be banished was, in fact, very, very bad. I steady myself, ready to come to his defense. Not only does he barely remember this place, but he's changed.

Though, something tells me we're not about to be sentenced to death or locked in a dungeon. No, something else is going on here.

"I am ready to pay for whatever crimes I have committed," Moth says.

He's *what* now? This had better be a part of the afore-mentioned plan.

"My only request is that you let the woman beside me go in peace."

Okay, no. Can we not do the whole hot self-sacrificing hero thing before I've had my second cup of coffee? But then Moth squeezes my hand like he did when I asked if he had a plan. He's buying us time; I just hope whatever he's planning works.

The queen squints her moss-colored eyes, her wings motionless as if she's frozen in time.

"Mother?" Moth's deep voice cracks.

His mother…

They have the same sharp cheekbones, dark eyes, tall frames, and sculpted chins. I see it now. The resemblance is so strong I'm surprised I didn't realize sooner.

"How... I..." Moth struggles to find the words. The queen descends the staircase, and Moth, as if in a trance, moves toward her. I'm not sure I've ever seen him look this uncertain.

Thud!

The door bursts open, revealing a woman with short periwinkle hair and soft round features racing toward us. Unlike the row of formal guards, she's dressed more casu-ally, wearing a chest plate on top of a billowing white linen dress. It is honestly a killer look and probably not what I should be fixated on right now.

"No, no, no, no, no," she groans, pointing toward the guards, who back away as if her gaze alone could cast them to stone. "Why is he here already? You were sup-posed to bring him to the east wing, and who briefed you on this? Was it Scarlet? I swear I will finally kick her off the patrol if she does not get—"

The young woman stiffens, her shiny silver armor creaking as she takes in the scene of Moth's mother standing inches away from the two of us. I'd guess she's around eighteen at the most, but knowing how old Moth is (or rather not knowing), appearances don't mean much. Iridescent butterfly wings in a gorgeous shade of blue flap at her back as she pivots toward Moth.

"Hello." Her voice takes a sheepish turn from the brash tone she had with the guards. I can't help but notice how her eyebrows quirk when she glances at me—another reminder that I am not supposed to be here.

"Holly, what is the meaning of all this?" The queen brushes a tear from her cheek.

Holly. Could this be another family member?

"This was all meant to be a surprise." Holly is short compared to the others, though they tower over me like elven royalty, which maybe isn't too far off.

She circles Moth as if inspecting him before throwing her arms around him—the very picture of a gleeful younger sibling. "Welcome home, brother!" she squeals.

Sweet, precious Moth stands with his arms stiffly at his sides with a look I can only read as *"Help me."*

Together, we had prepared for war, but nothing could have prepared us for a family reunion.

2.

"**I** ONLY EXPECTED DEATH," HOLLY turns her attention to me. "You are not supposed to be here."

I wince at the word: *Death*. It's not a threat, but a name. I sharply turn to Moth, who shrugs. Could that have been his name here?

"Heather will remain at my side or be safely returned to the mortal realm," Moth says. His body is as rigid as a statue. I can understand why he's unwilling to put his guard down—but this is his family, right? I'm sure they'll forgive him for being skeptical, but this is my first, and only, chance to make a good impression. From the way his sister is eyeing me as though I'm an unwelcome surprise, I think I'm already blowing it.

I straighten my posture, brush off my dress, and try my best to turn on any ounce of charm I can summon.

She clearly didn't think her beloved big brother was going to come home with a girlfriend. *I need to play it cool and win both her and the queen over.*

"Allow me to introduce my mother, Queen Plume of Eclipsica, and I am Princess Holly—First Knight in the Royal Guard." Holly steps forward, her tone and body language suddenly more formal.

"Heather! Hi, wow, it's like so nice to meet you!" I extend my hand to Queen Plume first—but that's not how you're supposed to greet royalty, is it? I fumble backward, folding myself into an awkward curtsy. Shakily, I repeat the gesture with Holly, who raises her eyebrows in a way that suggests I should have probably just stuck to the handshake. My darling cryptid boyfriend, however, does not budge.

"Moth," I whisper, placing my hand on his shoulder for support.

"Moth?" Holly tilts her head, the furrow of her brow deepening into two heavy lines. The way she said the word, *Death* rings in my ears. God, that really was his name, wasn't it? No matter the realm, it seems like he can't get away from being seen as this dark mysterious thing. *As if he isn't a total cinnamon roll!* I'm used to calling him Moth, but if he wants his old name back, I'll gladly adjust.

"I will not stand trial addressed as anything else." Moth laces his fingers in mine, pulling my body close to his side.

"Stand trial..." Holly repeats, but Queen Plume doesn't seem to hear.

"This name—*Moth*. It is what you call him?"

"Oh, oh yeah. I just—well I, um, last year he sort of landed on my house and, uh, wouldn't really give me a name. Which is like so fair because ... you know." I gesture vaguely to the castle. "So I asked if I could call him Moth, and he said he didn't mind, and I—"

Someone, for the love of God, please stop me from talking.

"It is the name she chose for me," Moth jumps in, giving me a moment to breathe. It's not a moment too soon because any more intense eye contact from Queen Plume is going to give me an actual heart attack.

"And it is also the name you choose for yourself?" she asks.

"It is." There's warmth in his eyes when they meet mine, causing a smile to curl on my lips. A name is something so personal. It's not like Moth was a creative choice, but I'm glad it feels like his.

"Then Moth you shall be." His mother clasps her hands together and nods—with approval or disapproval, I'm not sure. Her matter-of-fact way of speaking moves the conversation forward. With a wave of her hand, the guards are dismissed, and the four of us are left alone.

"Mother, do you not think that is a little on the nose?" Holly protests in a hushed tone. "Surely there is something more regal or—"

"It is not my choice to make." Queen Plume gives the same easy shrug as Moth, a twinkle gleaming at the corner of her green eyes. "And I like it."

"But—but—but—" Holly stammers, following at her mother's heels.

They bicker in a way that reminds me a little of my mom and me. I guess complicated mother-daughter relationships extend through every realm. The pair don't wait for us to head out of the throne room. Moth and I exchange glances, and at his nod, we follow. I need a coffee, a nap, and to check in with Moth before I feel ready for anything more, but we trudge down the ornate pathways of Moth's former home.

When I started dating a mysterious cryptid, I thought I'd avoid the whole "meet the parent" thing. On my end, at least. Mom is fully obsessed with my gorgeous, 7-foot-tall boyfriend. She's already planning a wedding and told me she wants her future grandchildren to call her "Glam-ma," which earned the first of many eye rolls from me over the holidays.

But that was a "bring your boyfriend home for Christmas" kind of thing. With Moth's family, someone has literally summoned us to a whole other world. Obviously, I want to be supportive, but this is kind of a lot for 2 p.m. on a Sunday.

With the grace of a ballerina, Moth's mother—Plume, the faerie queen, I'm still trying to grasp what I'm dealing with here—leads the way. I can't help but notice Moth is stiff and on edge, as if he's not ready to accept all of this. I can't blame him.

Everything is moving so fast. In one breath, the queen rattles off bits of history to me. I nod politely but honestly can't keep up with a thing she's saying. Suddenly, as if Moth is waking up from a daydream, he inhales a deep breath, glancing around at the tapestries and storybook windows. His ruby eyes widen with shock.

"Am I not to stand trial for my crimes?" he asks, an edge to his voice.

This again.

The hugs and tears should have been a good sign that we are in the clear, but I don't know their family dynamic. Would it be surprising to have this warm reunion end with a lavish personal tour of the dungeons? Yes. But what hasn't been surprising about today?

"My darling son." The queen finally gets the nerve to place her hand on Moth's shoulder. He visibly stiffens, his eyes widening as if he's fighting the urge to flee, but he stands strong. "What crimes could you have possibly committed?"

"I remember very little before my banishment," Moth says quietly, taking a step backward.

"*Banished*?!" Holly shouts, shaking her head. "Is that what you think happened?"

Moth's eyes glaze over, as blank as an old iPhone the day after the release of a new model. I give his large hands a squeeze as a signal that I'm going to try my best to help navigate this.

"He's been kinda rolling with the whole bad-guy-banished-to-another realm thing," I say, and *wow*, those are not the words I meant to choose.

Queen Plume's shoulders fall as she leads us farther into the castle.

"Come, let us find some place more comfortable to talk," Queen Plume says, and her slight smile reminds me of the way Moth looks when he's hiding something. "I think there's someone who will be even more pleased to see you."

My heart twists. Am I about to be confronted with a former lover? It's just been the two of us for so long, I'm not sure I'm ready for a romantic rival. My eyes dart to Moth, who is as stiff as ever. I shouldn't be worried. Heck this is the most stable, healthy relationship I've ever been in, but can love and comfort compete with history?

What if, as soon as he sees their face, he's overcome with a million memories of the greatest love he's ever known? I gulp, focusing on the clusters of pink flowers that climb the large, rounded columns in the great halls.

Together, I remind myself. Whoever is waiting—we'll face them together.

Moth's old bedroom.

If the castle was sunshine and flowers, this room would be the moon. The walls are dark wood, and the ceiling sparkles with painted stars that gleam in the flickering candlelight. But unlike the pristine beauty of the throne room, this room has been destroyed. Dark navy curtains hang in tatters, paintings hang askew, and the space seems robbed of anything personal...

"The magic to track someone through a portal requires a token," Holly explains, her wings tight against her back. "I apologize for the state of things. I have been searching for a very long time."

Queen Plume holds a hand to her chest. Could it be the first time she's been back since Moth disappeared?

The air is heavy; it's like a scrapbook that's been left in the rain or a wound torn open. But not everything here is lifeless. I spot a large, tufted couch with a black fur blanket in the corner, lush and cozy with pillows haphazardly arranged on the cushions. At least, that's what it looks like until it starts to *move*. A head reveals itself from the mess of fur, and two large beady eyes set their sights on Moth.

"Sprout?"

If you took the floof of a Pomeranian and scaled it up to the size of a Great Dane—and gave it two antennae on the top of its head—that would be Sprout.

He bounds up to Moth with thundering paws. Moth allows himself to be knocked over by the fluffy beast. It reminds me of those viral videos where soldiers return from war. After decades of sulking around this library, Sprout's person is finally here.

Queen Plume places a hand on my shoulder. When I look up, her eyes are dewy and bright. If she had any doubt in her mind that Moth was really her long-lost son, this moment has shown her everything she needed to see. People can deceive other people—but dogs? They always know what's up.

"Most of your time in this castle was spent in this room," Queen Plume murmurs softly "Do you recall it?"

The toothy grin on Moth's face wavers at the question. "I am sorry," he breathes, ruffling his large hands through Sprout's mountain of fur. Sprout's paws tap happily on the stone floors as the fluffy beast rolls from his back to his belly. There's a patch of white on his left paw and a light dusting of gray fur under his chin. Decades this cute giant furball has been waiting for Moth to return, and the urge to capture it all on video makes my palms itch to grab the phone from my pocket. But with a mood this heavy, I resist.

Not every moment is meant to be captured after all.

"It was underhanded enough to push you through a portal. Wiping your memory is downright cruel." Holly shifts, and the gentle rays of sunlight cast a beam of light off her silver chest plate and right into my eyes.

"Okay so..." I blink white spots from my vision before glancing at Moth. He is adorably distracted by the giant dog-like creature, and I assume he won't mind me taking over this conversation, so I ease myself into an nearby chair. Holly breaths out a deep sigh before both she and the queen sit opposite of me.

Right... Probably should have let the royalty sit first.

"What exactly happened?" I ask, cringing at the way I'm probably breaking every social expectation by doing so.

"Your father, the old king, passed away." Queen Plume addresses Moth rather than me. "I was not in a place to lead, Holly was far too young, and you were next in line."

"We had an uncle—Atlas. He wanted the throne." Holly picks up the story, fiddling with the hilt of the sword strapped to her belt.

"I must assume he faked your demise." Queen Plume spits out the words bitterly. "And I believed I buried my son and husband just weeks apart."

Holly pats her mother's knee in reassurance, but there are daggers in her sharp blue eyes. There's some part of this story she's not willing to tell yet.

"Uncle Atlas took the mantle," Holly says through gritted teeth, "after father died and you disappeared. He ruled until only a few years ago."

"After all of the work he did to take the throne..." Queen Plume gulps shaking her head. "He... he fell in love. It was someone who worked in the castle. They ran off in the night, and I took the mantle once again."

Huh. That's a twist on the classic evil uncle trope that I didn't expect. While I'm glad it landed Moth in my life, I feel sorry for the two of them.

"First off, that's horrible, and I am so sorry," I say, unsure who to address. They've both carried an unfair amount of grief all this time. "But this all started decades ago, right? How did you find Moth now?"

"I never stopped looking," Holly says, staring at Moth like he's some kind of superhero. "I knew you were still out there—somewhere."

How?

I want to ask, but I can't bring myself to be so bold, especially not when there are other things I'm curious about.

"Wait, wait, wait. If Moth is supposed to be dead, isn't it going to be weird if he's just kind of walking around the castle?"

"You will find the people of Eclipsica are nothing if not dramatic." Holly scoffs. "It will take more than a faked death to rattle the people here."

Queen Plume stands suddenly, and the three of us jump to rise with the queen.

"May we speak for just a moment?" She holds out her hand to Moth. After a long pause, he stands, clasping his clawed hand in hers. As stiff as a board, Moth follows the queen out to a small balcony. Despite how torn apart it is now, this must have been a beautiful room to have growing up.

I stretch my back, feeling the pressure of my wings aching to stretch wide across the room. It's large enough, but I don't want to knock over anything, so I wear the tension like a second skin. It's a trick I've been learning to master when I'm trying to be careful at home. I've broken more teacups than I can count, and I'm sure the items in this place cost more than I could ever pay.

"So, you opened the portal, right? Why send a letter and not just come yourself?"

Holly narrows her dark eyes. "Ah, well, with a letter I was able to be vague on the off-chance I missed my target." Holly fiddles with the hilt of her sword again, a child holding tight to their favorite stuffed animal while putting on a brave face.

"Wait, let me get this straight. You just threw random objects into a portal thingy, hoping it would find him?"

"Magic is not a skill I relish or, frankly, take pleasure in." She shrugs. In this moment, her cool indifference makes her look so much like her brother. "I can open small rifts in the veil, but the magic is crude and takes a considerable amount of effort."

"Well, I mean, I guess it worked, right?"

"Finally." The sigh of relief is a nice break from the tough girl vibes she's been giving off ever since Moth stepped away.

That explains all the random lost things he's squirreled away in his burrow. I want to ask her to explain further, but she's already glaring daggers at me—and holding a literal sword. I do my best to piece it all together.

"King Atlas is really gone?" I ask, unable to help myself. After all that work to get the crown, it seems strange he'd just run off, but then again, people do wild things when they're in love.

"Of course, love led him astray like it has for many others." She fiddles with her blade once more. "Running off with a servant in the middle of the night—it's such a romantic notion, isn't it?"

"But that's not what happened, is it?" I ask, leaning in closer. "Did you banish him, or is he going to show up for like an awkward family reunion thing?"

"Oh..." She looks up only slightly from her shining sword. "He will not be returning to the castle."

"Did you...?" I begin but can't bring myself to finish the sentence—not when she's smiling *like that.*

Welp, Holly has officially gone from cool and intimidating to terrifying. I don't know what the rules of this realm are, but I'd take a guess that murder is probably still a bad thing.

"Oh yeah, cool." I try—*and fail*—to sound unfazed. There's just one other thing that has been bothering me.

"How do *we* get back?" I ask, and that's when Holly's face shifts to something cold and deadpan.

"You can't."

"**W**E'RE STUCK HERE?" I SHOUT, my wings unfurling as I jump to my feet, knocking a few dozen books from a shelf. "Sorry, ah, um, no, no, no, that doesn't work for me."

"You are a *commoner* in a castle among royalty," Holly says, cocking a thick eyebrow.

Clearly I've offended her, but hello? She can't mean we're supposed to be here *forever-forever*, right?

"Okay, yes." I gesture around Moth's tattered bedroom. "This is all very impressive—"

Even in shambles, is it the most beautiful room I've ever seen? Yes. Would I have liked a little heads up before getting ripped from my cozy life in the woods? Also, yes.

"You will adjust." She acts as if this is something as simple as a missed flight or canceled hotel, not a life-altering decision neither Moth nor I had a say in. "I understand it must be a lot for you to take in."

"But you're saying we're going to be here... No—no, sorry! Oh my god. There are things from home I kind of like ... need."

Moth's heavy steps rattle the floorboards behind me. I turn and both he and the queen have finished their conversation and returned from the balcony.

"Surely that cannot be true." For a split second, I think he might be agreeing with Holly until he stands protectively at my side.

"We must return." From his lack of rage, I'm assuming he didn't hear the part where she called me a *commoner.* Still, it's good to know Moth has my back.

"Transporting you here took me years to master," Holly begins. "I'm sure whatever you need can be acquired."

"Do you have Synthroid, preferably in a 100-mcg dose?" I sigh, casting a painful glance at Moth.

"I'm sure our chefs can make whatever manner of delicacies from your world." Holly's voice is flat as if explaining this to me is a chore.

Queen Plume nods in approval. "I too would like to try this Synthroid."

Oh, my god.

"It is a medication," Moth interjects. "And it is taken daily."

"A medication?" Queen Plume cocks her head in my direction.

"It is impossible," Holly says, running her fingers through her short blue hair. "It took me years to master creating a portal in the first place, it's closed by now, and I'm without the resources to cast another spell."

"That is unacceptable." Moth's deep tone leaves little room to argue. Holly's eyes widen, as if the words caused a physical blow. She doesn't expect us to stay forever, does she?

"A week, " she finally relents. "Give me a week to gather the supplies I need."

Moth looks down at me for approval and I nod. A week. Yeah, we can do that. My thyroid has been pretty balanced, and I'm sure a few days without medication won't make me flare up. Not too badly, at least.

"One week," he agrees with a nod. It's not like we have much choice. Medication or no medication, this will be a good chance for Moth to finally get to see where he's from.

"Don't worry about me. Seriously, it's just one week," I insist before Moth has a chance to overthink this. "I'll be fine—probably—definitely."

We stand in an awkward huddle before going on another impromptu tour with the queen as our guide and Sprout at Moth's heels.

I hope Moth's sanity is faring better than mine because every moment in this castle feels like I'm being pulled deeper into a dream. I mean, how am I supposed to act in this situation? As rude as Holly's comment was, she's not wrong. I am a commoner and can't even begin to piece together the rules of this world.

Is Holly going to run me through with her sword if I don't stand ten paces behind Moth while we walk down the hallway? Is there going to be one of those long dinner tables with both of us sitting on opposite ends? Can she get us home by the end of the week?

"Heather." Moth's voice makes me squeak like a mouse caught in a trap of my own thoughts. His mouth picks up in a smile at the sound. Despite himself, he chuckles, pulling me close.

Okay, there goes the whole "walk ten paces behind" thing. I glance at Holly to gauge her disapproval, but she says nothing. Instead, she looks up at her older brother with stars in her eyes, like a child meeting a princess at their birthday party.

Behind the tough-murdery-sword girl thing, there's a lonely child who dearly missed her brother. I've always wondered what it would be like to have a sibling. In influencer world, it would have meant someone to collaborate, share ideas, and maybe even start a podcast with. And most of all, it would mean having a teammate when my mom was driving me crazy. By the way Holly stares up at him with awe, it's clear Holly missed her brother every day. It would be sweet if she wasn't so damn scary.

Honestly, the whole murder thing shouldn't put me off this much. I mean, Moth has done some *questionable things* in the time that he's been in the moral realm. But in the past year, we've stayed up late trading stories, regrets, and our dreams for the future. There's been a deep sadness in his eyes when he talks about his past. With Holly, there was no remorse. I didn't know King Atlas. Maybe he deserved it, maybe not. But in a weird way, I'll always be grateful to him. Moth getting transported to the moral realm is the reason we're together. If it had never happened, then, well, *we* would never have happened.

However complicated, a future without him isn't what I want to think about.

All that said, King Atlas did sound like a giant dick. If I were a stabby kind of person, maybe I would have taken the same route. Queen Plume seems more like the poisoning type, but if push came to shove, Moth would definitely claw someone's face off. I think—

"My flame..." Moth's urgent whisper shakes me out of my meandering thoughts, back to the ivory hallway. In an instant, I'm keenly aware of his iron grip at my waist.

"Hi, yes, sorry!" I squeak, hopping to attention. "I'm here. Sorry, long, long day."

"You two require rest." Queen Plume hums thoughtfully. "At the end of this week, we will have a ball to celebrate your return."

"Mother, you are just looking for an excuse to throw a ball." Holly groans, a hint of a smile on her lips. There's no bite to her words; if anything, she is amused. After all, her brother is home, why wouldn't she want to celebrate?

"The gesture is unnecessary," Moth protests. He doesn't like much of a fuss. My interest however is fully piqued. I mean hello, a *ball*? Despite my desire to keep life low-key, I have never been able to resist the sway of a fancy dress. Just throw me in a pile of chiffon and hand me a plate of hors d'oeuvres already.

"Nonsense." Moth's mother clasps his face in her elegant hands, placing a kiss on his forehead. For a moment, his angular face looks uncharacteristically boyish.

Her eyes glitter with tears as she looks at her son, seeming to study every crack and wrinkle that age has given him—which admittedly is not much. The deep mossy color of her eyes reminds me of a forest after a storm.

"We have much to celebrate," Queen Plume says, never taking her eyes from her long-lost son. It makes me wonder, how much have they all changed since the last time they saw each other?

If the day gets any weirder, I think I might pass out from exhaustion.

"I'm not usually that rambly, right? Like, I know I ramble, but that was bad. Like, bad-bad. That's my first impressions with your family just out the window." I groan. "I'm normally so cute and charming! What even *was* that?"

"At least you managed to say something." Moth covers his beak with his hands and sighs.

"Hey, you are allowed to be in shock, okay?" I take his rough hands in mine, stroking up and down the rows of downy feathers. He nuzzles me, pulling me down onto the bed next to him.

He transformed the minute we were alone. Considering everyone else was in human form, I don't blame him for waiting. Moth has said time and time again that both forms are equally comfortable, but I know that when I'm tense, I like to stretch my wings. It makes sense he'd like to flex his claws, wings, and feathers all at the same time.

I place a small kiss at the tip of his beak, and cozy into our mountain of pillows. The room is a far cry from our small cabin bedroom. Heck, our whole house could probably fit in this room. There's an arched stain glass window opposite the bed, its peak nearly reaching the tall ceilings. A dark blue tufted bench sits below it, decorated with flowers. The walls are light, with white wallpaper that reminds me of floating feathers after a pillow fight.

It's one of the dozens of guest rooms in the castle. Moth had little interest in his original room being restored. Considering the state of it, I'm sure it would take well over a week to fix. The servants brought up trays of snacks, similar to the charcuterie boards Moth makes at home. How many traces of this place live inside him, and neither of us even realized it?

"We have a dog now, so that's cool." As if on cue, Sprout's tail happily thuds against the mattress. "You think they'll let us take him home?"

"They will not have a choice."

I grin, imagining Sprout sprawled out across the faux fur rug in our living room.

"We're going to need to get a bigger bed." I stretch out my arms and bask in the sheer size of this bed. Moth coils an arm around my waist, holding me tightly in place on top of him. I relax, encompassed by his warmth and the cozy bedding.

"My flame..." I can tell from the measure of his voice that he's not buying how easygoing I'm being about all this, but how can you be upset in a bed this soft?

"And we were talking about wanting to do a little get-away, I guess?" I force a laugh, letting myself melt into his feathers. "It's all no big."

"It does not always have to be *no big*."

"I know."

But the way his claws graze up my back gives me pause. "It has been nearly a year since that night," he begins.

I cringe as my antennae poke into two sharp points at the top of my head. I'm not going to think about this—not here, not now. "Time has really been *flying by—*"

"—and we have yet to discuss everything that led to this moment." Even in this form, I can tell he's frowning. His beak is doing this downturned thing that would be ridiculously cute if it didn't look so sad. I'm fine. We're fine. I'm not sure why Moth is bringing this up again.

"There's nothing really to talk about. I look cute as hell with wings, have the best boyfriend in the world, and we're in a gorgeous room in an even more gorgeous castle. There's a bed you don't have to squeeze into, and a bathtub that could double as a swimming pool. I think life is going just fine. And like really, if we're going to be here for a week, we might as well turn it into a little staycation."

"I worry about what they will expect of me." He sighs, letting his head fall back onto the pillows.

Oh.

Moth is a prince who returned home after decades away. I'm sure they won't expect him to slip right into his old role. Queen Plume and Holly seem excited just to have him back at all.

"A week is plenty of time to take things slow, settle in, and have time with your family." *Even though one of them is a murderer.*

I haven't gotten around to sharing that tidbit of information with him Technically, she didn't confess anything, but still—no secrets. I've been holding tight to that promise and am not about to let it go. But considering Moth still appears to be buffering from all the newness of today, I'll wait. One more piece of information might make his head explode.

"They have not given us much of a choice." His owlish red eyes blink at me slowly before he finally nods. "But my origins have been a source of wonder for a long time. I suppose I would like some time to explore."

"How about this? We spend the morning with family tomorrow, and when it gets overwhelming, we can escape for a little picnic lunch. There's got to be a garden around here somewhere, right?"

"You are making all of this bearable."

"I love you too."

When we decided to have a "casual picnic" for lunch. I didn't expect a catered meal with blankets already laid out and an eager staff clustered nearby, waiting for Moth's next command.

"This is ... a lot." I sigh, trying to cast my gaze away from our curious audience to the landscape. The same white marble columns inside the castle arch over this space, making it feel like each section of the garden is its own room. Overflowing pots with pink and purple blooms decorate the space while climbing blossoms and ivy hang over our heads. Despite the flourishing plant life, nothing is overgrown or messy, unlike the wildflower field we frequent back home.

The gazebo in the distance looks like the perfect place to sneak away from the ballroom and steal a kiss under the stars.

"You are dismissed." Moth waves his hand and the group of servants scatter. Heaving a breath, he lies back onto the grass, pulling me down with him.

"A lot does not seem to cover it." Pinching the bridge of his nose, Moth squints his eyes tight. "You had much to *accept* about me before this. I hope it does not..."

"Change things?" I roll over so that I'm practically on top of him, brushing dark hair away from those ruby eyes I fell in love with. Moth is my person, and I accept everything that comes along with that—mystical fairy realm included. When will he realize there's nothing that's going to scare me away?

"Yes."

"You know it doesn't." There's a glimmer in his ruby eyes—soft and sweet, just like his lips which press lightly against my forehead.

"I suppose I should by now," he says, stroking the length of my jaw.

"So, are your memories totally back?"

"It feels as if I'm recalling a series of dreams..." After a thoughtful pause, his face crinkles in what looks a lot like a cringe.

I suddenly wish Sprout had joined us on this picnic. When we gathered ourselves to leave, he picked up his fluffy head for a moment before huffing dramatically, which like, honestly, #mood. But I can't help but think his old companion would be better at providing comfort than I am.

"Good dreams?" I press, wishing I knew what was going on in his head.

When I go back to visit my mom in Florida, the story of the two of us lives inside those walls. I feel the good times and bad the minute I stand on the front porch of her bungalow. How many memories are lurking in the shadows of his castle for him to discover?

With Holly's flippant attitude toward murder, the death of his father, the way his uncle betrayed him and the far-off look in Queen Plume's eyes, I have to hope the good will outweigh the bad.

"I—" he begins but stops short, shaking his head.

Slowly, I place my hand on top of his, squeezing tight.

"Let's just take this week a minute at a time." I hope my smile is reassuring enough. I meant what I said about trying to enjoy our week. A staycation is way overdue. While you can't beat the scenery and room service, even holding tight to my rose-tinted glasses, I know how complicated this is. In my world, he's a monster, but here he's a prince.

"Processing this can't be easy," I continue. "After years of hiding in the shadows, you can have anything you want at the snap of your fingers."

His eyebrows raise as he gives me a look I can't quite recognize. I'm wondering if I fumbled my words. When he elegantly raises his hand and a sharp snap fills the space between us, I freeze.

For a moment, I'm worried we're about to be circled by countless servants hoping to get a glimpse of Moth. But it remains just the two of us, the clicking of his fingertips still ringing in my ears.

"Well," he drawls, tapping a claw in the spot where my dress has ridden up my thighs. The sudden contact sends shivers down my bare skin. "I am waiting."

Oh.

Oh!

"If His Majesty insists..." I pounce, putting all my weight into his shoulders. Moth lets himself topple backward onto the soft bed of well-maintained grass.

I slide down his chest while stroking his quickly hardening length with my fingertips. The feeling of his desire building with only a thin piece of fabric between my fingers and his skin makes me tremble with anticipation. Soon, my head rests comfortably between his legs, and all barriers between my mouth and his cock are cast aside.

It starts with just a kiss. That's all it takes to make him moan. The sound is deep and pained and fills me with more power than I could have ever imagined.

"Is this what you wanted, *Your Highness?*" I ask, planting another kiss on his head while my fingers trail down his shaft. He shivers with anticipation at the curl of my tongue on his skin.

After a year of fumbling around the woods with no one around for miles, this is the first time there's ever been an actual threat of being caught. There's a small cover of trees, but people know where we are. Walking down the halls, it feels like there's always someone watching. I stretch my wings forward, giving us a shade of privacy.

The deep groan he emits sends shivers up my spine and gives me the reassurance I need to know I'm hitting all the right spots.

I teasingly spur him on. I want him to chase me through the woods and make me scream his name.

"I need you," I whisper, pulling myself up and straddling his hips. He takes me by the waist, flipping me onto the dewy grass, and holds himself steady. He kisses from my lips down to my shoulders before entering me at an agonizingly slow pace. I dig my nails into his shoulders, arching my back to let my wings unfurl under my body. I loudly moan and bite down hard on my bottom lip. As exciting as it is being out in the open like this, I don't want to give anyone a reason to investigate.

Moth's large, clawed hand moves to my mouth, clamping down just in time for me to let out a scream— and fuck, does it feel good to let go.

"Scream for me, my flame," he whispers, and my entire body responds to the command. Pleasure releases before I'm ready, and his strong clawed hands muffle the sound as I cry out his name. That little fantasy plays through me— he's caught me after chasing me through the woods—and I scream into the palm of his hand.

Moth bites the flesh of my shoulder, pulsing into me until he explodes, and we melt together, messy and satisfied. Blades of grass stick to every bit of exposed skin on our arms and legs.

"Wow," I breathe. "That was—wow."

"You are *wow*," he says sweetly, biting my earlobe ever so slightly. Heck, if I had more stamina, I'd be climbing right on top of this giant gorgeous man *again*. Instead, I curl my arm around his middle like he's a big sexy body pillow and kiss his shoulder. We lay like that for a long time. With the gentle rise and fall of Moth's chest, I think that he must have fallen asleep. But when I look up his glowing red eyes are distant, like he's got something on his mind. "Heather..."

"Yeah?"

"There is something you are thinking about."

"Well yeah, there's a lot going on..."

"No." He shakes his head. A firm hand pulls at my waist until our bodies are flush. "It is something between us."

"I don't—"

"My flame," he breathes the pet-name out in a sigh, "I want no desire unspoken."

Dammit, why does he have to be so perceptive? A blush warms the skin of my face until I'm sure I'm tomato red. *Okay*, I gulp, *here it goes.*

"There is one thing..." I begin. There's one little fantasy I haven't had the nerve to ask him about. It's been racing through my mind every single day since even before we got together. "It just feels like maybe it's too much." I sigh, hiding my face in my hands. "Besides, now is *so not* the time. Let's save the pitch meeting for my kinky sexual fantasies for after we get home."

"Spoken as if I do not need a distraction." His claws brush through my hair, and despite my mounting tension, I relax into his touch. "Nothing you could ask for will ever be too much," Moth whispers in a tone so earnest it would be silly to doubt him.

Sex has been nothing but incredible and taken pretty *extraordinary heights* since I got my wings. I don't know why this, in particular, has been such a hard request to make. How am I supposed to tell the man who makes love to me like a goddess that I want him to chase me down like prey?

"Do you remember when we first met?" I start, mostly to see how he responds. An amused murmur from smiling lips is a good sign for what I want to say next.

"I caught you from that tree."

"And I thought you were trying to eat me—so I ran. You were worried, so you chased me." My face burns. "I want to do that ... *but like,* sexy."

I wait for the judgment, the laughter, a perfectly sculpted eyebrow raised in disbelief. Instead, his eyes flash a deeper shade of red.

"And what will I do once I've caught you?" His deep voice lowers into something that sends tingles down my spine.

"Whatever you want." I swallow hard, gathering up my courage to say the next part. "But in that moment, I don't want to be Heather, your flower, your flame. I want to be your prey."

With clawed fingers, he pinches my chin between his thumb and index finger, forcing me to meet his glowing eyes. They darken with hunger with every passing second.

"And would you like me to be kind, to take pity on the pretty little creature I've found in my forest?"

I shake my head and am mesmerized by the way his Adam's apple bobbles in response. We have our safe word, and I know Moth will respect any boundary I lay down. "I think I might like if you're a little mean."

To this, he finally raises an eyebrow, but the look isn't judgmental—no, if anything, he looks fascinated. I can see the wheels in his head turning.

"And are there any other terms you'd like to set in our game of cat and mouse?" He hums thoughtfully as if mulling it over.

"I don't think I'm going to use my wings. I don't want you to tie me up—that's a pretty hard boundary." I like when he catches my wrists with his hands, but the idea of being bound in rope—even in a safe space makes my hair stand on end after getting kidnapped. Drawing in a deep breath, I draw my attention back to Moth and my long-brewing fantasy. When I picture it, I'm always running until the muscles in my legs ache, being held in his arms, and carried away. I want to feel his strength—his desire.

"Understood." He nods in agreement, and relief floods through me. "Is there anything else you would like?"

"Hmm, uh, no, I mean, other than that, I just kinda want you to fully have your way with me, you know? I want to like..." I blubber, unsure how to say the next part.

"Tell me."

"Struggle a little—or a lot. Unless I say 'pineapple,' I don't want you to stop. I'd like to be home, I think. I'm more comfortable in our woods."

The red of his eyes flickers once again.

"And this would please you?" he asks, his shoulders squared and hunched over in a way that looks like he's ready to pounce at any second.

I manage a nod.

"Heather," he presses, waiting for a verbal answer before allowing the conversation to continue.

"Yes, it definitely would. I've thought about it a lot."

"Have you?" Amusement dances like a song in his voice. The longer he looks at me *like that,* my cheeks grow redder.

I gulp, forcing myself to nod. "Not too weird?" I ask, hugging my knees to my chest. This fantasy has been building in my head for almost an entire year. I've imagined every reaction possible from Moth. I never thought he'd be this relaxed and accepting, but I should have known better. In our life together—sex included—he always makes me feel respected and safe. Maybe that's why I thought this would be too out of the box. The things Moth whispers can be playful and possessive, and I love that. He knows how to take control and tease me, but chasing me down in the forest? It's a bold request for anyone.

"No, my flame, it is not even close." He plants a kiss on the top of my head, and I snuggle into the warmth of his body.

"Hah, yeah, I'm sure in all our years together, much weirder will come, right?" I say the words still burrowed in his chest. When I look up, there's a spark of interest in his ruby eyes.

"Is that a promise?" he rumbles, raising an eyebrow.

"You'll have to wait and see."

We have forever together, after all.

4.

HEN WE FINALLY MAKE OUR WAY inside, we look like we've just rolled around in a field of flowers. I'm thankful we don't run into too many sets of prying eyes on the way back to our bedroom.

Moth fills the giant bathtub and sprinkles in white rose petals and bath salts from the tray on the vanity. He pulls me in to soak next to him, and we lie together until the water is cold and the clock strikes five o'clock. Yeah, we're slipping into vacation mode nice and easy.

I change into one of the beautiful dresses hanging in the wardrobe; it's a light pink chiffon-like fabric with two giant bell sleeves and bows at the shoulders and a skirt that flows in just the right way to my ankles. Moth is dressed like a prince from a fairytale in pants that fit his butt beautifully and a ruffled shirt that makes me think I should add "Pirate Roleplay" to my list.

The clothes, like everything in the castle, perfectly accommodate giant wings, and being as I'm still getting used to mine, it's something I appreciate. Moth must be loving that. At least that's my assumption until I see him walking around the room like a dog wearing socks. "What's going on?"

"They are too tight," he grumbles, pacing back and forth in front of the large gold-trim mirror.

"What? No, you look amazing."

Moth bends his knees, his nose crinkling in an expression I'm pretty sure he picked up from me. It's cute—he's cute. "The fabric is stiff." God, I love this man.

"You're just saying that because you hang out naked like ... all the time."

"I have heard very few complaints from you on the matter." His fangs poke out in a lazy smile.

"Oh, I'm not complaining." I lift my hands in the air. "I can personally attest to both wanting to admire the way your butt looks in those pants and rip them off of you."

"Then we will do the latter." He hooks an arm around my waist and begins leading me to the bed.

"Dinner! We are doing dinner with your family!"

He stops, letting out a sigh of defeat as if we didn't just fuck each other's brains out in the palace gardens. Is it flattering? Absolutely. But someone needs to keep us on task. Unfortunately, that person is going to have to be me.

"It is strange to see them," he admits after we've pried our arms off of each other.

"Pants after this long are going to take some time to get used to—"

"My family," he interrupts.

My face flushes. "Right, yes. I totally knew that."
I didn't.

"Maybe tonight will feel better," I add. After a day of keeping to ourselves, I'm hoping Moth's social battery is charged enough for whatever is to come.

"Perhaps..."

What a journey he's been on in the last 24 hours. Moth went from thinking he was utterly alone in the world to having assorted memories of being from another realm. The guy thought they'd banished him for unspeakable crimes. It's not like he's had many positive experiences with humans either. Anyone would feel rusty after so much time spent in the shadows.

I'm sure after a few *super* awkward family dinners, they'll be back to awkward family dinners, then maybe only moderately awkward family dinners as the universe intended.

I straighten, threading my arm in his and leading the way out of our room. Moth deserves to feel like he belongs somewhere, and tonight is the first step to making that happen.

If it's news that sounds like it came from a soap opera, the people of Eclipsica are totally here for it. Moth's tale of returning from the dead with amnesia is a typical Tuesday here. Still, gossip is as gossip does; regardless of how normal this kind of thing is, Moth is the long-lost prince. Holly enthusiastically informs us he's the topic of whispers in the hallways and songs in the tavern. I make a mental note that we absolutely have to check that out.

"It is unusual to have a private dinner like this during the social season," Queen Plume begins. "But I thought the occasion of your return called for a break in protocol. The rest of the court can have their fun with you tomorrow at tea. Tonight, it will remain just the four of us."

"That was gracious of you." Moth's nod is as stiff as ever. But I agree; easing into this world and the "social season" seems like the best idea for both of us.

"Perhaps afterward we can retire to the parlor together," Holly suggests, her eyes wide and filled with hope. "I'm sure you're aware that my brother is a brilliant pianist."

"Am I?" Moth's deep voice echoes across the dining room.

"Don't be so modest!" Holly exclaims. "I remember curling up in the parlor with a book while listening to you play when we were children. You had a way of playing exactly what the scene I was reading called for."

"How perceptive of me."

"Perhaps you could play us something after dinner," Queen Plume suggests, her tone measured with the grace and pose expected from a queen.

"Perhaps," Moth agrees, though I'm not sure he means it. Historically, I have had a thing for musicians, though the idea of Moth becoming even more attractive is almost intimidating.

"I believe it would be best if you two had some time apart." Holly leans close, so that the whisper is for my ears only. The clink of her dinner knife landing on the table sends a shiver through me.

"To jog my brother's memory, of course," she continues, leaning in even closer, and in response, my wings tense tightly in what feels like a knot. How is me staying away from Moth supposed to help?

"But I want to be there to support him," I whisper back, trying to keep my face neutral.

"And you will be," she continues. "Give me just a day or two to show him around the castle with no distractions."

Hang on, is she calling *me* a distraction? I don't know whether I want to puff up or sink into my chair. Moth regaining his memories would help him connect to his family again, and that's what we're here to do. If giving him space is what he needs, I can do that for him ... even if it's not what he wants.

"You really think it will make a difference?"

"I would like to try." The honesty of Holly's statement strikes me. At the end of the day, we're both just trying to do the best for someone we care about.

"If he agrees, you don't have to worry about me tagging along." I nod. "I want to help him any way I can."

"So, you think it's a good idea?"

"Sure, yes?" If she really thinks it will be good for Moth, I'm willing to try anything.

Holly clears her throat. "Heather has suggested it would be a good idea for Moth and I to tour the castle together tomorrow. A brother-sister day, if you will. Just like old times."

Okay, that's not exactly how the conversation went down, but sure.

"Is that so?" He raises an eyebrow.

"Yeah, totally. It's been decades, right? You're long overdue for some sibling hangouts."

After a long moment, he finally nods, which gives Holly the go-ahead to rattle off every little thing she's planning on showing him.

The ballroom, the gallery, the armory, the way she rattles off rooms makes me realize we've only scratched the surface of how big this place is. I'm a little jealous.

Queen Plume showed us around some of the halls, but I wouldn't mind going on a grand tour too.

But no, when they ask, Holly nudges me under the table, and I lie through my teeth saying it's "so no big" and to "have fun without me" and how much I would love a rest day. Moth doesn't look like he buys it but doesn't press the issue at the dinner table.

It's his sister.

It's his memories.

And all I have to do is spend a few afternoons without him.

For the man I love? Yeah, that's the least I can do.

"Oh, my darlings, I am sorry. We are hosting a picnic in the front gardens tomorrow." Queen Plume shakes her head. "You will have to wait until the next day. I'll have the staff clear the calendar. A few lunches and tea parties can wait, especially with such an important reunion." Her smile gleams across the dining table, and as always, her tone leaves no room for argument.

"Very well," Holly agrees with a dip of her head. "It will be the first time we'll be seen as a family in too long." She nods her head more enthusiastically after the realization.

Moth bites his bottom lip, rising from the table with a bow that suits him more naturally than I would have expected.

"'Til tomorrow then," he says simply. *Wait a second*, is he just going to leave me with them? No, no, no! I need him as a social buffer while I get to know his family!

I flash a grin, poking at the plate of salad greens and edible flowers. To my relief, the menu has been fully vegetarian, so I haven't had to make any special requests. The conversation is slow until the meal is over, and I dip out into the hallway in search of Moth.

When I find him, he is looming in the doorway of what I assume is the parlor. It's draped in a canopy of blue flowers, and a white piano sits in the center. Rows of books line the shelves, and in comfy chairs sit unfinished embroidery projects. *Huh.* I wonder if they belong to Holly or Queen Plume.

Moth traces the keys, an intense look on his face. If he sat down right now, would his fingers remember a long-gone melody?

"Do you want to play me something?"

"No, my flame, not now."

We don't discuss it for the rest of the night.

5.

THE BALL AT THE END OF THE WEEK isn't the only thing going on while we're stuck in the faerie realm. Moth's family neglected to mention that Eclipsica is in the height of its social season and The Moth Court is this year's host, which seems like *a lot to leave out.*

At breakfast, Queen Plume briefs us on the jam-packed week's activities and planning. Does it sound like it's going to be a stunning week filled with gowns, dessert, and dances? Yes. Am I fully swooning over the idea of Moth twirling me around a ballroom? Also, yes. But as we stand together on the front lawn, surrounded by banquet tables filled to the brim with teacakes and flowers, I'm grateful for all the moments we've stolen together so far. Not only do the memories of our picnic make my hair stand on end, but the evenings may be the only time we're alone until the week is over.

As Moth guides me through clusters of well-dressed nobles raising glasses of honey-colored wine to their lips, the smell of peony and cinnamon hangs heavy in the air.

Hungry gazes are cast in Moth's direction as we walk toward the head table. Queen Plume and Holly sit in two of the fanciest wicker chairs I've ever seen in my life. My heart catches at the sight of the creatures scattered throughout the crowd. Instead of focusing on the yellow eyes and sharp claws, I turn my attention to the crystal chandeliers dangling from tree branches.

When transformed, Moth is objectively more terrifying, but I've grown used to—even fond of—him in any skin. Seeing claws, beaks, feathers, and fangs in such numbers is more unnerving than I expected, but it's the ones hidden behind wide smiles and feather fans that circle Moth like he's a new dessert at the cake table that worry me.

"It seems I am to be gawked at, no matter what realm we land in," Moth says in a low voice.

"I honestly can't blame them for trying." I scan him from top to bottom. The way his biceps are screaming to be free of the sleeves of his white billowy shirt every time he bends his arms is criminally sexy—and those pants... *ugh.* "Not only are you the total package, but who wouldn't want to be royalty?"

"Do you?" He dips low and leans forward so that his breath tickles my ear.

"Do I what?"

"Want to be ... royalty?"

"I want to be with you," I say, squeezing him with a tight hug. "Whatever that means. I look good in a tiara, but let's be honest, royalty or not, I've already found excuses to wear those."

"You are one of a kind."

"And that's why you *looove* me."

"One of the many reasons." He plants a kiss on my cheek. "Now, shall we see why my sister is waving us over from the head table or feign ignorance?"

"You go ahead." I nudge him, not exactly eager to spend more time with Holly than I have to. "I'm going to inspect the snack table."

"A noble quest indeed," he says jovially, his fangs peeking out in my favorite goofy grin. "I would like to join you, but it has been said I wanted to rule this place." He glances at the crowd. "I would like to learn why."

"Then go play the part." I nod. He's been a cryptid in our world for so long, Moth's more than earned being a fancy pants prince for a week. Though he'd probably rather be a fancy pants-less prince.

I stand by that. The tight fabric makes his ass look fantastic, and I obviously make sure to get a good look at him walking away before I wander to the banquet table. It seems like a self-serve buffet situation, but I pause, unsure of what side to start at, if there's a line, and all the usual party anxieties I haven't felt in ages. Human mixers and events are stressful enough. Is it too much to ask for a tutorial on how this place works? Shuffling past a few guests, I dodge creatures whose animated speaking would be less terrifying if they didn't have giant stingers for hands. One accidental jab and I could seriously be *impaled.*

Swallowing my mounting anxiety, I grab a plate and fill it with pretty looking fruit and a few pastries for Moth. God, they're so temping. Would a little gluten really be that bad?

"It is unusual to meet someone new during the social season." Two women with beautiful ginger hair styled in curls stand before me, breaking me away from the temptation. I plaster on my best smile and extend my hand.

"Hi, I'm Heather. It's nice to meet you."

They exchange glances before throwing their heads back with laughter, their mouths filled with rows of sharp teeth... cute.

"She seems very odd." The second one circles me, eyeing me up and down. Her pale brow wrinkles into a deep burrow.

"Very odd indeed."

"Her teeth have no points."

"And her wings have no discernible pattern."

"Is one of your parents a part of the Dragonfly Court, perhaps? Someone we know, I'm sure."

"No—"

"A butterfly then."

What does that even mean? I curse myself for not asking Queen Plume more questions. Holly has butterfly wings, but she's part of the Moth court, I think? Oh my god, I'm so confused.

"Uh ... sure."

"And that's where our prince has been this whole time?" The first nods.

Do I bother to correct her? Rumors spread fast here, and Moth hiding in the *Butterfly Court* could be a better cover story than meeting me in the human realm, especially since I'm not sure how open I'm supposed to be about the whole human thing. Holly made it sound like portal travel is *hard*—I doubt it's all that common. "About that—"

"You must regale us with stories of your adventures."

"Of course." I smile. "You know, I don't think I caught either of your names, though. I'd love to know who I have the pleasure of entertaining."

The scorn radiating off the two identical faeries buzzes through the air, creating tension so thick you could swallow it.

"You mean to say you have no idea who we are?"

"Sister, she must be telling a joke."

"Sister, I do not believe she is."

"Sorry," I say, the weight of my wings heavy as I shrug my shoulders. It wasn't meant to be an insult, but clearly these two are micro-celebrities around here. Not knowing their names is a grave offense. I've had this happen a few times with fellow influencers. They either think you're pretending to not recognize them to be aloof or insult them. And while I wouldn't mind bringing these two down a peg, I haven't been here long enough to play those kinds of games.

"Odd and rude," the first sister huffs under her breath. The other elbows her in the ribs. If they're trying to use me to get to Moth, they're really blowing their chance.

"Well, this has been a real delight." I nod, awkwardly excusing myself from the Mean Girls of Eclipsica.

I had enough of that in the mortal realm, I'm *so* not dealing with it here. But when I turn to leave, the first sister's fingers grab hold of my arm, lightly guiding me back toward them. Her lips part in a sharp-toothed grin that is anything but comforting. "Now, now, the party has only just begun."

"Uhm." I look to Moth to signal an S.O.S, but sandwiched between his mom and sister, he looks just as trapped as I am.

"What good fortune you've fallen into by running into us."

"Mmm," I murmur, unsure I can agree. Studying the shape of their wings, they do appear to be more butterfly-like than moth-shaped. Does everyone here have some kind of winged insect cosplay? The hulking creatures with stingers for hands look a lot like bees, but where does it end? Is there a Ladybug Court? A Flying Cockroach court? The inner Floridian inside me cringes at the thought of a *Lovebug* Court. Two bugs attached at the butt gave me the creeps in our realm. I do not want to see a giant humanoid version. *Bleh.*

"I am Lady Vanessa of the Butterfly Court, *obviously*, and this is my sister Lady Annabella."

Hmm, for two people who raised their eyebrows at my name, they sound like they could be plucked right out of my world. It's giving classic Mean Girl vibes TBH, and I'm not here for it.

"Take a turn around the gardens with us, Heather," Vanessa says.

It wouldn't be a bad idea to try to learn more about the world, but I'm not sure how I feel about these two as my guide. Before I have a chance to protest, I have a butterfly sister at each side, parading me around the gardens like a new pet they've brought to school for show and tell. A few people whisper as we walk by, leading me to believe these ladies are just as well-known as they claimed. Whether it's for good or bad reasons is yet to be seen.

"So, *Heather*, are you the prince's attendant?" Annabella says my name like it causes her physical pain.

"I'm his girlfriend," I respond, making a mental note that she is the meaner of the sisters.

"His girlfriend, you say? Hm, what a quaint expression." Vanessa hums thoughtfully. "Hm, he has always had a taste for beauty."

"You ... know each other?"

"Not intimately," she says, stealing a glance in my boyfriend's direction. "But even in his absence, his portraits are admired by many."

"If I may be so bold, he has returned to us more handsome." Annabella pulls me closer to whisper in my ears, her breath smelling of wildflowers.

I want Moth's shadow to loom behind me while his large hand circles my waist. I want him to call me "my flame" right in front of them. More than that, I want them to see just *how* he looks at me because after that, they'd never be able to question how much he cares or kid themselves into thinking they have a chance to break us apart. But when I look for him, he's seated at the table with his mother and Holly. He's laughing, his pale cheeks flushed pink, his eyes bright. He's *happy,* so terribly happy.

I don't understand what happened. Two minutes ago, his biggest concern was how early we could leave, but now he appears as relaxed as he is during a cozy night in. I've tried to push down every serious thought about being here. It's a glamorous break in routine, a staycation in a castle, a family reunion, but it's also his *home.* What does that mean for our future?

"Heather." Vanessa beckons, holding out her hand. "Come, I think an audience with the prince is required."

6.

"How many of these affairs must we attend?" Moth asks, dragging his feet as I walk into the privacy of our bedroom. We have about four hours before family dinner, and after anxiously stuffing my face with a million tiny appetizers, a nap is necessary before consuming more food or conversation.

"Why? You looked pretty comfortable to me."

"I am exhausted," he huffs, casting off his cravat with a moan.

"Well, you did use a lot of people skills in the span of a few hours." I shrug. It makes sense he'd be feeling worn— even if he did seem to be having fun.

"Do my 'people skills' include having to be fashionable?" He arches his back, his body bending and cracking until feathers and bone replace his gold-speckled skin. His tight fitting garments are tatters on the bedroom floor.

He could have shimmied out of the pants before transforming. Sure, there are more in the wardrobe, but his ass really did look incredible all day.

"I definitely saw some transformed people in the crowd," I say. "You are the prince—I think that means you're going to set the trend whatever you decide."

"I am not accustomed to this."

Snatching up his clawed hand, I press my lips to the warm skin of his palm. "I get that—and as a former trendsetter, I admit it can be pretty exhausting being a style icon."

"I do not wish to be a style icon."

"Babe," I laugh. "They're going to want to do whatever you do."

"Then dare I rock the boat?"

"I feel like you're just trying to figure out how to stop wearing pants in polite society."

"I—" He begins, then presses his beak shut, closes his glowing red eyes. "Yes."

"Well," my hand trails up the soft downy feathers of his neck until they rest on the side of his face, "you're free now." My other hand finds its way up his legs. "And I for one like you fine just like this."

The bug-eyes I've become so accustomed to soften into an expression I recognize as the equivalent of a smile. "You do, don't you?"

"Did you want to take a nap or...?" Snuggling closer, I pull his large chest to mine. The fluff of his feathers tickling my skin, I relax into my own monster-sized teddy bear.

"*Or?*"

My fingers trail up and down the length of his strong thighs, and I feel him begin to shift under me. I tease the tip of his cock. The feeling of him growing impossibly large under my touch never gets old.

I swallow at the sight of him, bulging with need. His body relaxes into the pillows, wanting and waiting to see what I'll do next.

My stomach flip-flops as I remember the hungry eyes of the other partygoers as they looked at him.

This man is desired beyond belief, and he's here with me.

Shimmying down, I place a kiss on his hipbone, savoring the deep moan that pours from his lips—it's the exact moment I need to catch him by surprise. Wrapping my mouth around his large cock, I dive as far down as I can go. *God,* the sounds he makes are all I need to keep going, try harder, and go deeper than I ever have.

I want to press my nose to the bottom of his abdomen and hear the moans he'll make then. My wings move behind me as I get lost in the frenzy of him.

Pushing myself deep, I gag, sputtering backward. He tugs gently at my hair. Our eyes meet, and his gaze is soft and tender.

"Slowly, my flame," he says, sucking in a breath that sounds like he's close to unraveling. "I am not going anywhere."

I nod, relaxing. "Sorry, I—"

"*No,*" he moans, pulling me up by the waist until our lips meet. He kisses me firmly, holding his arm tight around my back. "I enjoy watching you get carried away."

"Well, then." I kiss him back, deepening it until we're in a full on make out sesh. My hands in his hair, his tongue in my mouth—god, he's just so perfect.

The people in the kingdom aren't going to give him up without a fight. But it's not fighting I want. When we're together, there's no one else.

At least, that's how it was back home.

Shaking off the anxiety, I take a deep breath, bringing myself back to this moment. I shimmy back down back down his body, and he tugs at my hair. I want all of him.

"Slowly," he reminds me. It sounds more like an order—and damn, it leaves tingles down my spine. I do as he directs, moving at an agonizingly slow pace, opening up to him inch by inch until I'm filled all the way to the back of my throat. I slowly—and carefully—bob my head and lose myself in the moment.

"You are taking me so deep, my flame." He groans, grabbing a fistful of hair. I moan and it spurs him to tug just a little harder.

He knows me so well, and it's just what I need. I use my mouth, my hands, and flick my tongue until he's writhing too hard to say a word. Clawing my fingers into his hips, I plunge as deep as I can, my own want building. He cums *hard,* dripping down the side of my mouth.

I swallow before smiling up at his dazed face. Clumsily, he pulls me back on top of him.

"You are a goddess," he moans, placing a messy kiss on my cheek.

"And you're very fun to play with." I kiss him back, cozying into his side. Moth turns to me with a wolfish grin, his fingers lowering from my chest to my hips.

"*Now,* I believe it's my turn."

7.

SPOILER ALERT: WE DID NOT MAKE IT to family dinner. After a few earth-shattering orgasms, I passed the heck out, and Moth requested to have dinner sent up to us, just like room service at a fancy hotel.

But then, when I woke in the middle of the night, he was just ... gone. And not like, "woke up to use the bathroom or get a snack" gone. I mean, "totally out of the room from around 2 a.m. 'til sunrise." It's odd. I mean, he's always been a night owl—er—moth. At home, he's sitting up in bed next to me, either reading or scribbling in a notebook. It's easy to fall asleep with his body next to mine. Not that being alone at night bothers me or anything. I definitely didn't lay awake until he crept back into the room.

Sprout plopping around the room like a sentient rug absolutely didn't make me jolt up multiple times.

We barely spent the morning together before he left again. Now, Moth and his possibly murderous sister are off having their adventure. But it's fine. I am determined to soak in some relaxing vibes after yesterday.

The breakfast tray arrives with a bunch of star-shaped grapes, flaky pastries, and a cup of strong-smelling break-fast tea with milk and sugar cubes on the side. Sprout happily steals a whole croissant and trots into a sunny spot by the window to enjoy his contraband. While I let the blankets fall away from my body and plop a few sugar cubes into my tea, I notice the pastries look ... amazing.

If Moth were here, he'd probably tell me a bite—even just a little tiny one—isn't worth the risk. I haven't knowingly consumed gluten in years; for all I know, I'm not even sensitive anymore, right? I raise the flaky pastry to my lips before setting it back down on the plate.

No, Heather. You have been so good. Now is not the time to break your medically prescribed diet.

But then again, when I was first diagnosed with Hashimoto's, I read a few blog posts about women who had awful reactions to gluten at home in the States but could magically eat all the pasta and bread they wanted when visiting Italy. It was a fantasy I didn't allow myself to indulge in when I went overseas for an influencer trip with my mom. Back then, I was too concerned about looking puffy in photos...

I probably don't want to be puffy for a grand ball either.

Gosh, just look at that golden crust. If there's anywhere I can attempt to eat gluten, it's a fantasy world, right?

Yes.

No.

Yes, no—

Crunch.

The first bite is crisp and buttery. If Moth was around to hear the moan that escaped my lips, he'd either laugh, or his lips would be locked on mine. It's filled with some kind of spinach and olive blend; the latticework covering the top is so beautiful, I almost regret eating it.

Almost.

Next, I grab a moon-shaped bun with some kind of peachy filling. It is equally delicious and gone before I'd like.

I wait for a minute. I know it's not like I'm going to burst into flames or anything. I'll wait a little while to make sure my body doesn't freak out, but if this doesn't cause any pain? Hah, then maybe we should just stay. Moth can be with his family, and I can eat bread—a literal fairytale for all parties involved.

It's only when my plate is filled with crumbs, and Sprout paces around the room that my mind wanders to non-pastry-related topics. I hope everything is going well in the sibling bonding department.

I walk to the mirror, letting my light-green wings span behind me. I'm the same Heather that got overwhelmed by her online life and moved to the middle of the woods, the same silly burnt out influencer who dragged a literal cryptid into her house and fell in love with him. Still, I wonder if more than just my exterior has changed. My wings flutter as I continue to study myself. What was it those mean girls said? My wings have no "discernible pattern" ... like I'm a shape that can't quiet fit into a box here or in the mortal realm.

Like this fairytale I've been pulled into is something I was never supposed to be apart of and—nope! That's enough deep contemplation for the morning.

Pulling on one of the frilly dressing gowns from the wardrobe, I snag my phone—which happened to be in my pocket when we arrived here and switch it to camera-mode.

One photo a day was the promise I made to myself. I don't post most of them, and I'm sure as heck not going to post whatever I decide to take today. The bottom of the robe billows over the ornate rug—it's backless, just like all the other clothing in the wardrobe, to accommodate my wings. I let my wings open, tracing the green veins and cheerful yellow spots; the sun shining through the window makes the thin skin look like the crinkly tissue paper at the bottom of a gift bag.

Arranging myself in front of the tall mirror, I call Sprout over to sit beside me. The giant pile of floof happily plops himself at my side like an enthusiastic throw rug. The flowers strung high on the ceiling frame our reflection as if I'd spent hours arranging them *just so*. Former me would have lost it at just how picture-perfect all of this is.

"Alright, Sprout, you ready for your first mirror selfie?"

He yawns in response, placing his giant furry head in my lap, which I think is a yes. I snap a few, ruffling his impossibly soft fur in between shots. I notice we have matching crumbs across our faces, and one stray hair keeps getting caught on my left antenna. It's less than perfect, and I have to remind myself these photos are about memories. Plus, who am I kidding? We're adorable.

Sprout and I are low key and lazy for the rest of the morning hours. I run another bath, eat lunch in said bathtub, and snuggle with Sprout. I'm starting to realize why Rosie and Clara have been peer-pressuring me to get a dog. He's an icon, *even if he hogs the entire bed.* It must have been lonely flopping around this castle for decades. I'm glad that he decided to stay cozy with me instead of tagging along with Moth and Holly, though. All this time alone is making me realize I don't spend much time by myself anymore.

Still, by mid-afternoon, I'm too antsy to stay in my room. Despite not knowing anything about this place, I dress in a white cotton bell-sleeved dress, pull my hair up in a braid crown, and show myself around.

It's a long shot, but maybe I can find a phone signal somewhere. It would be nice to tell Rosie and Clara we didn't mean to blow off our double-date and ask if they could water the plants and stuff while we're gone.

"You're where?" Rosie shrieks through the phone. "Heather, no—this is too much."

"I know, I know, it sounds impossible but—"

"Nothing sounds impossible coming from you anymore."

"Thank you?"

Finding bars was difficult, but near the large bridge at the entrance of the castle where we landed, I do manage to find a weak signal. It's not 5G but leads me to believe the connection between worlds is still open. Though Rosie's stunned silence makes me question if she's still on the line.

"You there?"

"Yeah, yeah, sorry. It's just—"

"I know, I know! My head is literally spinning, okay? I will fill you in on everything when—"

"No, no, it's not that you're in the ... fae realm?" She cuts me off with a heavy sigh into the receiver that sounds like a gust of wind.

"Then what?" I ask, feeling every bone in my body tense. I hope she's okay...

"Honestly, you being away this week is kind of good timing." She groans, and I can picture her nervously tucking strands of red hair behind her ear.

"Oh, yeah?"

"Chris is in town," she whispers. I straighten at the sound of her brother's name. Chris—the monster hunter who had dedicated his teens and entire adult life to hunting down Moth—, the man who became so obsessed he used me as live-bait to try to finally catch him.

Chris—the man who almost killed me. Yeah, the wings are cool, but I would have preferred getting them in a less near-death experience kind of way. As far as I was aware, he's been living with their parents out of state and seeing a therapist after the entire ordeal. No one besides the five of us knows what really happened that night, and admittedly, I was lighter on the details with Rosie than I should have been. Who knew a life-altering moment would be *this hard* to talk about?

I had told her I'm glad he's getting help, and I should be happy—I mean, everyone is capable of change, right? He can work on himself if he wants to. It just needs to be as far away from me as possible.

"He wants to meet me for coffee," she continues.

"Are you going to?"

"He is my brother... so, yes? I don't know. Clara says I shouldn't bother, but—ah no, I shouldn't be talking to you about this."

"No, it's my fault. I asked."

"At least you won't have to worry about running into him in town. "

"You won't tell him about this, right?"

"God, no, and he's still banned from The General Store. No matter how this conversation goes, the store is a safe space for everyone."

"Thanks, Rosie."

"Literally the least I can do."

I've been telling myself that maybe—just maybe Chris could earn my forgiveness one day. Friendship? Never. But isn't forgiving him supposed to stop my stomach from tying in knots when I hear his name? Rosie is right: being transported to another world couldn't have come at a better time.

"Could I trouble you to water the plants? Also, I think there are some cinnamon rolls that are probably attracting flies on the counter."

"You got it," she chirps. "Do you still have the same code for the lockbox?"

"Yeah, just make sure you lock up afterward," I say, flexing my free hand open and closed.

And don't tell your brother where the key is.

"You know it's okay to be dealing with lots of emotions, right? What you've been through is—"

"In the past! I'm totally good! Do not worry about me," I say in one breath. I don't want to talk about this with her—or anyone. I tap my fingers across my phone, trying to focus on the raised texture of the decorative flowers on the case. It's been a year. Why does everyone keep asking if I'm okay? Realistically, as long as I don't think about that night, I'm great. I can just keep living in the moment.

"Okay, okay, if you say so."

"Whatever you decide to do with the whole coffee thing, I hope it goes well."

And by "well," I mean I hope she tells her brother to move out of the country and never come back.

"Yeah, sure. Be safe, okay?"

"I'll do my best." Given my track record, I'm not making any promises.

With a click of my finger, the call ends, and I tap my nails on the screen, craving the numbing effect of a good scrolling session. As if my phone could handle loading up a meme in this state! Switching it into airplane mode, I curse myself for not having more music or a few games downloaded.

I guess I could go back to the library. Shuffling back to the castle, I spot Queen Plume, her fangs worrying her bottom lip—did something happen? In our few interactions, she always seems effortlessly put together.

"Hey!" I call, jogging toward her.

The sharp turn of her guards causes me to stop in my tracks. Right, yep, probably should have thought ahead before running up to the queen like an old friend at a coffee shop.

"Sorry—hello, Your Majesty." I bow, lipping "sorry" to the guards. Out of the corner of my eye, I'm pretty sure one of them smirks.

"Ah, Heather, I trust you have had a relaxing morning?"

"Oh absolutely. Thank you so much," I reply with as much formality as I can muster. "Um, but is there anything I can help you with?"

"Me?" Her eyes widen. Uh oh—maybe that was too bold of me.

"Sorry. I just mean with the ball coming up." I fiddle with a loose tendril of hair that's slipped out of my braid crown, trying to busy my hands. "As nice as the leisure is, I wouldn't mind a project."

"I cannot ask—"

That's when I notice the soft pastel stationery clasped in her right hand. Before I can think, I cut her off. *Again,* probably not something I should be doing to royalty or my boyfriend's mother.

"I took a calligraphy class in high school," I state, pulling my shoulders back. "And honestly, it would be nice to get to know you better."

"In that case," Queen Plume gives me a once over as if she can read my resume with a simple glance, "I will take all the help I can get."

8.

THERE'S NOTHING LIKE A DISASTER to add some excitement to a last-minute event, and this one is a doozy. Queen Plume's invitations to the ball were supposed to go out *yesterday*, but after a mishap with a new maid with nervous hands and a very full pot of tea... well, here we are. A pile of stationery sits on the left of the table, far away from the silver tea set. An E-vite from my world can't get wet, but they're also not even half as pretty as this.

My handwriting is nice, like *really* nice. But the queen's letters have more aesthetic loops than a rollercoaster. I try to copy the style, but who am I kidding? No amount of decorative bullet journal layouts could have prepared me for sweeping cursive calligraphy—and with an actual quill? I've only used them as props in photos. What I wouldn't give for a glitter gel pen. Though I'm not sure that's the vibe she is going for.

As I copy the names and titles over, I find that most are Moth-, Butterfly-, or Dragonfly-related, which I sense is a theme. But the next page feels like it's got to be a joke—Queen Plume must be playing the "mess with the human" game.

"As if there's a Goblin Court!" The shock causes me to drop all decorum.

"Oh no, not in Eclipsica. Their Court is quite a distance from our borders. I do not expect them to attend." She hums, reaching for a piece of paper to pen her next letter. "We had a flimsy alliance a few millennia ago. It pleases them to have the opportunity to reject our hospitality, so they remain on my list."

"So ... goblins." I swallow hard. I've barely adjusted to the idea that faeries are real, and my boyfriend is one of them. "Sorry. I so thought you were trolling me."

"No, trolls do not take to parties and high society." Her forehead wrinkles as she speaks. "I suspect our guests will mostly be of the winged courts; however, all kingdoms are welcome."

The queen's attendant shoots me a look as if to say, "Why do you keep bothering our queen with your silly questions?" I bite my tongue. There will be plenty of time for answers later. Right now, I just need to get through this list.

Drawing in a deep breath, I try to mimic Queen Plume's serene expression as I write, ignoring the strange names and titles and focusing on my penmanship. As far as settings go, this is about as regal as it gets. Instead of a record player, a live musician—fully transformed into a Moth-creature with iridescent blue feathers—plucks a harp in the corner with sharpened claws. They sway to the rhythm of the music they are creating, their glowing eyes closed. When I try not to stare and miserably fail, the creature simply winks at me.

I turn my attention to the large family portrait hanging above the fireplace. I thought Moth took after his mother, but *whoa*. The scary looking man standing next to Queen Plume must be Moth's father. He's the mirror image of my boyfriend, right down to the pale gold-flecked skin, red eyes, and scowl—only there's no warmth radiating from him. Even in an intimate family painting surrounded by his wife and children, the former king is distant.

"Moth is the spitting image of his father, is he not?" The queen raises her eyes to the portrait for just a moment. I imagine anything more than that is just too painful.

"I don't know..." I begin, tilting my head. "The more I look, the less and less alike they seem."

With the way Queen Plume still mourns him, I thought Moth's father would look kinder, but then again, I'm no stranger to a snapshot not reflecting reality. Who knows what their day-to-day life was like? He could have been "#1 Dad" for all I know...

"Sorry, that was probably an insensitive thing to say." I shake my head. "I've been living out in the middle of nowhere for a year, and I think it's whittled away some of my social skills." I hope the shred of honesty will break the tension between us.

"No, I did not mind." She glances up at the portrait again, for longer this time. "I wish I could see what you speak of—it seems unfair to lump the two together."

I nod politely, focusing on Moth's portrait. He's only a few feet tall and his antennae are too big for him; he wears the faintest of smiles: young, boyish and adorable. Holly is a toddler no older than two and is being held lovingly in Queen Plume's arms.

What a couple of cuties. It's probably too much to hope that there's a baby book filled with pictures of tiny Moth around here somewhere. I'm dying to see more of what he looked like as a kid.

"Can you believe I almost had it removed—the portrait that is," Queen Plume begins. "There are days it was too painful to even look at."

"I'm so sorry," I say, knowing those words will never be enough. "You've all been through so much."

"Yes—to mourn a king, a prince, and an engagement all at once." The queen stares at the portrait as if it's a portal to a lost moment in time.

"An engagement?" I croak. "Moth was engaged?"

"Oh, ages ago, my dear." Queen Plume waves away my obvious concern with a serene smile. I gulp, trying to force my now ridged back to relax into the seat cushion. With delicate hands, she carries on with her work.

Engaged…

"Were they in love?" I ask, taking a hard swallow of tea, ignoring the way it burns going down my throat.

"The two were betrothed since birth. Lady Ruby was his best friend, and yes, I suppose they loved each other. She mourned for years after his disappearance. Ruby always cared for my son more than the idea of taking the throne, but I dare say she would have been a more enthusiastic ruler than I. As would Moth back then—he wanted to be king more than anything."

I shouldn't be upset; I mean, I know he's had relationships before me, including a few unique sounding dalliances in the mortal realm. Of course, someone like him would have suitors upon suitors here, but love is different.

I've been bracing myself for something like this ever since we arrived, but *childhood best friends?* When they see each other again, will sparks fly?

"You have other questions?" she asks, though she doesn't raise her eyes from her work.

Other questions? Hmm, that's an understatement. I glance at the harp player in the corner, who gives me a nod. Oh my god, I need to stop staring at them. "I'm sorry if this is like ... totally ignorant, but are there any rules for transforming?" I ask, quickly turning my attention back to my pile of envelopes.

"You can take whichever form you are most comfortable in," she says, furrowing her brow. "An odd question. Have you also suffered from your memories being taken?"

"Oh no, no, I was human before ... Moth saved me."

The music stops and so does Queen Plume's quill.

"Oh?" She tucks her legs up on the sofa and reaches for her teacup and saucer. I thought it was obvious considering my request for human medication, and the fact we met in the mortal realm, but I guess those are details she overlooked. "Then it seems my hands are in need of a break, and my ears are in need of a story."

"Oh yeah, no, totally."

So much for not thinking about it.

Queen Plume dismisses her attendants, leaving the two of us alone in the large sitting room. She refills both our teacups by hand and leans back against her cushioned seat.

"Moth and I met in the human realm when I fell out of a tree—and then later he fell on top of my roof. I nursed him back to health, and the two of us fell in love..." I say. "Those are the basics at least."

"So, you ... tended his wounds yourself?"

"Yeah, I mean ... I had to try, right?" I grimace, remembering the sight of his wing bending backward. "It took a while for his wings to heal, but that also gave us time to get to know each other." Warmth blooms in my chest at the thought of those early moments together; we've come so far. I figure that's enough to satisfy her curiosity. But Queen Plume isn't interested in the Cliffs Notes version, which doesn't explain how I had been transformed.

So deeper I go, pressing on a bruise I wasn't sure still hurt until unshed tears cause a funny lump in the back of my throat.

"Obviously, Moth saved me," I say as casually as I can manage, "and when I woke up, I had wings. Pretty cool, right?"

"Cool ... yes." Queen Plume nods with a heaviness in her eyes that I try not to notice. "I caution you not to mention this to anyone." She purses her lips together. "Though, your human nature does explain your need for this ... synth-a-roid."

"I can't be the first chronically ill former human who got transported here."

Queen Plume's lips turn downward in an apologetic expression that suggests that I, in fact, *am*.

"Our kingdom is not prone to illness, though it does exist. Perhaps not this same condition, but I will talk to our healers. Herbs and spices can do wonders—"

I cringe, suddenly transported back to millions of "Have you tried Brazil nuts?" comments in posts that so much as mentioned Hashimoto's. It's not that I don't believe in natural remedies. The whole reason I'm gluten and dairy free is to try to fight inflammation. But my body needs modern, *human* medicine to deal with this very human problem.

Besides, Moth's father was sick, wasn't he? I swear Queen Plume said he had fallen ill when we spoke about him in the library. If healers, herbs, and spices couldn't fix a fae king's health problems, I don't think they'll do much for me.

"There really aren't any other humans here?" I press. It seems unlikely that I'm truly the only one.

"'None' would be an understatement, and 'some' would be generous."

Yes, thank you for the very clear answer.

"I guess with the wings and stuff, it's hard to tell who started out human, huh?" My wings flutter slightly.

"Oh..." She sets her teacup down on its saucer with a thud, waving her hand. "No, my darling, the way Moth healed you? It is not a power shared by everyone."

"It's not?"

"It is passed down from the royal family. You may have noticed the pattern of Moth's wings: a Death's Head marking, black with yellow spots, and a skull at his shoulder blades—his father had the same."

I always thought it just looked like some big dots. Clearly, I would have failed an ink blob test for creativity.

"Claws to kill—and the power to save. The mark of Death has always meant new beginnings." She clasps my hands in hers. "I'm glad I'm here to see yours."

"So, if Moth wasn't—I mean, um..."

"You likely would not be seated next to me."

I've known how lucky I was that Moth found me, but the gravity of just *how lucky* hits me right in the stomach; it stirs up an unwanted feeling too big to acknowledge while surrounded by floral stationery and tea.

I steel myself as I look up at the family portrait. Moth's father glares down with the same dark wings as Moth, but Holly's are an iridescent blue.

If she was the one who tried to rescue me, I'd be dead.

"My mother is of the Butterfly Court. Holly takes after her," Queen Plume explains, following my gaze. "To have them both under one roof again..." She shakes her head, dismissing tears before they have a chance to fully form.

"So, is everyone named after their wing pattern?" I ask, eager to change the topic before more tears fall. Before last year, I never really spent much time in nature, so bug types are more than a little lost on me.

"Here and in the Butterfly Courts it is tradition." She wipes a few rogue tears from her eyes before an award-winning smile spreads across her lips. "The others have their own way of doing things."

Others.

"So, Moth and his father..."

"Were both called Death, yes." She nods "Though the king preferred to be addressed as *your highness.*"

Huh.

That's surprising considering how informal Holly and Queen Plume are with each other.

"Even by you?" The question spills out before I can catch it. Her face falls. Shit, I totally overstepped on that one.

"I would say we've done enough work for today." She reaches for a silver bell on the end table, and with one small jangle, a group of maids file out of the hallway, a spring in their step. Queen Plume instructs her attendants to finish off the rest of the invitations and help themselves to the teacakes—which the girls seem delighted by.

"Let's see what those children of mine are up to, shall we?" The queen clasps my hand, and as we rise from the couch, she lets out a laugh that sounds more like a sob. "I never thought I would say those words again."

Well, we find them—but not how I expect.

Moth sits on the floor with a tiny wooden teacup that looks even smaller in his massive hands. Gathered around him are equally adorable children dressed like they're from a regency novel. As a group, they seem to be having a very a very serious discussion about—*well, honestly, I have no idea.* It's mostly high-pitched babbles with a few random words thrown in, but straight-faced Moth seems to be keeping up. Sprout lays nearby, his tail thudding every once in a while as if agreeing. I blink, struggling to take in the cozy—yet somewhat chaotic—scene.

Then I see *her*.

My breath is caught in a giant lump in my throat.

On the couch next to Holly sits the most beautiful woman I've ever seen—and mind you, *I've been to fashion week.*

Her skin is a warm dark brown, and her black hair is styled in an intricate updo. She swoops up a rogue toddler, who cozies onto her lap. The murmured "mama" confirms that they're her children. There's a twinkle in her amber eyes when she takes in the scene that causes a pang of jealousy to settle in my chest.

Just who is this beautiful woman?

"My sweet Lady Ruby!" Queen Plum extends her arms. Oh my god, *this* is Moth's ex. "You were greatly missed at tea yesterday. It seems you have not wasted time becoming reacquainted."

"I can barely believe my eyes," Ruby's voice is light and airy. "But it really is him."

"Ah yes, I hoped Ruby's appearance might help my brother's memory. You see, they were inseparable growing up."

"So I've heard," I reply, smiling as sweetly as I can manage. A sibling day, huh? Seems Holly and I may be on opposite teams after all.

Moth excuses himself from the tea party—well, sort of. There's now a toddler with pigtails riding on his tall shoulders, giggling as he approaches. Standing next to Ruby, they are an image of what could have been: a picture-perfect royal family. In our world, their collectable coronation plates would be out of stock in minutes.

"Hi! Oh my gosh, it's so nice to meet you," I greet Ruby, extending my hand and swallowing my pride. Years of networking events haven't only taught me to navigate awkward dinners, they've also taught me to keep my enemies close. With those killer legs and bright red wings, Ruby is absolutely a threat, a threat ... who is currently hugging me.

Why is she hugging me?

"Oh, it is wonderful to meet you!" Ruby says. Wow, her hair smells a spring afternoon after a light rainstorm. "No wonder the eyes of our prince light up each time he speaks your name."

"Whaaat?" I blurt out, my face warming at the unexpected compliment. "Oh my gosh, stop."

But don't because I could use the ego boost.

"My admiration should not come as a surprise to you." Moth punctuates the sentence by placing a kiss on my hand. It would sound almost cold if I couldn't see the smirk on his face.

The adorable toddler riding on his shoulders shrieks and waves as he moves around the room—and wow, he's good with kids too? *#Swoon.* It might not be something that's on my mind right now, but I've always felt like you can tell a lot from a person's character by the way they treat kids and animals. In my former life as an influencer, a few of my ex's were annoyed when toddlers would mistake me for a Disney princess in public. It's something that I always thought was adorable. Living in Central Florida with a penchant for floofy dresses meant it came with the territory. The way Moth looked holding a tiny teacup in his claws is proof that he would have had way more patience in that sort of situation—not that we can go trapsing around in public back home.

"The children have taken to him quite well," Queen Plume says with an amused hum. She leans in close so she can whisper in my ear. "Perhaps you are right about the lack of resemblance to his father."

I press my lips shut. *What is that supposed to mean?* Maybe Moth's father was just as cold and distant as he looked in the painting after all.

"Darling!" Ruby comes to life at the sight of someone else in the doorway.

"*Baba!*" The children race toward the figure, and the toddler who was resting on Moth's shoulder launches herself into the air, flying toward her parent on adorably tiny wings.

Within seconds, I'm no longer looking at a person. I'm looking at a fae jungle gym. They're around my height, with tan skin, black and white speckled wings, and hair to match.

"This is Pepper—my partner," Ruby introduces us with a small laugh. "Moth, you must remember them from the royal guard."

Moth gives them a polite nod, but the tight smile leads me to believe it's another memory lost in time.

"Oh, uh ... hello." Pepper pauses, unsure how to greet us all, but lands on a causal-looking bow, which is impressive considering they're balancing a fairy child on each hip while another flies in circles around their head.

"Sorry for not giving you a more proper greeting, Your Highnesses."

"I believe your hands are a little too full to worry about such things," Queen Plume says with a warm, motherly smile. "Tea will be served shortly. Until then, I wonder if a few little fairies might join me for a story." She plucks a large picture book off an end table, and with a few squeals of delight, the children rush to gather around her skirt.

"Mother, surely there are preparations you must return to..." Holly protests.

I smile. I don't think her little reunion is going how she expected.

"I cannot think of a better way to spend my break." Watching the way they flock to her, I have a feeling this is a fairly regular occurrence—or a welcome change in routine. Her musical voice makes for a calm soundscape as the rest of us gather at the far end of the room as to not disturb them.

When tea arrives, she remains with the children, chatting and feeding them countless sugary treats, just like a grandmother might. On our side of the room, Pepper closes their eyes, drinking their second cup of strong black tea.

"Long may the queen reign." Pepper raises their glass in Queen Plume's direction while Ruby snuggles against their shoulder. The two seem more than happy to have this moment to themselves, and their contentment allows me to relax.

If Moth ever had a romantic place in Ruby's heart, it's clear that Pepper has taken it.

"So how did you two meet?" I ask, breathing in the scent of vanilla and cherry from the gorgeous tea service set before us.

"It was ten seasons ago—"

"Eleven," Pepper corrects her as they snag a scone off the tray, giving their partner a cheeky half-smile.

"I had mourned you for a decade," she addresses Moth with a solemn nod. "But I was not looking for love. That season was being hosted by the Dragonfly Court, and Pepper was assigned as my guard."

"We had a whole carriage ride to get to know each other."

"I thought they despised me," Ruby says, clutching a hand to her chest.

"I was quite shy." Pepper taps thoughtfully at their chin.

"The carriage broke down in the middle of our journey—and the rest..." Ruby glances at the children who are attentively listening to Queen Plume's story. "The rest is history."

Her hand slides into Pepper's and the pair lock eyes, glowing with affection for each other.

The more the four of us chat, the sillier I feel that the pang of jealousy just won't go away. If Ruby and Pepper were anymore head-over-heels for each other, they'd have literal hearts in their eyes. Still, the image I saw of Moth and Ruby, and all of these kids running around is burned into my mind—a constant "what could have been." The feeling follows me like a ghost for the rest of the day.

Moth loves me, I know that. But would he have been happier if he was in Pepper's place? It's a question I should be happy I'll never know the answer to, but I can't help but wonder: if he could have any future, would he really choose one with me?

"She's very beautiful," I say once we're alone in our room.

"Who?"

"Your ex-fiancée—obviously."

"Ah yes, she is." He nods. "Though Pepper is equally appealing..."

"You're not making this better."

"I find your jealousy ... cute," he says with a sideways grin. How dare he be so smug! It's not as if I have a lot of opportunities to get jealous back home. We live in the middle of nowhere, and the only people we hang out with are married. Sure, I've seen him get checked out on the rare occasion we're disguised in public, but that's different.

"You two looked good together," I say, hating the venom in my voice. It's not just that she's pretty—heck, I'm pretty too. Maybe not supermodel, drop-dead gorgeous like Ruby, but that's not the problem. No, what's bothering me is how they fit together like puzzle pieces. Yes, their lives have gone in completely different directions, but I can't help but think she's always going to be the one that got away.

Moth spins me around so that our reflections meet in the mirror. He towers over me, his frilly shirt unbuttoned while his strong hands trail down my shoulders to the soft curves of my body. "*We* look good together."

He's clearly not looking in the same mirror.

"You're built like a god, and I'm like a ... cupcake."

He bends, kissing—no, *biting*—my neck. My tension releases at the sensation of just the right kind of pain radiating down my spine.

"Is that why I crave you so badly?" He cups my chin, tilting my face just enough so that I'm staring in the mirror again. His wings sprawl out, wrapping me in their darkness. I lean into each kiss, relishing the feeling of being wanted.

His claws brush across the floppy strap of my dress that, despite my best efforts, has been sliding down my shoulder all day. "And this dress..."

"You like it?" I playfully let the straps fall, exposing the top of my chest. "I was thinking about changing before dinner. The lacing on the back was giving me trouble earlier."

It wasn't. Not that it matters. Moth knows exactly what I'm playing at here.

"Mmm." He presses a kiss to my newly exposed shoulder. Seizing me by the waist, Moth carefully unlaces the back of my dress, threatening to unravel me right along with the decorative ribbons.

The garment falls away, and he stands tall behind me, running his fingers from my waist to my shoulders. The tip of his claws trace my jawline.

"What a beautiful confection..." There is nothing teasing about the admiration in his voice. He holds my bare body to his, feasting on me with his eyes alone.

My breath hitches. He makes his way down the length of my arm, biting and kissing, and food is the last thing on my mind.

"Are you hungry?" I ask, my voice weak and breathy, leaning into his touch.

"Starved." Moth's fingers slide from my hips until his hand presses right against my core.

He dips a large finger inside me with ease. A moan escapes me as I melt into the firm weight of his chest. Moth pauses. Raising his hand, he licks from his knuckle to his fingertip.

"So sweet," he purrs. *Fuck*, if that doesn't make me weak in the knees. Moth eases me onto the edge of the fainting couch, and by the time his head is between my legs, I'm shaking. The simple touch of his hand on my inner thigh causes me to bite my bottom lip.

"You are trembling." He breathes the words against my skin, leaving kisses farther and farther up my leg. "Would you like me to stop?"

"*No!*"

Moth's laugh is dark. His hands leave my body, and without warning, he stands.

"There is a request I forgot to mention..." He pauses for long enough to cross the room.

"Oh?"

"I would like you to watch."

He picks up the large full-length mirror with one hand and drags it right in front of the fainting couch I'm sitting on. I gulp. "May I show you just how well we fit together, my flame?"

Oh. Heat rises to my face when I realize just *what* he's asking.

I manage to nod, and he spreads me across the furniture like a delicacy. When I peek up into the mirror, I have the perfect view of my 7-foot-tall monster boyfriend between my legs. The warmth of his tongue heavenly caresses my core, sending waves of pleasure through me with every skillful movement. How is it possible that he keeps getting better at this? He works his mouth until I groan, clawing my nails into his shoulders. I never want this to be over, but I'm not sure I'm able to take any more.

Resisting the urge to throw my head back, I keep my gaze locked on our reflection. I watch the way my hands look, grabbing a fistful of Moth's dark curls to pull him closer. I find myself transfixed by the way the curve of my leg looks hooked around Moth's broad shoulder.

"We look perfect." I whisper the words, and he moans into me, sending vibrations all the way up to my chest.

His claws dig into my hips, pulling me toward him until I'm nearly hanging off the cushions. His tongue flicks in and out, and in and out; it twists and laps at the most sensitive spots and—

Oh my god, wow.

Wow, *wow*.

He moves to bite my inner thigh while his fingers take the place of his tongue. I moan at the sudden increase in pressure deeper and deeper. Finally, he drives me off the edge.

"You're so ... *wow*." I guide him up until his head is resting on my chest.

"And you are perfect." He kisses my exposed skin, sending another shiver through my body. "There is no one else I want."

"Same," I breathe, kicking myself for not saying something more romantic.

Again, as the evening falls, we don't go down for dinner. Nope, a "headache" very sadly keeps us bound to our bed for the rest of the night.

Something neither of us minds one bit.

9.

I'M THANKFUL FOR THE *HEADACHE* last night because the moment we come down for breakfast, all of Moth's time seems to be occupied. There are nobles to shake hands with, paperwork to fill out, new portraits to commission, and more seemingly trivial things that don't seem to have room for me—according to the meticulous itinerary Holly has crafted, at least.

Moth has invited me along, and honestly, I'll probably try to see what the portrait thing is all about, but I want to give him space. After my little jealous outburst, I'd hate for him to think I feel like I need to watch over him 24/7. Considering he disappeared *again* last night, my trust is really being tested.

But I feel for him. For a long-lost prince, they're certainly putting him to work, and maybe that's good—maybe it will help with his memories. Though, I really hoped we could have some time together to explore.

My morning is spent helping Queen Plume pick out linens and flower arrangements until lunch, where we sit in a room filled with noble ladies who not-so-subtly arrange the conversation around what a good match they would be for Moth.

Pedigree

Musical Talent

Connections

And unspeakable beauty.

I make small talk with my head held high, nibbling at my rose petal salad. It's been a long time since I've had to smile and laugh on cue, and the performance leaves me exhausted.

A break couldn't come soon enough. After being dismissed, I take refuge in the library—of course a place like this would have a library.

If the floor to ceiling books weren't impressive enough, there's one of those cool rolling ladders. Everything is warm earth tones with ivy and other climbing plants dancing up the columns, their leaves creating shadows upon the tall windows. The pink flowers that hang around the castle look especially beautiful in here, bright against the dark wood and dusty shelves. The ceilings are large enough for someone to spread their wings and fly all the way up to the tallest shelf. There are even a few high alcoves that suggest people might perch among the books like birds in a tree—needless to say, I love it here.

Sprout lays at my feet while I curl up on a large sofa with a stack of books I don't have the attention span to read.

The light highlights the suspended chair-swing in the corner, and I watch the flower-covered wicker seat swing idly back and forth between the dark wood bookshelves.

Looks like I've found my Photo of the Day.

Hopping to my feet, I snag my phone out of my pocket and power it on. I balance it on some shelves near the window. The suspended chair is perfectly showcased in the corner of the shot. I arrange a stack of books towering a few feet above the ground. Clicking the timer, I rush to the swing, crashing onto it just in time to pull a book into my lap. Repeating the process a few times, I end up with a handful of photos I love—the best are the ones where Sprout sprawls across the floor just in frame. I couldn't ask for a better furry friend to keep my company—even if I miss Moth more with every passing second.

"What are you doing?" The sound of Holly's voice causes me to jump and let out a scream—which is totally not embarrassing in the slightest.

"Sorry! Oh my god, I didn't hear you come in. Are you two all wrapped up?"

Holly narrows her eyes, snatching the phone from its place on the shelves, which is *one*, rude, and *two*, makes uncertainty bubble in my chest. Cell phones obviously aren't a thing here, and neither are cameras.

"What is this?" She holds it with just the tips of her fingers as if it will bite her if she gets too close.

"Oh, it's like..." How do I describe this to someone who has idea what a phone is?

"It's like a communication device, and this here," I point to the camera, "takes pictures, like a very fast real-life portrait."

"And you have been taking these around Eclipsica?"

"Just the castle, really." I bite my bottom lip. "Is that okay? I can delete them obviously. I'm not planning on sharing them with anyone or anything like that."

She blinks, as if still not being able to understand the concept. I flip the screen toward her, swiping across the photos from the library.

"How did you accomplish this?"

"Oh!" I grin. "If you want, I could show you. We could take a picture of you now, or we could get a little artsy and have you dressed in full armor with a row of swords behind you."

"Why would you do that?"

"Oh, to create an interesting composition, I guess. Training seems really important to you so—"

"No." She raises her hand to signal me to stop talking—and I do, clamping my lips together. "Why would you do any of it?"

"Oh..." I hesitate, pushing down the sinking feeling that's building in my chest. "Well, I used to take pictures for a lot of different reasons. It was my job to make all sorts of content, but now, it's kinda like a scrapbook."

"A what?"

"Like a very personal portrait gallery?" I offer, trying not to let my frustration show. Holly is probably not *trying* to insult me. She just wants to understand this hobby of mine better, and I should try to show her with a little more patience. She's never seen a camera before, let alone an entire phone. Of course she has a million questions—even if they do seem a little bit judgy.

"Do you have any more?" I let the tension fall from my shoulders at the genuine curiosity in her voice. "I would like to see where my brother spent his life without us."

"Yes, totally!" I hop up, sliding close to her on the couch, and place the phone between us to give her the best view. While I can't show Holly what Moth's entire life in the mortal realm has been like, I can show her a few snapshots of this last year—which, in my opinion, has been *a pretty spectacular one.* It's hard to decide where to start, so I pull up an album of my absolute favorite shots.

"You're going to love these," I gush. Not only are the compositions effortless, but they're just so *cozy.*

In the first photo, Moth sits at our small dining nook, his red eyes just peeking over the rim of a large floral mug. Behind him, sunshine from the windows casts golden light across the dark wooden walls. Breathing in, it's almost like I can smell the warm scent of cinnamon as it wafts from the kitchen.

"This was from the morning before you brought us here. I had just pulled homemade cinnamon rolls out of the oven, and there was this incredible cool breeze coming through the windows. I took an instant photo but couldn't help grabbing one on my phone too."

"That is where you live?" She moves closer, grabbing the phone and squinting at the screen, no doubt taking in every whimsical detail of the home we created together.

"Cute, huh? And it hardly ever leaks when it rains anymore, which is a definite plus," I ramble before flipping to the next shot.

Ah, this one is nice too.

Moth and I are piled on the loveseat. He's reading Jane Austen, and I'm sipping a cup of homemade hot chocolate, overflowing with marshmallows. My legs are draped over top of his—it's sweet and intimate, and the only way the two of us fit on that piece of furniture together. My blue tinsel Christmas tree shines in the background. Moth called it an "insult to the woods," as if he hadn't admired the lights all season long.

Whether or not he likes to admit it, he has a thing for sparkly things, which is probably why he loves me.

"He is so..."

Happy.

Relaxed

In love.

"...cramped." Holly grimaces. *Wow,* not the adjective I expected. "I found you both not a moment too soon."

Yikes. Sure, it's not a big house. But it's packed with love, and in my humble option, we do just fine in it.

These photos are some of my favorite glimpses into our life together. When I look at them, I'm filled to the brim with warmth.

"We don't need much space," I murmur, trying to sort out my thoughts.

"*You* may not, but he is—"

"A prince." I cut in. As if she'd ever let me forget.

"I was going to say 7 feet tall—with a wingspan that appears to be wider than your entire kitchen."

Well, I can't argue with that.

She flicks through a few more pictures, her thumb sliding so quickly I barely register the blurred pixels as images. In seconds, she's blasted through the entire curated gallery with little commentary. These pictures are just for me—I didn't take them for anyone's approval, but I feel like I just got 0 likes on a new post.

"This is what you spend your time doing?" Holly asks. Wow, with the way she looks down at me from the end of her nose, I have a strong feeling she doesn't approve of or even like what she sees.

"I mean, some of it?" I manage, ignoring the stab of anxiety.

"Tomorrow I'll teach you how to use a sword," Holly says, leaving no room for argument.

"I'm not really a weapons kind of girly."

"You will learn."

I guess that settles that. Breathing out a heavy sigh, I search my mind for something—anything—to talk about.

"There's a portrait being done of Moth today, right?"

"Yes. Mother mentioned you expressed an interest in watching." She sighs. "I came to collect you, so that we could head to the throne room together."

"Aw!" I cheer, as if she didn't fully insult my home and my hobbies. "That's so nice."

Holly stiffens as though I've horribly insulted her. She stands, practically marching out of the room.

"Hey! Wait up!" I chase the angry fae out into the hallway.

The walk to the throne room is different without being flanked by dozens of guards. Holly moves casually through the overgrown walkways, her shiny armor gleaming in the sun.

Damn, if I don't just want to snap a photo of everything—including Moth, the moment the heavy doors open to reveal him.

Holly gives me a knowing smile.

"This is how a king should be portrayed," she whispers, which I assume is another insult about my photos. I knew a royal portrait session would be serious. I don't know what I was expecting, but it certainly wasn't *this*.

Moth's armor is heavy and black; he holds a helmet in one hand and a sword in the other. This must have been what he changed into before sparring with Holly, who suddenly comes to life with compliments for her brother.

"It is going to be absolutely perfect. Wait 'til Mother sees." She clasps her hands together in a gleeful, almost childish gesture, before stiffening her hands at her sides. I peek at the unfinished painting, and my jaw goes slack. It's even more severe than he looks in front of me.

He looks just like his father in that portrait hanging over the fireplace. His posture is stiff and his lips a straight line. This is the picture of a warrior—a king. Someone ruthless, scary and ... not Moth.

"What do you think, my flame?" Moth's voice floats down the staircase. Even his tone sounds prickly, which isn't too different from the man I fell in love with. He tilts his eyes toward me while remaining perfectly posed—and there's that softness I recognize.

"It's different," I say, earning a glare from both Holly and the artist, who like everyone I've met so far is model-level gorgeous. "I mean, you look great." *You just don't look like you.*

"And you think you could do better," Holly scoffs, her wings fluttering.

"No, it's looking amazing. It's just—"

God, how do I explain this?

"Just?" The painter interrupts our brewing argument by blowing out a sigh. Stepping around his canvas, he tucks the paint brush behind his ear, awaiting my next word.

"It's not him," I add a little more gently. "And like ... that is *so not* your fault."

The artist squints between the canvas and Moth and lets out a defeated sigh. "I will admit it is appearing ... stiff." With a hand on his hip, the artist swivels toward me. "What would you suggest?"

"First, the armor has got to go."

Moth wastes no time unclipping the heavy chest plate to reveal another frilly shirt with sleeves that cling to his biceps in just the right way. I blink to try to regain focus but ... nope, he's too damn sexy. Yes, he's dark and brooding but also delicate—someone more suited to holding a flower while surrounded by greenery, not a sword.

"Then what if we moved this outside?" I muse. "Some more greenery would totally brighten things up and add a nice contrast." Clasping my hands together in front of my body, I rock on my heels, awaiting a response.

"There is plenty of greenery in this space," the painter argues, gesturing with the tip of his paintbrush to the ivy and flowers that flow into the white open space. "However, I am beginning to agree—something does feel *off*."

Despite the beautiful setting, there's something cold in this room I can't explain. I'm glad the artist is starting to see it too.

"I would be willing to move," Moth says, looking to me for approval. I love how he trusts my artistic direction.

"Wait!" Holly shouts, holding out her arm as if to block the doorway. "Brother, this cannot truly be what you want." Her eyes flick from the canvas to the discarded armor.

"Is there any significance of this particular background?" Moth asks with genuine curiosity.

"It is where we are always painted." Holly's response is matter-a-fact, but I have a feeling that this outburst is about more than just tradition. "I do not understand."

Are her eyes watering? Her hard exterior begins to crack, and I'm reminded that she's just a girl who missed the heck out of her older brother. This is supposed to be a gift, and she probably feels like I've totally messed it up.

"Then perhaps it is time for a change," the painter suggests gently, sparing a hopeful glance toward Holly.

"I will hear no more of this," Holly says, shaking her head. "No, no. We will do it once, and we will do it properly."

Moth has moved off the platform to *literally* take my side. Before he can open his mouth to speak, Holly throws her hands in the air then points a sharpened claw at the artist's chest.

"I have called you here for a portrait. I expect it to be done before the ball. Now, if you'll excuse me..." With heavy footsteps and thud of the door, the three of us are alone. The room falls silent.

"I am so sorry." It seem like ever since I got here, I can't stop putting my foot in my mouth.

"The princess said she would hear no more of those fanciful ideas of yours, " the artist says, sucking air through his pointed teeth. "But I made no such promise." He places his hand in mine. "Oak." The young man bows slightly, a glint of mischief dancing lightly in his eyes.

"Heather." I return the firm handshake.

"My prince." Oak stands at his full height. He's the closest person to my height I've met. Though I note that his heeled shoes might be what's giving him an edge. "May we move this session to the gardens?" Oak asks, bowing with more formality than I was granted—which like, *fair*, Moth is a prince after all.

Moth looks at me and grins. His claws trail up the small of my back, and my knees quake in response. "I will follow her lead."

It's been a long time since I've had a creative collaborator. Despite working with photographers all over the world, I've never played art director to a painter before. Oak, with his brown mop-like hair and subtly striped wings, nods in approval at the set we've pulled together. "This is very interesting indeed."

"You like it?"

"No one would have thought to use such a soft setting for a royal portrait."

"And why is that?" I ask, glad Oak doesn't seem to mind a little conversation while he paints.

"King Death liked to show a strong front, as did the rulers before him," Oak says, shifting slightly to paint the outline of Moth's jaw.

"Okay, I'm new here so bear with me. Why all the armor, training, and serious stuff? Is there a war I haven't heard about?"

"Not in centuries," he says, more to Moth than me. He is the one who lost his memory, after all. "But you would know that, my lady, if you had been residing in the Butterfly Court as the rumors suggest."

"You can't always believe rumors..." I trail off. Oak seems nice, but considering Queen Plume's warning, I probably shouldn't just tell him the truth.

"No, I suppose not." Oak nods with a knowing smile. "Regardless, visiting a new kingdom, even one as humble as ours, can certainly cause confusion."

"Honestly, I have no idea what's going on," I admit. Wow, does it feel good to be truthful. A *pfffft* of laughter escapes Moth, who is doing his best to stand still, and Oak, who I like more and more by the second.

I glare at Moth, who has about a teaspoon more knowledge of this place than I do but decide not to tease him. It's bad enough that everyone knows Moth is suffering from partial memory loss. I don't need to rub it in.

I know there are different types of fae, and their wings seem to mimic winged insects from the human world, and everyone—and their mothers—wants a taste of the long-lost prince.

Other than that, I'm totally lost.

"Now, how can that be?" Oak asks, giving me a side eye. "I did not realize your memories had also been affected."

"Hah, surprise." I choke out a less than convincing reply, earning another laugh from Moth. Oak narrows his eyes.

"Right, well, my lady, what would you like to know?"

Tutorial mode unlocked. Thank you, Oak.

"Everything," Moth answers, and the painter's suspicion seems to lessen at the sound of his low voice.

"You stand in the Moth Court, filled with the most attractive and talented members. As you can see, art is showcased from the highest of stations to the night markets, where you can find all manner of creation." He skillfully moves his brush across the canvas, marking out Moth's outline.

"This year, we are the hosts of the social season. It is early yet, but members of the Dragonfly Court, Butterfly Court, and the Bumble Court will all be in attendance at the ball. You have no doubt already seen them at various social events this season."

"The Bumble Court... right." I nod. I remember most of these titles from addressing invitations and from getting thrown in the deep end of society at the garden party.

"Correct. Their territory encompasses most of the crystal caverns. We have only one cavern on our side of the border, but it is enough for us to drown in silk and sparkle."

"Does everyone try to one up each other? Like, I'm guessing they have the fanciest clothing—"

"Oh no, the Bumble Court will take to their 'true forms.'" He makes air quotes while rolling his eyes. "They will not debase themselves with something as lowly as skin."

That confirms the fuzzy bee-like creatures I saw in the crowd during the lawn party.

"Unlike those of the Dragonfly Court, who hardly ever transform. Can you believe Lady Emerald's family set a match between her and some unknown Bumble count?" He scoffs. "I pity her, moving from her lily pad palace to their crystal hives in the mountain."

"Oh, yeah, that's awful." I nod, trying to soak in this first taste of Court gossip. "So, okay. Bumbles like to stay in their bee forms. Dragonflies live on—I'm sorry, did you say lily pads? Please tell me the Butterfly Court lives in the sky and raise flying unicorns."

"They are called alicorns," Moth says in a low voice, angling his head to the side.

"And you aren't supposed to be moving." Oak shakes his brush at Moth before his attention returns to both the painting and the conversation.

"I'm not hearing a 'no.'" I pipe in, holding out some level of hope that alicorns exist.

"Ah, it is a no," Oak says musically with another wave of his brush.

Dammit.

"So, all the regions are pretty cool with each other?"

"There's other manner of warfare than battle and bloodshed."

Believe me, I know. I grew up on the internet. I bite back the words, knowing they'll have no meaning to Oak.

"Besides, traditions are hard to break. I doubt the princess will be pleased when she sees this piece," Oak continues.

"If strength is so important, why not paint him in his other form?"

"Ah yes, the queen is not known to transform in public. As such, wearing this form has been—what's the word?—*more fashionable* since she took the throne."

A frown crosses Moth's lips.

"So, if I were to transform..." Moth begins, and I wish I could tell what he was about to ask. After our conversation last night, I can't help but wonder—is he worried the people here won't accept him as anything but their beautiful, stoic prince?

"I told you—you'd be a trend setter."

"That, and it would be very thrilling." Oak nods in agreement, and I think I sense the slightest amount of flirtation in his voice. "And nothing I haven't seen before."

Oh, not *this* again.

"We were acquainted?" Moth asks, squinting his eyes at the man I now suspect is more than a long-forgotten friend.

"Yes, my prince," Oak replies with a wicked grin. "That is one word for it."

A blush rises to Moth's cheeks, suggesting something is resurfacing in his memory.

"All in the past." Oak winks at me, and dear lord, is everyone I meet in this realm going to be someone he had an entanglement with? I hop up to brush a stray hair from Moth's brow, my jaw clenched tight.

"Is that jealousy I sense from you, my flame?" Moth asks quietly.

"Oh my god—me? *Never*."

"A pity," he whispers, leaning in close. Suddenly, his hand is warm on my lower back. "I would be happy to remind you just how well we fit together."

Heat radiates from my chest to my stomach. Dear god, does this man have any idea what he does to me?

"As tantalizing as your bedroom talk is, you are not supposed to be moving," Oak shouts, throwing a spare paintbrush in our direction.

"Paint us together then," Moth commands, positioning me in front of his body.

"Hah!" Oak exclaims. "As if you two would actually stand still! No, I will not risk Holly's wrath for that fool's mission."

"That's okay. We have a ton of artsy portraits together," I remind Moth, helping him get back into his original pose before walking behind the canvas.

"Very intriguing." Oak raises his eyebrow. Oh my god, not *those* kinds of photos.

My ears burn red at the thought of capturing our entanglement on film. His strong shoulders, my soft curves, skin on skin with a few well-placed props to give interest.

Maybe that's another thing to add to my list.

While Oak is hard at work, and not paying attention, I snap my own little photo of Moth. With the pink of the flowers, and the pop of red from his eyes, he looks like my own personal valentine. I settle into a spot in the garden, hoping this is all worth Holly's wrath. With every brushstroke Oak lays on the canvas, Moth—*my Moth*—comes to life. That authenticity has to be worth something.

I huff, letting my body fall onto the soft blades of grass. Is Holly's tension seriously just for the sake of appearances? I mean, I get it, but *come on*. There's got to be more to Moth's porcupine of a sister than she's letting on. I know what it's like to put on a performance in front of people. How much of all of this decorum does she actually care about?

I have a feeling that, this week, we're going to find out.

10.

IKE I TOLD HOLLY, I'M NOT A WEAPONS
kind of girly, but there is something about holding
a giant sword that makes you feel cool. That is,
until I try to move around with it. No one tells you how
heavy swords are. God, this looks way easier in the movies.

It's awkward and heavy and, like anything, takes a god-
awful amount of practice. Drill after drill assures me it's not
a skill I'm looking to add to my library. The movements
Holly shows me are like a very precise line dance—something I'm *also* not very good at. Adding something sharp
to the mix only increases my stress around the situation.

"You are holding it wrong," Holly says, helping me to
grip the handle differently.

"I thought it was fine as long as I wasn't touching the
pokey bit," I say, trying my best to keep my stance and
position like she'd shown me.

"Be thankful we are not practicing with real swords."

"You think I would have gotten hurt?"

"I think you would be dead."

"Oh..." I flex the blunted sword in my hand, and a full body shudder runs through me. "Maybe that's enough swordplay for today."

"Hah, I expect you to keep doing these drills. The hour is getting late, and I should check on how the preparations are going with Mother."

"I can—"

"—do the drills until I've returned," she cuts me off, leaving no room for argument.

"Yeah, sure."

"Pepper will assist you."

"I will?" Pepper, watching on the sidelines, sighs. At the lift of Holly's eyebrows, they rise from beside Ruby and drift into the training area with no more prompting. Usually having an audience would add to my nerves, but Pepper's presence has been reassuring. Holly is much less likely to murder me if there is a witness.

"Not that there's much hope," she says under her breath.

"I heard that!" I shout after Holly, raising my weapon in the air.

I swing the sword the way she showed me—at least I think it's the way she showed me.

"I'm not actually going to make you practice," Pepper whispers once Holly has disappeared from view. "Skills are better taught when one isn't exhausted."

"Some serious parent energy."

"Yes, next I will offer you a cup of juice and a snack." They nudge me toward Ruby's picnic blanket, topped with a basket filled with the aforementioned snacks—an offer I don't have the energy to refuse.

"Besides," Pepper continues, the sun glinting off their light brown skin; flecks of gold shimmer. "We can leave the battle to Moth. Though, I believe he might be losing."

Moth has never needed a sword. No, his claws suit him better than any blade and strike just as sharply. However, he's not flexing them at the moment.

In the courtyard, giggles erupt as Moth dramatically falls to his knees as a blunt wooden sword collides with his chest. Ruby looks up from the book she was reading to cheer on her children as they pummel Moth to an untimely demise.

"Ooof!" Pepper groans, watching Moth flop to the ground. "My back hurts just watching that."

"Ah, he'll bounce back." I shrug. Except he doesn't. Moth fully commits to the bit with the resolve of a high school drama student.

"My flame—" he chokes. There's the barest hint of a smile at the edge of his lips. "I have been vanquished."

"I see that."

"My foes were many—and fierce." Clutching his chest, Moth begins to cough dramatically. So cute. The children eat it up, bursting into giggles.

"Should I avenge you?" I ask, Pepper's chuckles resonating at my side.

"*Fiercely.*"

I let my wings span behind me and let out my best battle cry. Grappling for the discarded wooden sword, I chase a dozen laughing children around the courtyard until Holly returns, her presence replacing my joy with tension. Her arms are crossed, but wait a second—is that a smirk on her face?

"Your form was better that time," she muses, giving Pepper a knowing look. "Mother is calling for both of you."

"Alas, with my dying breath, I will send my regrets." Moth coughs a few times before letting his head fall to the side.

"Charming." Holly sticks her nose up, but the smirk remains.

"I think so," I giggle, offering his faux-lifeless body my hand. To everyone's relief, he makes a miraculous recovery. "Come on, let's get some tiny cakes to revive you."

We wave our goodbyes, getting ready to make our way back to the castle.

"Well, they're adorable," I say, stealing a glance back at Moth's plentiful foes.

"Yes," Moth responds, with an undeniable glint in his eye. Maybe one day the two of us will have a little winged horde of our own—okay, probably not *that many*. But I could imagine us as super cute parents in a decade or so.

I lace my fingers in his, giving his hand a light squeeze. It's a future that's fun to think about, though right now, I'm happy with just Sprout.

A girl toddles over—Ruby and Pepper's youngest I think, the same who had been riding on Moth's shoulders the day we met. She holds out her hand and gives Moth a piece of paper. When he leans down, she whispers something that causes him to shake with unexpected laughter before nodding at her. Gleefully, the girl jumps, returning to the rest of the group.

"What is that?"

"A formal request for honey cakes at the party."

"Ooh, she even added in a leaf."

"We must take this request before the queen."

"*We must.*"

"We are stealing you two as full-time babysitters," Ruby shouts across the field while Pepper nods in agreement.

I'm suddenly glad I agreed to blow off another tea party to be here—though I don't expect I'll want to pick up a sword anytime soon.

"Duty calls," Moth shouts back, the light fading from his dewy eyes.

"Why don't you just hang out?" I ask. "I'm sure your old friends wouldn't mind the help, and I can work on stuff with your mom. We're probably going to be talking about décor for an hour again anyway."

"Do you doubt my knowledge of centerpieces?"

"I would never," I gasp, holding my hand to my heart. Stretching my wings, I flutter up to his cheek, planting a kiss on his warm skin. "Seriously, have fun, okay?"

"Do not work too hard," he says, holding out the leaf to me. "And remember to honor this request."

"I'm on it." I wink, waving a last goodbye before heading off in search of Queen Plume. The laughter fades, but my smile doesn't. It's good to see Moth with friends—I just wish we could take them all back home with us.

THIS AFTERNOON, IT SEEMS LIKE Queen Plume wants company more than help. I ignore the way her shoulders shrink just a fraction when she realizes Moth isn't with me. Her son—I can't imagine how she feels after seeing him again. Did he once run around the training grounds armed with a wooden sword and a sharp-toothed smile? Or was he in the library with a book held tightly to his chest?

I wish I had more than these formal portraits of him to go off of. Sadly, there aren't any family scrapbooks or cloud storage in the fae realm. All we have to go off of are the stories, and those seem to be few and far between. From his place above the fireplace, the king's portrait stares silently, judging my every move.

"And how did you and your husband—the king—meet?" I ask, the urge to know more about Moth and his family overshadowing formality once again. I'm glad Queen Plume doesn't seem to mind.

"Oh, the usual. He kidnapped me," she says in her usual sunny way. I *must* have misheard her.

"I'm sorry—what?"

She tilts her head as if baffled by my confusion. "He was known for his dramatic flair." She shakes her head. "As is most of Eclipsica, as you'll find."

"And he was a total stranger?"

"Oh no, we shared a dance—"

"One dance?"

"That was enough for him to whisk me away to this castle."

Kidnapped. Goosebumps prickle across my skin at the idea of being "whisked away" by anyone except Moth...

"I'm sorry. Does this happen frequently here?" I ask, trying to shake the tension from my body.

"Oh no. Not in earnest, at least. Proposals have gotten dull in the past few years. And no one is ever forced to marry—not anymore, thank goodness." Her smile thins at the words. From everything she's said, I had assumed she was madly in love with Moth's father—but maybe there's more to the story than I realized. "But, no dear, I think royals just like putting on a show."

"So, princesses do this too?"

"All manner of noble, it matters very little." A far-off expression overtakes her green eyes "Death—my former husband—I thought he was an absolute brute at first, but as predicted, it only took two weeks' time for me to fall for his charms."

"And you loved him?"

"Yes, I did. Ah, forgive me for changing the subject." Her hands jump to the small pouch hooked to her belt. "I believe this is for you."

An orange prescription bottle rests in her palm. My head spins at the sight of something so modern in this antique world. But that's not the most surprising part.

SYNTHROID: 100mcg

It reads at the top, followed by my full name and address. This isn't just a random prescription, it's mine, and should be sitting on my nightstand next to a neglected bottle of water—not here in Queen Plume's hands.

"How did you get this?"

"A queen has her ways."

Oh, absolutely not. Sure, she's my boyfriend's mom and the queen of this realm, but there's no way I'm letting this slide.

"Do *those ways* include a portal back home?"

She pinches her mouth shut. "I thought you would be pleased."

"I am. Very pleased, *and very, very confused.*"

She sighs, as if deciding something after a silent conversation. The queen rises from her chair. "Come," she commands, "I would like to show you something."

"This is where I go when I need to relax."

Relax.

I'm not sure I could use that word to describe the place I'm standing in.

We've climbed to the tower attached to Queen Plume's chambers. The space is large and rounded with storybook windows and ivy covering the roof. Walls painted a deep blue echo the night's sky and camouflage the cracks in the stone. Unlike the rest of the castle, this place has not been well-maintained but is instead well-loved.

Well, *love* might not be the right word.

I expect the sound of ticking to fill my ears; large cuckoo and grandfather clocks fill the space, though they are silent and the hands unmoving. There is a collection of other oddities, like antique dolls, figures, and other lonely things that you'd find left behind at a thrift shop.

For a room filled with clocks, it's eerily silent. The absence of ticking makes me wonder how long the two of us have been standing together in this room. Every second that passes, a sense of unknown urgency builds inside me.

My uncle had always fiddled with old clocks and other trinkets, but I've never seen anything like these. I think they're all broken beyond repair but beautiful.

Being here reminds me in a way of Moth's hollow. In his years spent living in the mortal realm, he'd squirreled away more shiny little trinkets than a magpie. It must be a family trait, though Moth's collection is less ... creepy.

Queen Plume stands frozen in time and, I imagine, sorrow. It's terrible that my first urge after wanting to offer her a hug is to take a photo. Imagine how stunning this photograph would be with the clocks blurred in the background and a clockface reflected in the queen's eyes. Goosebumps prickle across my skin.

It's a stunning image I don't dare capture with anything other than my memories. In her rage and grief, Queen Plume created *art,* and I don't think she even realizes it.

"Moments frozen in time," she says with a small hum. "They're one of my favorite things to collect from the mortal realm. The image of stopped time has provided a strange comfort since ... everything."

"Since you lost your husband—and your son." I gulp, unsure how to comfort her in this deeply personal place; the woman has been through more tragedy than I can possibly imagine.

"And as a result, Holly lost her mother and the kingdom their queen. At least for a while," she continues. Unsure of what to do, I place my hand on her shoulder and am surprised when she reaches up to give me a small squeeze.

"Atlas seemed to swoop in just when I needed help most. It's funny—no one ever talks about how fickle he was—a man who longed for adventure away from the castle, or so he said. The terrible thing is, he was an outstanding leader: patient, generous to the villagers, and always careful to not create ripples. To think that, all along, he was the cause of my misery." She paces the length of the space. "I do not understand why he would do such a thing..."

"Did you love him?"

"He was a friend. I *thought* he was a friend." She stares off before finally nodding. "It was not a romantic love, but yes, I cared for him deeply. I thought he felt the same for me—and the children. To think it was all a lie..."

"You never really know some people." The bitter words flow out before I can stop them. The more I think about two-faced assholes, the more Chris echoes through my mind. I wonder if King Atlas thought he was the hero when he damned Moth to live a life as a monster in the mortal realm.

"There is more to see."

She takes my arm, leading me farther into the tower where ivy creates a curtain between this space and the next. Behind the makeshift curtain is the most beautiful mirror I've ever seen with carved birds and flowers decorating the full-length frame. The glass ripples and moves like something from a funhouse.

My heart catches in my chest—this must be a portal.

"Atlas knew I wanted a way out. In secret, he commissioned this piece from the Dragonfly Court just for me. Now I wonder if he hoped I'd leave for good."

"How does it work?"

"Do you see the way it moves?" She traces the surface, and it ripples as if she's skimming her fingers through the water. "The Dragonfly Court live in marshy waters that are said to have magical properties. They're the ones who created—and ultimately banned—travel through portals..."

"Banned it?"

"It is like anything," she says with a roll of her eyes. "Those with means can still grant access. I am no stranger to this privilege as you can see. Though many of my fellow rulers do more harm than good when they visit."

"So..." I begin, tilting my head as I stare at the mirror. "Where do you go?"

"I walk around a city where I am not queen and revel in the obscurity, perhaps do a little shopping." Her mauve lips pick up in a genuine grin. "That is something I believe you can relate to?"

I spin the prescription bottle in my hand from its place in my pocket. "You went to my house."

"I admit, apart from wanting to help you with your ailment, I was curious about your dwellings. It has been such a long time since I've seen my son."

"But how did you find it?"

"Would it be too chilling to admit I used a lock of your hair?"

Oh my gosh, *what?*

"Maybe?" I squeak, hoping she's not serious.

"Then I cannot say." Her lips quirk. Oh my god, she *did*.

"I don't understand anything about this." I sigh, holding my fingers to my temple. "For most of my life, I didn't even know magic was real."

"All new things are learned with time," she says in a soft, low voice. There's something so effortlessly warm and charming about her that the tension in my shoulders relaxes with just a few words.

"Magic like this needs something: a token of desire, an intention to command. I took hair from your brush, and as I stepped through the portal, I imagined I was entering the woods you described."

"And that's all it took?"

"We shall say the portal is the train, and everything else is the ticket." She nods. "I apologize for the invasion of your privacy."

"No big—seriously." I shake the bottle of Synthroid in my hands. "And thank. Wow, wait 'til Moth sees this..."

This seemingly normal comment is enough to wipe the smile from Queen Plume's face. With all the authority of a queen, she raises a hand indicating me to stop. "Oh, you mustn't tell him."

"I can't just keep a secret like this."

"His sister is so happy to have him returned. I'm not asking you to keep this place locked away from him forever, just 'til the end of the week. These years have been hard on her. To think she was playing with transportation magic behind my back!"

I mean, you're literally hiding a portal, so you can't really be mad, I think. Obviously, I don't say so out loud.

She sighs. Her head bows and her hands fall to her sides.

"My son wanted nothing more than to be king when he was here." For a moment, her gaze is distant as if the memories are playing before her eyes. "There is so little he remembers of his past and some I hope he never recovers."

"Uh, what?" That's obviously not what I meant to say, but more secrets? *Please no.* I love Moth with everything in my being, but can't a girl catch a break?

"It is not my place to say more." She gives the mirror another touch of her long fingers.

"Moth's past is his past," I tell her firmly, forcing myself to make eye contact. Her green eyes are unflinching in a way that's uncomfortable.

She clasps my hands tightly in hers, giving them a small motherly squeeze. "And I hope," she says tucking a loose strand of hair behind my ear, "that his future will be yours."

As the two of us move through the small space, I can't help but notice the unnatural movement of her wings. I wonder if the all the fabric she decorates them with weighs them down.

"You are a real treasure, Heather." She laces her arm in mine as she guides us past the ivy curtain and down the steps toward the rest of the castle. "We will do good work together."

We slip out of the tower, quickly moving ahead of the guards who were waiting at the bottom of the staircase.

Is this place really a secret if the guards are standing watch?

"Thanks for talking with me about, well, everything. I like, honestly, super appreciate it."

I think I have experience putting on good events. None of my experience putting together influencer parties—or going to them—could have prepared me for a ball in Eclipsica.

I don't know what the logistics would be of my mom meeting Queen Plume, but something tells me they'd really hit it off.

They both love people, parties, and pushing me to my limit with an endless list of tasks. The queen asks me questions about everything from table settings to floral decorations to which song should accompany the first dance.

I don't know anything about the customs here. Without Moth next to me, it feels like I've been thrown into the deep end, but somehow, I'm keeping my head above water. There's something fun about planning something this grand. I just wish we had more time to do it.

Though, all I really want to do is find Moth and tell him everything. Heck, I still need to mention the whole "your sister might be a murderer" thing. But what if keeping my mouth shut is honestly in his best interest?

For now, all I can do is wait for the right time. Maybe after all the festivities tonight we can stay up late and trade notes from the week. After so much time apart, I think we'd both really like that.

12.

TIME HAS SHIFTED WHILE QUEEN Plume and I stood in her hiding space. The new secrets weigh heavily on my chest. My eyes dart around the corners looking for Moth until I remember he's sitting for the rest of his portrait with Oak out in the garden. Good. Until I can swallow all this new information, I'd rather not have to face him.

Free from the tasks of the day, I head to what's becoming my new favorite place: the library with its sprawling dark wood shelves and endless stories. I just want to sink into the tufted couch and get lost—preferably in a nap instead of a book.

I freeze in the doorway, spying a stressed-out looking Holly behind the old mahogany desk. In front of her grimacing face sits a mountain of paperwork. Upon further inspection, it isn't her usual scowl, no, her eyes gloss over like she's cramming for a last minute test; all she's missing is a mountain of energy drinks and a few stray candy wrappers.

"Ooof, I hate paperwork. I always had to hire an accountant because like what even *is* a write-off when everything you do is a part of your job, you know?" I ramble, sliding into the seat across from her.

Holly flinches, straightening in her chair before briefly regarding me. "What a shame. I would not mind handing this task off to *anyone* at this point."

"Even me? You must be desperate," I tease, leaning over the desk to inspect the piles. Holly has been nothing if not cryptic, a trait that must run in the family. I'm shocked when she doesn't swat my hand away.

"Mother does not care much for bookkeeping." She points to a section that *I think* is supposed to be about accounting. "An adequate amount," it reads in flowing cursive script under a heading that says "finances."

Ooof—and I thought independent business taxes were bad. This... this is a hot mess.

"Would it help if I sorted them into piles for you?" I scan through the documents, snatching two up in my hands that seem to match and piling them together.

"Fine." She huffs. "Just don't misplace anything."

"How would you even be able to tell?" I ask, trying banter on for size, and while I can't tell if she's annoyed, it's a better dynamic than when I was trying to be friendly.

"You have a point." Holly groans, placing her hands over her face long enough for me to admire her blue iridescent nails. "Do your best—or worse—it matters very little."

With that vote of confidence, I get to work finding anything that looks vaguely similar and piling it together. Usually I'd put on music while doing a task like this, but since I don't want to drain my phone battery, and dragging a harp player into the library seems a little much, we work in silence. Okay, *mostly* silence.

I try, okay?

"So, what do you like about embroidery?" I ask, noticing the little project she has off to the side. "That is yours, right?"

"Pardon?"

"Oh, um, what do you like about embroidery, like as a hobby?" I ask again.

"Oh. Well, similar to training on the field, how do I put this..." She wrinkles her nose, tapping her quill to her cheek.

"Is it the stabbing?"

"I was going to say repetition." She hums in the melodic way both Moth and Queen Plume speak.

"Oh yeah, that totally makes sense—"

"But the stabbing doesn't hurt." She picks up the embroidery hoop, turning it over in her hands before violently shoving a needle through the fabric. "In this instance, at least." My blood runs cold at the sight of the repetitive and *very, very stabby* motion.

God, she is so freaking scary—but warming up to me, I think? I should try to keep this momentum going. What else can we talk about?

"So, your mom told me—"

"The queen."

"Yes, your mother, *the queen*, mentioned that, there are other kingdoms in this realm," I say as I sort through the stacks of papers. "Anything I should know about?"

"About what?"

"I don't know... the goblins and stuff!"

"Are you worried about things that go bump in the night, former human?" She raises a thick eyebrow, not bothering to look up from the paperwork.

"No—yes—wait." I draw in a deep breath, steeling my nerves. "Why do I feel like you're about to tell me you're expecting a hoard of vampires?"

She blinks before confusion turns to a sly smile. "Yes, and?"

"*No.*" I gasp. I can accept faeries, goblins, and trolls, but vampires? No, no, that's ridiculous. "You've got to be kidding."

"Why would I be?"

"I'm sorry. It just seems a little..."

"*What?*"

"Silly."

Her eyebrows raise. "Remember that when a vampire bleeds you dry for your carelessness," she huffs. "Not that my brother would let that happen."

But you would.

"If it makes you feel better, the vampires and were-wolves mostly keep to the mortal realm. When the king-doms were split, most had the unfortunate luck of being stuck with your lot."

"And that's supposed to make me feel better because...?"

"You're in Eclipsica now," she grins, her fangs on full display, "and we are all so much worse."

"Thank you for that," I grumble, stretching my arms behind my back and letting my wing-span follow as an attempt to rid myself of the building tension. "Is that what all the swordplay was for?"

"No—"

"Then why?" I tilt my head. "Don't tell me you just wanted to spend some time together."

"Sharing a hobby is ... a way to bond, is it not?" she asks. "As strange and silly a human you are, you seem to have captured my brother's attention..."

Wait.

Wait.

Am I hearing her right? Does Holly totally want to be my BFF?

She clears her throat. "As for threats from other kingdoms, all I meant to say is that you will be protected."

"Oh." I breathe out a sigh, unable to shake the warmth in my chest that Moth's baby sister might be warming up to me—as murdery as she is. But not wanting to push it, I change the subject.

"So, there will be even more creatures than just fae at the ball?"

She shrugs. "A few will come, but unless they are married into a winged court or traveling through, most will not bother with our social season in favor of their own. The invitations are more of a formality, especially on such short notice."

Right. Queen Plume mentioned something similar. I guess that makes sense. It's like traveling to Burbank to go to a theme park when you live in Orlando. I'm sure they all have their own events and seasons to worry about.

"The Gill People were in attendance when the Dragonfly Court hosted a few years ago, and I must admit, I wrongly assumed their webbed feet would affect their dancing abilities. Alas, we are too far inland to witness any of their skills."

Is she ... *blushing* right now? The rosy expression suggests she did more than just dance with someone she met at the Dragonfly Court. But I can't focus on an assumed love affair with a swamp person right now, not when I'm wrapping my head around the idea that there *really are* more than just humans and fae.

"So are all our unexplained creatures just..."

"Just *what*?" She throws down her quill to look at me, clearly losing her patience with all my questions.

"People from this world who can't get home?" A pang of sadness rests in my stomach, and Holly's face falls. I don't know what she was expecting me to ask, but it wasn't that.

"There are undoubtedly more like my brother," she says with a small nod that lacks any sympathy. "But he's back. I can't worry myself with anyone else."

"Right—no, of course," I reply, and the chatter between us runs thin.

The sun has shifted by the time I turn the giant pile into five slightly less giant piles.

"Adequate. Thank you." Holly briefly inspects my work before scribbling into the columns she'd been poring over for the last ten minutes.

"Anything else?" None of this is in my wheelhouse, but I managed to sort everything out. I can try to dive a little further into the greatly confusing world of Eclipsica treaties and finance if she'd like me to. As expected, Holly waves me away with a flick of her wrist.

"Run along. I'm sure my brother will be finished soon—"

A note on the piano rings quietly through the library, followed by a few more notes to a song muffled by the heavy wooden door.

As if possessed, Holly rises to her feet, wandering out into the hallway. Queen Plume stands in the doorway to the parlor, her jaw slack and eyes focused on the source of the sound.

Moth.

He does play beautifully. His long fingers stroke the keys while he hums, quietly focused and unaware of the growing audience that has been drawn to him.

It's a song I don't recognize, but by the way Queen Plume's eyes water, she does. Holly moves into the room, humming the tune quietly at first. When she starts to sing, I can't pick my jaw up off the floor. Her gentle voice is bright and youthful; it's a surprise that it's coming from Moth's thorny younger sister.

Moth's mouth hitches into a smile, but he doesn't join in, not right away at least. His eyes roll to the side as if searching the lost part of his memory for the words.

When they reach the second verse, the rich tone of his voice knocks me back; the low humming tone sends shivers through my body. Is there nothing that this man can't do?

Queen Plume joins in next. Her voice is not as polished. She sounds very much like a mom singing a lullaby in a sing-song tone, but it's as comforting as blanket tucking you in to sleep.

Still seemingly in a trance, she and Holly make their way to the piano bench.

Their voices blend like a choir until the song is done. Their laughter afterward is somehow even more beautiful. The feeling that I'm intruding on a family moment strikes me, and I begin to retreat to the large arched doorway.

Queen Plume looks up, extending her arms toward me. "Heather," she says. "There is room for you."

Holly says nothing but doesn't protest. I'm still not sure she likes me very much, but when Moth joins his mother in beckoning me forward, I don't hesitate.

"I am so happy you're home, my darling," Queen Plume says softly. "And you have brought such a wonderful bride."

His what now?

"Your bride?!" The words fly out of my mouth the minute Moth and I are alone. "Your bride?" I giggle, unsure which emotion to latch onto. Honestly, I don't know why I'm freaking out. Moth's mother calling me his bride causes a tingle to move all the way from my head to my toes.

But for it to just be assumed like this? I don't know—I don't know!

"Is that not where this is headed?"

"You haven't asked me! How can I be your bride when you haven't even asked?"

"Will you—"

"No, not like this." I shake my head. "People dream about their proposal. You can't just ask me because your mom—"

"That is *not* why."

"Is that what this ball at the end of the week is?! Am I planning our wedding, Moth?"

"Of course not."

"But she called me your 'bride'!"

"Do you not wish to be?"

"Yes—no—yes. Moth, don't ask me like this." I flush pink. He—I—*what is even happening*? I giggle again and fully hate myself for being both unspeakably angry and happy at the same time. What is with me?

Moth's deep laugh fills the room and fuels the negative side of my emotions.

"I was under the impression we wanted the same things." He chuckles, amused at my state of distress.

"We do!"

"So what, may I ask, is the problem?"

"I don't know!" I yell. Would I like to marry Moth? Yes, obviously, of course. He's everything I've ever wanted in a partner and more, but it's just that after the last few days... "It feels like there's so much we don't know about each other."

"Because of my past? My flame, I barely know of it..."

"And the future I guess too, right?" I look around at the ornate walls of the castle and think back to our shabby little cabin in the woods.

Holly was right. Our house is a shoebox compared to this place, and I don't know what that means for our future. How is he possibly going to go back? I don't know why I'm overthinking. I have my prince, a four-poster bed, and I just helped make arrangements for a freaking grand ball.

This could be home.

This life is the one he was born into. It's perfect, glamorous, and has a 24-hour staff. There's no sneaking around, no hiding in the shadows. After a lifetime of hiding, he deserves this.

It just doesn't feel right yet, but maybe it could? It took a while to adjust to living in the middle of the woods, and now I can't picture myself anywhere else. Maybe that's part of the problem: I've gotten too comfortable. I'm losing my sense of adventure.

"Do you ever feel like we skipped the big conversations?" I ask, flopping onto the giant bed with a thud. He follows my lead, turning so we're looking into each other's eyes.

"My favorite color is that of your eyes, my favorite sound is your laughter. You are my flame, my heart. What more do you wish to know?"

"Do you want kids?" I blurt out. If we're going to get married someday, that's probably something we should talk about. Even after my mom hounded us over the holidays, we haven't had a conversation about it.

There's a thoughtful pause before he answers. "Do you?"

"I don't want my answer to influence yours," I say honestly. The truth is, despite how strange my relationship can be with my mom, I always pictured raising a family *eventually*.

"I ... never thought it would be possible."

"Oh?" I ask, sitting up a little straighter.

"Not in the physical sense. It is just... who in the human world would look at me and think, 'Yes, that forest monster would make an excellent father'?" He laughs, but there's an edge to his tone; I think it might be the pain of thinking there was a future he wanted that he could never have. Except, now I'm here, and everything is different. As I've seen in the last few days, he's great with kids, but that doesn't mean he wants them.

We fall back into the bed, laying in silence for a long time. It's an effort to keep myself from blurting out every single passing thought I have. I'm not super great at patience or quiet, but I want to hear what he really thinks about this.

"Yes," he says quietly. "I would—at the right time—very much consider it."

"Me too," I answer, feeling a little relieved. "Not now, I mean. But yeah, I want to be a mom someday. I don't know if that means trying to get pregnant or adopting; there are so many kids who need a safe place, you know? But I'm not like ... in that headspace or whatever."

"We are in agreement then." He nods, his fingers lazily trailing down the line of my jaw. "I am also in no rush. Now, what else do you want to ask me?"

Where do you want to raise this hypothetical family?

I push the question down, forcing a smile. We just got here a few days ago. He's still recovering his memories and settling into everything. I don't want to put more pressure on the situation. Maybe just knowing that we both align with that small slice of the future is enough.

"Are there any special dances I need to know for the ball?" I ask. "I feel like I've stepped into some historical fantasy world—like if Jane Austen wrote *Lord of The Rings* or something."

His eyes crinkle into half-moons when he laughs, and I savor the relief on his face.

"Perhaps you can teach everyone the Cupid Shuffle you required me to learn during our Valentine's party with Clara and Rosie."

"I mean, *if* they're lucky." I snort, thinking of the four of us blasting the wedding reception hit after too many glasses of punch. I'm still not a big drinker, but it was Rosie's special recipe, and every cup tasted like straw-berry jam. Side effects included: teaching West Virginia's beloved cryptid how to do an organized dance and later, a monster hangover. Looking back, it was worth it.

"I love you, my flame."

"I love you too." I pull him closer, breathing in the familiar scent of autumn leaves and oak. As long as we're together, everything is going to be fine.

"Now about this proposal." He chuckles. I just about throw a pillow at him before I notice the sincerity in his eyes. "How do you imagine it happening?" He tilts his head, looking more owlish than human.

"First off, you have to be down on one knee."

A sly smile creeps around his handsome face.

"And if I would like to fall to both my knees?" he purrs, his claws trailing the length of my body.

"Not for our marriage proposal, but um, if you're suggesting what I think you are, that would be a definite *I do*..."

It doesn't take much more than that for Moth to be on his knees in front of me. Gripping his shoulders, I pull him onto the bed, laying myself out as if the silk sheets were a plate at the dining hall.

"Devour me." It's a plea and an order all wrapped in one, and Moth does not hesitate, pulling up multiple layers of tulle until my dress bunches at my knees and obscures my view of him.

I usually like to watch, but there's something in feeling his kiss slide up my leg never knowing where the next will land that's equally fun.

Left ankle

Right knee

The fleshy part of my thighs

A bite to my skin—a kiss that follows. I moan, unable to anticipate where he'll be next. Who needs a blindfold when you have a ballgown?

He traces the lines of my body, slipping my bloomers off and casting them aside.

"Do you realize how wanted you are?" he whispers, kissing, biting, and kissing again. "How seeing the light in your eyes has been a balm to my soul?"

A finger teases just the right spot, working in small rhythmic circles until my hands are clutching the bedsheets.

"I need more," I beg, reaching down to pull his hair, but under all the tulle, it's *impossible* to find him.

"And I intend to give you everything," he says like a vow in the night. His tongue replaces his fingers, and the sensation of pleasure changes. The rhythm is the same—slow and steady—but the warmth of his mouth sends shivers through me.

"I want you inside me," I gasp, attempting to flatten the dress so I can see him. Moth angles himself, his head appearing above a cloud of tulle. I can't help but laugh. He's dark and sexy, but also so, *so* cute.

"You may have whatever you wish," he whispers, climbing up. I take in the sight of him; Moth's bare chest is as pale as the moon sparkling with flecks of gold. Well-defined muscles glint with sweat in the dim light. His wings span out across the ceiling, and I gasp at the sight of my dark angel. His hips grind down onto mine, teasing and temping until he's pressed lightly against my entrance. I push my body up, enveloping as much of his cock as he allows before he meets me in the middle with a smooth thrust, peppering my shoulders with the same bites and kisses he showered over my legs.

With the rhythm of two dancers at the end of the night who lean into each beat of the music, our bodies intertwine.

"My flame," he whispers and it's honey sweet. His body leads our dance to a place only the two of us know.

I pull him down, his body heavy on mine, pressing me deep into the fluffy mattress.

Grabbing his jaw, our lips crash with a hungry desperation. This kiss is the only thing that will keep my lips from spilling the newfound secrets that sit at the edge of my tongue, waiting for just the right moment to escape.

Each time our bodies meet, the melody between us grows stronger and stronger. Finally, he screams out my name, and we collapse onto the pillows, my head spinning, and skin aching from the countless blissful bites.

God, he's good at this.

"So next time," he begins with a smile, "it is only one knee I am supposed to get down on?"

"I'll be honest." I cuddle in closer. "That was also great."

13.

I **CHOOSE A HIGH-COLLARED DRESS IN**
the morning. It bells out like the petals of a flower
at the top of my neck, which is not only adorable
but also perfectly hides the bite marks on my neck. They'll
be gone by the evening—#thankyouhealingpowers. But for
now, they remain a delicious reminder of last night.

Walking down the halls, I can't believe I got so worked
up about the idea of a surprise wedding. Not only could
my gown double as a wedding dress, but this place is
prettier than any wedding venue I've ever swooned over
on Pinterest. God, the flowers alone! If I attempted to get
even half of these arrangements back home, I'd blow my
entire savings. If I wasn't the sort of person who'd been
dreaming about their wedding since middle school, maybe
I'd consider a surprise elopement. But for all her drama,

it wouldn't be right without my Mom walking me down the aisle, and my favorite aunts and uncles in attendance.

Rosie and Clara would have to be there too—they've become such regulars in our lives, it wouldn't be right to have a big event without them. I pause, breathing a little heavier with each step, the joints in my arms and legs throbbing with signs of exhaustion I choose to ignore.

"There you are, my darling." Queen Plume opens her arms, beckoning me close. The surrounding guards stiffen at our embrace but say nothing "Are you sure you are up to the task today? You looked unwell last night in the drawing room."

"Ah yeah, no, I'm sorry. I'm ready to go today. No worries!"

"Of course." She claps her hands and the castle attendants scatter, some *literally* flying into the wind to complete today's tasks. "Then let us begin."

In the past week, I've consumed more gluten than in my entire life. I don't think it's affecting me. I mean, I'm extra tired, and extra foggy, and honestly uncomfortably bloated, but that could be just normal stress, right? Wouldn't it be rude not to accept the countless treats offered by nobility? I've always hated talking to chefs and asking questions about menus. When I was an influencer, it was often part of the job, but now? I'm in too deep and feel like it would be weird to say something.

Not to mention, everything tastes *so good.*

Queen Plume takes me around each event; when she introduces me, I feel like either her beloved future daughter-in-law, personal assistant, or a puppy who dares not stray too far—not that I'd want to. I'm getting used to being in the Moth Court, but that doesn't mean I'm getting used to the lords and ladies and their looks of disapproval. Holding my head high and standing in my place next to Queen Plume is hard when they're all sneering and whispering under their breath.

You're not worthy of him.

It's the subtext of every look and snide comment. The people have accepted Moth back into their world with open arms, but me? I'm no one here. And sure, I can keep proving myself to Queen Plume, but what good is that going to do if my public approval is at an all-time low? It's not just Moth's family I have to impress—it's an entire kingdom. I've seen how relationships in my realm work for royal families, and I have a feeling it's going to be a million times worse in Eclipsica. Whatever the equivalent to a gossip blog is here, I'm sure it's not pretty. But for Moth's sake, it's all going to be worth it.

Helping Queen Plume plan the ball is tiring, but no worse than planning one of my mom's elaborate holiday parties. Plus, it's brought us close enough for her to share some massive secrets with me. Secrets that are making my insides feel like an energy drink that's been shaken and will explode when the tab is pulled.

Just a few more days, I remind myself.

It's a long morning of overseeing décor, responding to letters, and selecting gowns for the next events. Everything for the queen is custom with her wings always covered in the same detailed fabrics. I've seen fellow ladies of the Court do the same, but why? I understand fashion doesn't always make sense *(hello, skinny jeans)* but why this style? I'd understand if it were a custom, religious practice, or cultural belief, but this seems purely aesthetic. Maybe it's just me being new here, but I can't get over how weighed down everyone looks. My wings are heavy enough as it is.

When Moth finds the two of us taste-testing cakes in the kitchen and attempts to steal me away, I'm surprised when his mother protests. I was sure I must be getting on her nerves with the countless questions I've had about ... well, everything. There's still so much about this world I don't know about, and god forbid I make a fool of myself at the grand ball.

"Heather has had a long day," Moth says, his arm encompassing my waist in a feeble attempt to pull me away from my newfound party planning duties.

"It's no big! Your mom and I have been having a blast," I say, trying to wave away his concerns. "Plus, I'm sure there are more embarrassing childhood stories I need to hear."

A gentle sigh leaves his lips. "With the gaps in my memory, I fear I will not be able to defend myself."

His mother laughs, laying her gold-freckled hand on his. "Perfect."

Oh, I like her.

She comes to life with each story. She laughs as she tells me about Moth and Holly running down the halls of the castle; they'd climb trees and perform skits and songs, him on the piano, of course. The two spent hours in the library—Moth scribbling in his journals and Holly building castles with old tomes about magic. Sometimes, Pepper and Ruby would be around, but honestly? It sounds like the two of them spent a lot of time together.

No wonder Holly fought so hard to get her older brother back. It sounds like she really looked up to him.

"They'd run all over the crystal caves, bringing me back little gemstones that had fallen astray." She smiles, and I can't help but wish I could see it all. They had a lively life in these halls together. As someone with no siblings, I find myself a little wistful while listening to their adventures.

"That's the second time I've heard about these caverns. I'm having a hard time picturing them. I don't think we really have anything like that back home."

"Then it would be my delight to show you." She squeezes my hand in a motherly gesture that makes me feel comfortable and homesick all at the same time.

"I will join you." Moth walks in step with the two of us. Queen Plume's smile does not waver, but I catch a flash of something I can't place in her eyes. Shouldn't she be excited to spend more time with her son?

"Very well," she murmurs, offering an arm to each of us. "Let us go."

14.

THE CRYSTAL CAVES ARE MORE hive-like than I expected. As we enter the massive opening of the cavern, tiny bee-like insects sparkle around us. They would be cute if they weren't so big and pokey.

"This is ... wow." And *wow* is an understatement.

Honeycomb structures climb to the tops of the caves with bright gold outlines and crystals glistening from every angle. God, I wish I had my camera. It would make for one hell of a Photo of the Day.

"You used to love exploring here with your sister. Oak and Lady Ruby would join you occasionally if my memory serves me." Queen Plume guides us through the entryway. "Lady Ruby more often. Oak spent even his earliest days apprenticing under his father—a painter he has long surpassed with his talents." A few workers harvesting crystals stop to bow as we pass them, but unlike a mining cave, the sounds that fill the space are the quiet buzzing of bees and conversation.

"I wish I could recall." Moth's usually confident posture is hunched while those ruby eyes I love search for something in the distance—a dot to connect, a spark of recollection—but even among the glitter and glitz of these caves, he continues to search.

"You may still," Queen Plume hums. I may be imagining things, but is there an edge to her voice?

"And if I do not?"

"There will be more memories to have." She tugs both of our hands so that Moth and I knock together lightly. "Something tells me they will be sweeter with you at each other's side."

My heart swells at the approval. Queen Plume is one of the only people Moth has even the foggiest memories of—the fact that she likes me isn't something I'm taking for granted. I'm glad all my work is paying off because honestly? I really do like her too.

We continue into the cavern. I'm mesmerized by the sheer size of the gem-encrusted honeycomb the farther on we go. The iridescent shapes create prisms of rainbow light while the impossibly fluffy bumble bees float from each cluster.

"What are the gems used for?"

"Everything from ornamentation to commerce. They are our biggest commodity and something I take great pride in." She angles her head, and her amethyst earrings twinkle like purple stars in the night.

"Is there a way to mimic this?"

"Pardon?"

"Oh! On the dance floor. You said you were trying to add a unique spin, and I love all the floral, but if we added a few crystals to the ceiling to replicate the sort of rainbow vibes we're getting in this cave, it could create a very cool atmosphere."

"An inspired idea, as always, Heather."

Beaming, I turn to Moth to see what he thinks but he's no longer at my side. He's wandered ahead and paces between two big gemstone hives with his brow furrowed.

"There isn't much to see beyond this cave." Queen Plume moves to lead the two of us away, but Moth doesn't budge. His eyes are unfocused and distant. Could he finally be remembering something from his past? I whirl to stand in front of him, eager to hear stories about what he, Ruby, and Oak got up to in these caves. Instead, his lips fall into a straight line.

"Moth?" I place my hand on his forearm, but he doesn't budge.

"I hid behind this cluster," Moth says slowly. "I was small... frightened.?" He looks at Queen Plume. "You found me, then you were frightened, too."

"You played here as a child."

"But this was not some childish game," he snaps. Moth's red eyes gleam as he stares at his mother, but it's sorrow that has a hold of him, not anger.

"No, it was not." Transfixed, the queen checks to see if there's anyone who could overhear.

"Moth, what's going on?" I ask, gently placing my hand on his bicep.

"The memory is hazy, and I... I fear I need a moment."

"Alone?"

"No." He pulls me close as we walk out of the cavern. "That is the last thing I desire."

"Okay, okay, I got you."

Queen Plume is stunned but doesn't block our way. I throw her a look that tries to convey an apology; it probably just looks like an awkward smile, but appearances aren't my priority right now. Moth is. I lead him past the glittering crystals back to the main path, and my powerful man trembles with every step.

"It's going to be okay," I tell him, fighting the urge to walk us straight up to the portal and back to our cozy slice of home in the woods. Another secret might be too much to digest.

"I love you," I say, but he's a million miles away.

And for the first time in forever, he doesn't say it back.

We take to the bedroom for the rest of the day and soak in the bathtub until our skin prunes before lying entangled beneath the covers.

I study the tension on his face, hoping to see his long lashes flutter shut; instead, his gaze remains unfocused on the ceiling. I stroke the length of his arm in a repetitive motion I can only hope is comforting. What memories are playing inside his head? I'm bursting at the seams to know, but when I open my mouth, it's to fill the space with idle chatter.

There's nothing I can do to help him. Useless, everything I'm doing is useless. He's lying here having an existential crisis, and I'm talking about the way the flowers arc with the curve of the windows and musing about what we should wear to the ball.

A pest. That's what any of my past relationships would have called me.

"Why can't you just give me space?"
"Can you be quiet for once?"

Moth's hand squeezes mine *hard.* The gesture pulls me away from my building anxiety and into his arms.

"Thank you." He squeezes my body to his, tucking my head beneath his chin. I exhale, leaning into this moment of security. Suddenly I'm safe and warm, snuggled as if I'm his own personal teddy bear.

"I literally haven't done anything," I whine. He's the one who should be taken care of right now, not me. But then he cups my chin with the tip of his finger and thumb, forcing me to meet his eyes.

"Yes." He strokes the line of my jaw with the pad of his thumb. "You have."

I want to believe him. I really do. But how can just being near him really be enough? There's got to be something else I can do to help.

It's nightfall when we finally pull ourselves out of bed. It's absolute torture not to ask Moth a million questions about his past. The fact that I haven't eaten motivates him to sneak down to the kitchens alongside me.

"If you want some time, I can go alone," I offer, but he shakes his head and follows me down the long hallways.

The bustling castle has stilled, and there's an eerie sort of beauty that each empty corridor holds.

Though devoid of activity, the kitchen is still warm, and the scent of freshly baked cake fills my nose. It reminds me of Saturdays at my mom's house, eating offcuts of cake while she tried to make something flawless enough to post. For all her flaws, she's never been a *handful of almonds* kind of mom. We'd have slices of "ugly cake" with creamer-sweetened coffee for breakfast while watching some terrible reality show. The scent of flour and vanilla in the air makes me ache for the simplicity of those imperfect moments. But there's no leftover cake here, so we'll have to find something else.

Moth moves through the pantry with the ease of someone who's been here a million times. I watch as he assembles an all-too-familiar plate of berries, chocolate, and sparkling elderflower water—our new favorite drink.

Moth raises a goblet to his lips, drinking deeply before letting his shoulders fall. This is the most relaxed I've seen him since we arrived. Was this a place he often escaped to when he lived here?

"You have been very patient." His deep voice is welcome after the long stretches of silence. *Patient.* I'm glad he thinks so because the mounting questions feel like they're going to burst from my lips at any moment. I tense my shoulders, plucking what looks like a golden strawberry off the tray.

Rocking back on my heels, I try to figure out just how to respond to him. I'm his girlfriend, and I want him to know he can come to me with anything, but I also don't want to be pushy. "You know you can share anything with me, right?" I begin. "What you remembered in the cavern— if you want to talk about it, you know I'll listen, right?"

"It is still hazy. I worry that if I speak now, I'll only be correcting myself in a day's time." He holds his head, squinting as if trying to see into the past. "But thank you, my flame. If you could continue to distract me..."

"Oooh, is that what I'm supposed to be doing?" I put my hands on my hips, leaning in close. I wrap my arms around him, relieved when his strong arms envelop me.

He loves me back.

He obviously loves me.

So, why am I still feeling so freaking sensitive that he didn't say it back earlier?

It's not like he isn't going through a million other things right now. Still, when he kisses the top of my head, I melt into him, savoring the feeling of being wanted and close.

"How should I distract you?"

"However you'd like."

Hmm, that's a challenge. Considering he seems to be remembering a traumatic event, seducing him doesn't feel like the right move. We've been cooped up in the castle ever since we got back from the caverns—maybe a change of scenery is what we need. "Then let's go on a date!"

"At this hour?"

"We could check out the night markets Oak mentioned. It might be nice to stretch our legs, get out of the castle for a little while—only if you're feeling up to it." I'm sure retail therapy does wonders for a troubled soul, no matter what realm you're in.

"Yes," he says abruptly. "I would like that."

WE SNEAK OUT OF THE CASTLE LIKE two bandits in the night. Donning heavy capes over our clothes, we creep down each corridor until we're out of the castle and into the fresh night air. The moon hangs low and pink in the sky, and stars seem larger than the ones back home. They shine in the same shade of gold that washes up on Moth's pale skin. We move through crowds, erupting in giggles. In this moment, we're not a girl in her early twenties and a long-lost faerie prince. We're just two people in love having a rebellious night on the town. By the wide smile on Moth's face, it's safe to say that this was the right call. We should have gotten out of the castle days ago.

The farther into town we walk, the more the air smells like fried food and honey. Music seeps into every crevice of the bustling market. I reach out and fireflies dance around my hand. The villages are dressed in simple garments in a variety of muted pastels, making our disguises stand out more than we had intended. A few curious glances are cast in our direction, but most folks—both monster and faerie alike—go about their business. Laughter mingles with the beautiful music played by a small band in the market's center.

"It is beautiful," Moth says, looking around. Together, we experience this place like tourists getting off a bus.

"What should we do first?"

He swoops his arms around me, and before I know it, we're dancing in the middle of the street. The fireflies swarm around us, casting a beautiful glow across Moth's face before dissipating into the crowd. Everyone dances, cheers, and *stares* at us.

"Do you think the capes are overkill?" I whisper, feeling more and more like a celebrity hiding behind an enormous hat and oversized sunglasses. "Everyone is looking at us."

"Are they?" He takes another turn around the makeshift dance floor. "I hadn't noticed."

I giggle with every whirl and spin, all of my worries drifting away until the song ends. Afterward, we stand on the outskirts of the dance floor, gazing into each other's eyes. It's only then that I see the sadness creeping back over him

"What next? Food stalls, shopping, or... oh, a tavern!" I squeal, pulling him toward a dimly lit building. In the human realm, I always wanted to check out a Renaissance Fair. But with event obligations, content to plan, and not knowing how to fit that particular aesthetic into my social media feed, it was never a priority.

"No freaking way," I whisper as we walk through the door. We're surrounded by boisterous laughter and pints of ale and honey mead. Vines twined with fairy lights are strung across the rough-hewn ceilings while rustic-looking meals are ushered to tables, leaving the heavenly scent of vegetables and herbs behind.

Oh shit, I did not bring any money.

"My flame," Moth whispers, patting a pouch at his hip with a toothy smile on his lips. "Tonight is my chance to finally pay you back for all our outings to the diner."

He does know I'm the one that's supposed to be cheering him up, right?

Despite myself, I smile back. I guess in a fantasy world, a tavern is the closest thing to a 24-hour diner, so it seems like a pretty fair trade. We work our way through the crowd, managing to snag two empty seats by the bar.

"Good evening." The barkeeper, a tall heavyset man with a dimpled smile and green dragonfly wings greets us. "What may I get you this evening?"

Moth and I exchange looks. We've mostly sipped tea and sparkling ciders at the castle, but what if that's like ordering a Manhattan at Denny's?

"Is there something you would recommend?" Moth asks, tilting his gaze curiously to the other patrons who drink from wooden steins, cheering with lively songs.

"The pear cider is popular," he muses, glancing between the two of us. "I could also recommend our mead, but it is quite strong."

I frown. How does this guy know I'm a lightweight?

"Two ciders would be lovely." I resign myself. As much as I'd like to cut loose, the last thing either Moth or I need is a hangover.

I nod, watching him hop into action and pour two frothy drinks from a tap. Then, he slides them across the wooden bar, and they stop perfectly in front of us.

"Have you been enjoying the season?" I ask. "I bet it's bringing in lots of tourists—er, travelers."

Moth stifles a laugh. I really need to stop talking to strangers.

"No, my lady." He dips into a bow, as if the question itself is a sign that, despite my *moth-ly* appearance, I'm not from here. An assumption he's right to have.

"Folks from the High Courts do not tend to visit our humble town."

I take a sip of my cider; the bright fruity notes have a sweet floral quality. It's one of the best drinks I've had since we arrived.

"Well, they are missing out!"

"Agreed," Moth says, raising his glass in the air. The barkeep gathers his own cup to cheers the two of us. Instead of going back to the other patrons, he lingers, obviously curious about what brings us to his tavern.

Doesn't anyone from the High Courts have a fun night on the town? Oak recommended the markets, but come to think of it, I don't think he's nobility, just an artist with close ties to the royal family. Maybe he has more freedom.

There must be a difference, but I'm too new here to know what it is.

"Tell me," the barkeeper asks, leaning closer to us, "do they serve tiny sandwiches and cakes all day?"

I nod. The way his eyes shine is so darn wistful. Glancing around the tavern, I wonder how many people here are allowed to attend the prestigious social events at the Court.

"What I would give to see it!"

"Well then," Moth brings his wooden stein to his lips, taking a deep drink, "you may come to the ball, of course— all of you!"

He gestures vaguely to the room filled with people—not that anyone is paying attention to our conversation in the midst of their own.

"And who are you to extend such an invitation?"

"Oh." Moth's downcast gaze is sheepish. In this light, his lashes somehow seem even longer than I remember. "I'm the prince."

The bar erupted into chaos as soon as Moth admitted who he was; we escaped after the third song to his glory was performed by a traveling musician. Though Moth doesn't do well under the spotlight, he was gracious the entire time, never letting the smile leave his face. Queen Plume told me all Moth ever wanted was to be king, and seeing him like this confirms it—he'd be great.

On our walk, we snack on lavender candy floss. Our bodies drift into a sort of spin as we pass more musicians, who he makes sure to tip with a few gems. Maybe it's all the cider, but he seems so alive and vibrant in this space.

As we stroll arm in arm, a shop window catches my eye. The mannequins are dressed in gorgeous, layered tulle skirts, covered in floral applique. The sleeves range from dainty baby's breath spaghetti straps to large poofy clouds. I've been lucky to have an entire wardrobe to pick from courtesy of Queen Plume and Holly, but there's something about the motion of these designs that's like a breeze on a spring day. Even in a window display, they spark something new and exciting. I sigh, letting myself drink in the sight of them. At my heart, I will always be a fashion blogger.

The dress in the center makes my heart ache. It's the same shade of light green as my wings with a giant billowing skirt and full tulle sleeves that look like something from an 80's wedding photo. Tiny silk flowers are dotted across the fabric, making the whole thing look like it's been freshly grown in a garden.

A gown fit for a princess.

"Any of those garments would be lucky to be draped over your skin." Moth's breath is hot on my neck. When I turn to face him, the tension has finally released from his shoulders, and the gleam is back in his ruby eyes. As he looks down at me, I flush from the tip of my head to my toes.

Here's the thing about being with someone like Moth. Just when I think we've hit our peak romantic stride, he gives me *that look,* and my chest flutters—just like the first time I saw him asleep on my couch, transformed into this beautiful man.

"I think you might have a crush on me or something," I say, keeping a bounce in my step as I twirl lightly around the square.

"Or something." He gathers my hand in his, pressing a kiss to my palm. "There does not seem to be a word strong enough to describe my feelings for you."

"Love?" I bat my lashes dramatically, fluttering off the ground just enough to swoop my arms around his neck.

"It does not even scratch the surface," Moth whispers, pressing his forehead to mine. "But nonetheless, I love you, my flame."

"I love you too."

In our world, Moth is something to be feared and hunted—but here? We can finally walk hand in hand down the street. I can't imagine how freeing that must be.

Sure, there's been something fun about flying around the shadows together, but how long has it been since he could just exist without hiding?

I squeeze his hand as the two of us walk through the market together. My head is fuzzy from the warm cider we drank at the tavern, and honestly, I don't hate it. I like this, I like being together with Moth.

I pull him close, cuddling his soft feathers as we walk.

"It's so good here..." I begin, pausing for a moment to watch the golden lightning bugs swarm around us, as if they're doing an intricate dance.

"I am glad you have enjoyed yourself."

"You have too, right?"

"Tonight has been just what I needed."

The warmth of his body, the smell of the street food—everything is warm and floral with notes of cinnamon. It is as if Eclipsica can't decide if it's spring or autumn. Two seasons I love mixed together in perfect harmony.

"What if we stayed?" I ask.

"What?"

"You wouldn't have to hide anymore."

"No... no I suppose I would not."

"And we could go on dates like this all the time." I loop my arm in his, pulling him down the street. "You had fun, didn't you? I mean, you said you had fun."

"I did." He catches my hand, placing a tender kiss on my wrist. "I've heard tell that craftsmen in the Butterfly Court specialize in glamours. If I were to procure one, it would not be out of the question to go on dates back home."

"But you'd be hiding again."

"No more than this." He smiles, pulling at his cape. I guess he does kind of have a point.

"Right?!" I launch the two of us into a skip. "Plus, it would be great for your memories, don't you think?"

Moth is suddenly dead weight on my arm, and the lack of momentum jerks me backward as if I've been trying to drag a statue down the street.

"Moth?"

"There are things I wish could stay forgotten."

"No, of course. I know whatever happened in those caves was bad, but—"

"No, you *do not* know."

"Right, because you haven't told me!" I half-shout, forgetting we're in public. "Which is fine! But also... how am I supposed to help if I don't know what's going on?"

"I do not need help." He raises an eyebrow. "You, on the other hand, seem to be running from something. Since we arrived, you have been jumping from task to task."

"Well, yeah, the whole grand ball thing—"

"—is not the source of your troubles."

Spoken like someone who's never planned an event in his life.

"Heather, my flower, my flame, I have taken notice." He moves toward me, and I bristle away from his touch, feeling that newly familiar tension at the base of my wings build until it has me shaking out my shoulders.

"Well stop. I'm good! Why are we talking about *me* all of a sudden?" I shout. Ugh I didn't mean to shout. Tonight, was going so well! The whole reason I wanted to go out was to cheer up Moth, and now I'm fighting with him.

"You have given me an impossible task."

"To trust me?"

"To *ignore* you."

"Oh my god." I bury my face in my hands. "You know that's not what I meant."

"I cannot gather your meaning regarding anything at the moment."

"I told you to stop worrying about me."

"And I told you—"

"Something dark and sexy and romantic, and like ... I get it, okay? You're super hot, and you don't want to talk about your problems, but that doesn't mean you need to project them onto me—*I'm fine*."

"Which is why you are yelling at me?"

"Yes! No! Ugh!" I stomp ahead, leaving him in the dust—for a moment, at least. He catches up with me within a few strides on those long, muscular legs—that I definitely didn't just ogle. "Just ignore me."

"As you desire."

Moth says nothing, so neither do I, and we walk in total silence back through the gates and down the long hall-ways. We silently change and get under the sheets. This isn't the sort of tension that makes us want to jump each other—quite the opposite. I'm as far on my side of the bed as possible, and I still wish I could create more distance.

I pretend to sleep, and like clockwork, Moth sneaks out of the room. This time, I creep down the dimly lit hall-ways until we reach the library. Because the heck if I'm not going to find out where he's been going all these nights. Pausing at the door, I listen for voices, hearing only the scratch of a quill on parchment.

He's hunched at the large desk, his dark curls pinned away from his face. Whatever he's writing is taking his whole focus. Transfixed on his beauty, I stand frozen in the doorway, noting the way the shade of the ribbon that holds back his hair matches his eyes. Moth writes as if the whole world has fallen away. With every stroke of the quill, the creases in his brow fade. I gulp. Is he angry journaling?

I stand in the hallway until my legs ache, and my curiosity gets the best of me.

"So, this is what you've been up to every night?" I say, breezing through the door. When it closes behind me, I expect something—anything—but a pin could drop in this room, and it would sound as loud as a firework.

"You didn't say a word to me all night—and now you're what?" I move toward the desk, and he snaps his notebook shut with a growl.

"I merely honored your request."

"You're *like* so stubborn." I stomp, giving him a sharp look. I cannot believe this. "*And* did you seriously just growl at me?"

"You normally like it when I growl," he muses thoughtfully—arrogantly. *Jerk.*

"That is not the vibe right now!"

"Heather—"

"You know what? *I'm* going to bed."

"Fine," he says through pursed lips.

"Fine!" I snap, puffing my wings out as I stomp back toward our room, secretly hoping he follows me so we can talk through whatever is going on.

But since he's so good at honoring my requests, he doesn't. And when he creeps back into the room after writing god knows what, he sleeps like a rock. *Rude.*

Meanwhile, I toss and turn, shifting my wings back and forth, unable to find a comfortable spot. The front of my ankles pop with each movement, but nothing gives the sore joints or my tense wings relief.

I rise into a sitting position, letting a giant sigh fall out of my mouth. I hate this.

As pissed at I am at Moth for uh... I don't even know anymore, I'd rather not disrupt his rest. His day sucked before our fight. The least I can do is let him sleep some of the stress off. Slinking out of bed, I gather up my pillow and blanket, my joints screaming with each step and the dizziness building at the base of my forehead.

I snuggle up on the chaise by the window. The glow of the night sky blazes through the curtains, creating a cool light across my skin. Except, when I catch myself in the mirror, I don't bask in the beauty of the moment.

The girl in my reflection is way too tired for that.

16.

"**A**RGH!" I GROAN, MY WEAPON ONCE again cast aside by Holly. I came back out here thinking maybe swinging a sword around would be good stress relief. But wow, no. After getting knocked on my back for the third time in the last fifteen minutes, I think I'll keep online shopping as my vice.

"Your moves are more reckless than last time," she says, unimpressed as usual.

"I think it's time for us to both call it—the sword girl life is not for me."

"I did not assume it would be," she says, giving me a pointed look. "And might I remind you, you're the one who called me out here."

Well, thanks for the encouragement.

"Perhaps next time your unexplained rage can be taken out on a embroidery," she says with a shrug. "Besides, when my brother is king, you will not be without guards for even a moment. This is not a skill you need to trouble yourself with—unless you find it amusing, and clearly you do not."

"But what about you?"

Her lips pick up into a grin. "I enjoy the dance." Holly pivots before gesturing for me to attack. Ugh, I *thought* we were done.

"That's the only reason?" I press, swinging—and missing—before dodging another one of her attacks. Geez, she's fast!

"I do not have a second form I can use—should there be a battle," she answers. The honesty—and her quick strike—knocks me off balance. "But even those who do sometimes choose not to fight. We have guarded Mother like a jewel for as long as I can remember."

I pause. Now that I think about it, even when Queen Plume sends her guards away, they're always just outside the door. The constant security might be comforting, but what about privacy? Knowing there's always someone outside our bedroom listening might put a damper on our sex life. Unless you're into that sort of thing, and the guards are too... "What if Moth doesn't *want* to be king?"

"Why bother ourselves with that idea?" Holly says, repositioning herself to fight.

She lazily comes at me like a hawk lunging at a small animal.

"Well," I raise my sword, thinking of how upset he was when I asked if he might want to stay here, "we built a life before coming here."

"Ha! That was not a life... merely an interlude." Holly spins backward, her short hair flipping. She looks cool but leaves herself completely open to my attack. I swing—

—and she blocks. *Ugh.*

"It's just ... being a king is a big change of pace," I shout through gritted teeth, swinging more sideways than intended.

"It is his birthright." She blocks my attack with ease. My legs stumble backward, the wooden sword once again cast aside. "You would deny him that?"

"Of course not," I huff, holding my knees, drawing in a few deep breaths. From what Queen Plume told me, Moth desperately wanted to be king in his life here, but goals change, and so do people. But then I think of that caring spark he showed at the dress shop and the tavern, the way his eyes lit up at the sight of the city—his city. He still wants this. It's there in his heart, and I need to support whatever path he chooses.

"Now, if you'll excuse me," Holly says, "I must take my leave. Some of us have bigger responsibilities than just planning a ball."

"Oh?" I move to match her stride "What are you—"

"Heather." She sighs, shaking her head. "How do I put this? Despite what my Mother would have you believe, there is not an invitation for you at every event this season. I am sorry."

"Oh..."

"I trust you'll find another way to occupy your time." Her eyes flick to the sword in my hand. "Preferably without stabbing yourself."

"Yeah hah—of course."

So much for blowing off steam. After that conversation, I feel worse than ever. It's not like Moth and I never fight. He leaves half-finished teacups on every surface of the house. I can never bother to pick up my shoes. We bicker about what we want to eat for dinner or binge watch on TV, but that's just normal couple stuff.

We haven't had a big fight since that time he tore apart the hunting lodge, and honestly, considering how everything turned out with Chris, his rampage was maybe not as uncalled for as I originally thought. Was I in the wrong this time too? I pick the sword up and heave it into a straw practice dummy, letting out a battle cry that sounds more like an angry housecat whose tail got stepped on than a warrior.

My joints ache, signaling me to rest—a call I've been ignoring for longer than I should. But how am I supposed to take a depressed nap when Moth is right there in the room?

"Well, if it isn't my new favorite faerie in Eclipsica," Ruby calls. She's dressed casually in a gold slip dress with sleeves that cascade to the ground and a neckline just off her shoulders. Oak walks beside her, a paintbrush tucked behind his ear and a splotch of paint across his cheeks.

"Working today?"

"Oh, this?" He spins, shoving his hands in his wide-leg trousers. "It's all a part of the look."

Finally, I've found my people.

I give him a nod of approval. I had a whole lens-free glasses phase in high school for the aesthetic. At least Oak actually paints, and the disheveled artist look works well for him. Ruby is the picture-perfect muse.

"What do you say you hang up that sword and join us for a shopping trip?" Ruby asks. *Thank god.* They are absolutely speaking my language. After that training session, and that massive fight, I could use a little retail therapy.

"Ugh, please!" I nod enthusiastically. "Where are we going?"

"The dressmaker." Ruby heaves a sigh, looping her arm in mine. "Though I don't know if she'll have time to fit us in."

"If I can't wear something new, I may take a break from this form and stretch my claws on the dancefloor," Oak says, taking my other arm with a wicked grin. I wonder what he looks like transformed.

"I suppose that is an option, but I would rather be draped in chiffon," Ruby muses, tilting her head to each side while she ponders.

"Can't you do both?" I've yet to see anyone in their monster form wearing anything intricate... or anything at all, really. My cheeks redden at the realization that naked fae have surrounded me almost 24/7, not that it's all that different from being back at home with Moth—but like, he's *my* naked fae.

"Then no one would see my gorgeous red feathers." She sticks her tongue out, and dear god, if my heart wasn't taken—and she wasn't married with kids! No, no... as mad as I am at Moth, I don't actually want anyone else, even if this entire realm is the definition of Bi Panic.

We walk together, getting more than our fair share of looks on our way to the dress shop. Unlike the night markets, it's on what seems like a ritzier side of town, closer to the castle, with a light floral scent in the street.

The pair lead me to a different dress shop than the one Moth and I passed yesterday. It's sleek white with a splattering of pink blooms that arch around the doorway. Fabric is neatly displayed in rows, and as we suspected, the shop is busting at the seams with customers. Oak and Ruby search the store for the seamstress while I busy myself looking at the displays of buttons and ribbons.

"What an interesting antique you are wearing," a voice says. I turn and find two familiar red-headed faeries with butterfly wings. Their appearance scratches at my hazy memory in the most annoying way, but no matter how hard I try, I can't seem to place the two ginger twins in front of me. I know I've met them somewhere—I just don't know where.

"A hand-me-down, no doubt."

"Some friendly advice: you may find the prices in this shop out of reach," the first sneers.

"And the gowns are far too fine for a night at the tavern," the second joins in, holding a fan in front of her lips. Though, it doesn't hide her laughter or smug grin.

"We're actually shopping for the grand ball," I say as I continue to browse, not bothering to get defensive or give either of them my full attention.

Ignore the trolls, Heather. Ignore the trolls.

"So, it's true. They're just letting anyone in." The sisters speak in unison, bursting into giggles as they exchange glances. To say that these two are identical with matching dresses and hairstyles and voices that harmonize when they speak feels like I'm seeing double.

"The prince thought..." I bite my tongue. So much for not letting them get a rise out of me. Besides, after last night, I'm not sure I'm the right person to presume Moth's thoughts at all.

They laugh, covering their mouths with fans as if the ruffly features do anything to muffle the sound.

"As if you could speak for the prince," one says as the pair circles, more wolflike than butterfly. "Or catch his eye in that." They continue to speak, deliberately trading places every other sentence making it hard to keep track of the conversation, and I'm sure they're messing with me on purpose.

"Yes, well," I clasp my hands together, "I like this old dress. Trends may come and go, but style will always set you apart from the crowd."

"What is that about your dress?" Oak sidles up, sliding his arm around my shoulder. For some reason, my body stiffens under his touch. It's different from the way he and Ruby playfully pulled me along—he's being protective. The last time anyone other than Moth acted this way, they shot me by accident. But Oak's vibe is not possessive. His fingers trace the sleeves of my shoulder like an artist at work until he's spun me around, taking in each detail of the applique.

"Forgive me, but I cannot stop staring. I've seen it somewhere."

"Seasons ago, certainly." The sisters once again harmonize their insults. Under my new friend's focus, the pair begin to fade into the background.

"Yes, but that is not why it plagues me." Oak clutches his chest dramatically before recognition meets his eyes.

"Did Queen Plume not wear it for one of the portraits your father painted?" Ruby pipes up, joining us.

"Oh, I believe she did!" Oak nods, keeping his arm tight on my shoulder. Ruby laces her hand in mine, swinging our arms to and fro.

"Lunch after this, don't you think?" she asks. It's not flirtation—no, I've heard her use this tone with her children. She's trying to pull me back to the present moment.

"Oh, absolutely. Did you want to do something out?" I ask ignoring the prying eyes of our audience.

"I think perhaps back at the palace," Oak says with a small nudge. *Ah,* I see what's going on here. These casual little gestures are a show of my place in this world's inner circle. At the realization, I relax into the friendly choreography.

"How did you come to be in possession of such a garment?" one of the twins asks, narrowing her eyes as though trying to place the three of us. For two beings so in touch with high society, it's strange they haven't seen me following Queen Plume around like a lost puppy. Huh, maybe they're not as well-to-do as they're leading me to believe.

"Oh, did I not say?" I twirl a lock of my hair between my fingers. "It's a part of her personal collection. My bags got lost on the way here, and Queen Plume and Princess Holly have been good enough to dress me in their finest."

"...and you are?"

"Did you not realize?" Oak cracks a smile. "This is the fair fae who stole the affections of our dear prince."

"You—"

"She's that same odd fae from the picnic," the first says, and it clicks together—these are those two mean girls who were trying to get to Moth through me. Rebecca and Annabella or something? God, of course I would run into them today. But Ruby and Oak have me in a protective friendship sandwich, and honestly, I couldn't care less what they think. Though, I wouldn't mind a little revenge.

"I'm sorry," I say, biting back a smile. "I don't believe we've met before. I *never* forget a face." They gape, and I savor the bitter shock on both of their faces. "But I'll be glad to tell the prince what an odd choice you think he made for a partner."

"Oh. Oh my lady, you must know that we—"

"—are so terribly sorry—"

"We did not realize—"

"Please, take our place in line. It's only right."

"Oh, it's no big. In fact, we're going to hit up another dress shop after this, but you probably wouldn't have heard of it—too antique for your taste. We'll see you at the ball?"

I turn on my heel and leave, not waiting for a response.

"As much as I love a good exit, you know that was the only suitable tailor," Oak huffs, untangling himself from me to cross his arms.

"Relax," I say, leading us down the path to the night market. "I know exactly where to go!"

I lead Oak and Ruby to the shop downtown that Moth and I discovered. To my disappointment, the dress from the window is gone, replaced with an equally stunning—but different—gown. Unlike the stuffy shop we fled from, this place has the distinct feeling of walking into someone's home.

Black tea and honey mingle in the air alongside the scent of lavender and fresh-baked cookies; loose ribbon and silk hang from the ceiling like fresh garland the morning of a birthday party. A tall woman with curled blonde hair and red lips sits behind a sewing machine near the back of the shop. She's beautiful with long lashes and a strong nose and dragonfly wings adorn her back.

"Welcome!" The woman stands to a height that rivals even Moth. Taking in the sight of the three of us, her smile is as easy as if she were welcoming a group of old friends back home after a long time away. She moves to a modest counter with a register and a display of home-made confections.

"Hi! Is it appointment only? Sorry if we're interrupting," I bumble, glancing around the shop to see if the green dress is anywhere on display.

"Ah, first time in? Well, welcome!" Her rich voice has a musicality that instantly sets me at ease. "I'm Widow. This is my little slice of paradise."

"Aw, I love that." The idea of being surrounded by beautiful dresses and treats definitely sounds like paradise to me. "I'm Heather, this is Ruby—er—*Lady* Ruby and Oak."

"Just Ruby is fine," Ruby says, extending her hand. I cringe at myself, hoping she wasn't trying to be low key. This whole week I've been trying to wrap my head around status and titles and I'd hate to upset anyone without meaning to. Oak offers a quick greeting. I can't help but notice the soft blush on his cheeks when Widow brings his hands to her lips in a kiss instead of just a handshake.

#swoon

"There was a dress in the window—a gorgeous sort of light moss green. Do you still have it anywhere?" I ask. I'm not trying to kill the moment, but I really, *really* want that dress.

"I'm sorry." Widow's red-painted lips dip into a frown. "Someone bought that one this morning—it's been through alterations and everything." Her warm hands clasp mine as her face lights up with the stunning smile of a saleswoman. "But I'm sure I have just the thing for you."

And she does—*multiple* things, in fact. But none of them give me the same rush as that gorgeous gown I caught a glimpse of last night. But they're pretty, fit like a glove, and conveniently go on the castle's tab, so two are wrapped in tissue paper and tied up with ribbons while Oak and Ruby make their choices.

Within the hour, the three of us have had a full-on shopping montage. Exhausted, we sit in a small pillow-filled nook at the front of the shop, a large round window at our backs. With cups of tea and homemade cookies, I yearn for Rosie and Clara's farmhouse with a humble plate in front of us.

I pluck a cookie from the plate, and the crumbly texture combined with the overwhelming flavor of butter and what tastes like lemon and basil is surprisingly addictive. I'll have to ask for the recipe. Clara would love these.

It's only been a few days, and I miss them. Have I ever had friends I miss like this?

"How dare you discover such a hidden gem in less than a weeks' time," Oak grumbles. "I cannot believe I've passed this place without notice for years." To be fair, it is nestled in a fairly secluded little alcove off the main path. Foot traffic must be hard to come by, which explains why we have the entire shop to ourselves.

"I am maddened by how many times I've suffered shopping elsewhere when I could have been enjoying a visit here," Ruby says, taking a sip of her tea and letting out a relaxed sigh.

"Truly. How devious of you, Heather, to be a world away from us." Oak puts his arm around me and pulls our shoulders together. Normally, I'd be worried about him getting the wrong idea, but with the glances he keeps stealing at Widow, I am *so* not worried.

"May it never happen again." Ruby raises her cup and Oak lifts his. I hesitate for a moment, unsure if I can allow myself to cheer to that. As it stands now, we're only going to be here for two more days, but I don't want to put a damper on the moment.

"Cheers." I clink my cup to theirs. It's not lost on me how strange it is that the two friends I have managed to make have both dated my boyfriend, but whatever jealousy I felt has settled. Not only do I genuinely like these two, but they might be the only people that can help me fill in the gaps about what his life was like before—and why he was so upset when I suggested staying.

"You appear to have gotten your footing since earlier this week."

"I'll say. Until Oak told me, I had no idea you also suffered from memory loss," Ruby says. Her voice drops to a whisper as she moves just a little closer.

"Oh no." I bite my bottom lip. I like Ruby and Oak, but the whole "I'm from the human realm" thing isn't something I should let slip in the middle of a dress shop. "I'm getting used to things, for sure, but honestly, I feel like I'm faking it ninety percent of the time."

"Aren't we all?" Ruby lets out a sigh, her shoulders relaxing back into her seat. "The season is always exciting."

"And so dreamy," Oak whispers, very obviously starring at Widow who is back to work behind the sewing machine, taking in the lavender suit coat he's picked out.

"It honestly does feel like a dream." I swallow hard. Even with this fairytale setting, Moth and I still got into the biggest fight we've ever had since we started dating.

"Ah, yes." Ruby's smile becomes just a little sad. "'This world might seem like a paradise," she begins, "but it has threats, the same as any. It would be wise to be careful."

"Mm." Oak nods. "We would hate for you to do something unthinkable—like show up for the ball in something *'so last season.'*"

The two burst into laughter while I struggle to shake the irritation with the twins off.

"What is their deal, by the way?" I ask. "They seem like stock character bullies from a teen movie."

They blink at me for a moment, and I freeze. Crap, I need to stay guarded for a little longer. Comments like that will not do much to keep my secret safe.

"Like many, they are fighting for their place in high society and, might I add, not doing a very good job. Befriending you as an attempt to rise to the top would be much better than making you an enemy," Oak says. I'm glad he was able to parse my meaning.

"Is that what you're doing?" I ask.

"As if I need to rise any higher," he says with a sideways smile. "Contrary to popular belief, I live to paint the portraits in the grand hall, not to be depicted in one."

The portraits... Moth's innocent eyes and his father's cold stare come to the forefront of my mind. If anyone is going to tell me what it was really like growing up with him, it would be these two.

"So ... Moth, what was he like here?" I ask, even though I probably shouldn't.

Hesitating, they exchange looks.

"When he was young?" I clarify. "Look, there's only one person here who hasn't dated the Crown Prince of Eclipsica." I point at Widow. Without any further prompting, the woman halts her sewing and moves to take a seat next to Oak.

"Oh, hi," I greet her. Widow seems great, but this wasn't a conversation I was expecting to have with anyone outside of my boyfriend's exes.

"I suppose I can give my testimony," she says. Dear Lord, he has dated everyone.

"Fine." I grab my teacup and take a large sip. "Might as well spill the tea."

"Why would we spill—" Ruby begins, but a wild sweep of Widow's arms cuts her off.

"Please contain yourself. The sofa is new," she scolds, and you know what? Maybe that's enough talking for me today.

"I believe the lady would like us to gossip about her royal lover," Oak says, raising his own cup to his lips. A knowing look sharpens his gaze as our eyes lock, causing me to wonder if he has either traveled beyond the realm or is just very good at context.

"Curious, very compassionate, a little bossy, but what tiny prince isn't?" Oak shrugs before snagging another cookie from the tray. His hand brushes Widow's as she reaches to do the same, and I catch the pair blushing at each other. I ship this.

"He was always kind, though. I remember he'd always save me my favorite tarts if I was late for tea." Ruby smiles. It may not be romantic love, but the affection for Moth is still there. Shockingly, it puts me at ease instead of sparking my jealousy. There are people who care about him.

"I guess his sweet tooth is something that hasn't changed." I laugh.

"Definitely not." Ruby laughs. "Though it might have gotten worse."

"What about when he was older...?"

"Angry," Oak blurts out, taking another long sip of tea. "Oak!"

"What? He was! All the time." Oak huffs, crossing his arms in front of his chest.

"Not all the time..." Widow pipes in, her Adam's apple bopping as she taps her fingers on the handle of the teacup she's claimed. "That sounds like the prince was stomping around the castle barking orders. He wasn't like that, not with me at least."

"Not with any of us," Oak agrees, not bothering to set his cup down on its saucer.

"A silent rage. I suppose I have to admit that," Ruby concedes. "Though he was never angry at us."

"Then at who?"

"Everyone else."

I guess even Moth isn't immune to a teenage emo phase. I wonder what the equivalent to blasting angsty music in your room is here? I can't imagine the harp, or the lute, have the same effect as an old punk record.

"He consumed himself with the idea of being a king who made change," Ruby says. "All the old traditions, the hunting, the hierarchy—he wanted to turn it all on its head."

"He would have been a radical king." Widow nods. "He never let things like status come between his feelings."

"Is that bad?"

"Well, at least King Atlas knew how to play the game." Ruby drums her fingertips on the edge of her mug. Ugh, the evil uncle again; he really does have a hold on the people who live here.

"The kingdom really loved him, didn't they?"

"They did. He was fair and kind, but firm." Ruby nods. "He really wanted what was best everyone in the kingdom, which made it even more shocking when he left."

"And Moth's father?" I press, still trying to put the missing pieces of this world and family together in my head.

Oak and Ruby exchange looks, frowns appearing on each of their faces. Widow takes the moment to excuse herself, and the hum of her sewing machine cushions the growing silence.

Queen Plume had a hard time talking about him too. He must really be missed.

"How do you think you'll style your hair for the ball?" Ruby changes the subject after the long pause. "With your dress, I'd suggest something with waves, and perhaps flowers strewn through it."

"Oooh, yeah I like that."

We fill the conversation with small talk about different ways to adorn ourselves. Widow pipes in now and then, upselling bows, cufflinks, and hair clips to go along with our new ensembles. Body shimmer seems to be popular, and I think of the way Moth's skin shines with natural gold freckles. On the way home, I pick up a jar in silver for myself with plans to use it as a highlight on my nose and cheeks.

Once through the castle walls, we run into Pepper—who, as usual, has their hands full. The kids circle around Ruby, who shows the little cuties what she picked up at the market.

"Unfortunately, I'd better get going," I say, a pang of sadness radiating through my chest at the thought of having to get back to normal—whatever normal is these days.

"You are welcome to join us for dinner," Ruby offers, scooping a toddler up in her arms and planting a kiss on her squishy cheek.

"It will be absolute chaos," Pepper adds with a nod.

"In all the best ways."

"Food will be thrown."

"As appreciation for the fine meal," Ruby notes seriously.

"Of course." Pepper stiffens in mock formality before the pair share a private laugh.

"Okay, as much as I hate to say no to a good time, I really should get back to the castle. There's a big fancy dinner tonight with a whole bunch of nobles who are in town for the ball, and I don't want to throw Moth into their clutches alone." As much as he might deserve it.

"You are better than me. I always found it cute to watch him squirm."

"Does his eye still twitch when he's in the spotlight?" Oak asks.

"Or that vein on his forehead." Ruby laughs.

"Oh, I uh–"

"We have made you uncomfortable." Ruby frowns. "Oh, I'm sorry. I know it must be strange—"

"No, no no it's not that."

It's just I have honestly never noticed either of those things. I love his little crooked smile, and the way he narrows his eyes and clicks his claws across the table. Wouldn't I have seen if he was vainy or twitchy? Maybe we're not as close as I thought. Couples are supposed to notice that kind of thing about each other.

"Honestly, it would have been nice to chat with one person who hasn't had a love affair with my boyfriend," I joke in a low voice for the grownups only. Pepper visibly flushes.

"Oh my god—you too?"

"A summertime fling."

There seem to be a lot of those.

"Well, at least we all have something in common. I'll see you later, okay?" I laugh it off, giving them all a beaming smile—which, if their expressions are any indication, they're not buying. "Enjoy the imminent food fight."

"We get to play food fight?" a tiny voice pipes up. Pepper's eyes widen in my direction, as if to say *thanks a lot.*

Sorry, I lip, hurrying away before I accidentally cause any more damage. With every step, I want to turn around and join their chaos, but instead, I'll have to face up to my own. I can't keep avoiding Moth forever.

I **THOUGHT DINNER WITH JUST THE** four of us was fancy.

But this? Ooof.

We sit at a long and dramatic dining table with a spread I haven't seen the likes of since Christmas dinner at my mom's house. Strings of ivy and glowing tea lights in pink-tinted glasses act as a table runner. To my delight, an array of vegetable dishes look just as pretty as they are delicious.

Moth is late, which isn't like him. Maybe sulking off this morning without talking was a worse idea than I thought.

"How lucky I am to be seated next to such a beauty." A man with dark red hair and a cutting smile snatches up my hand. He's different than the other nobles: no wings sprout from his back, his skin is as pale as a ghost, and instead of a row of fangs, the only teeth that are sharp are his canines.

Holy shit, it's a vampire.

"King Magnus, you were so good to join us," Queen Plume interjects, a subtle reminder of the man's name and title.

The vampire king.

He raises my hand to his lips, poised to kiss my wrist, and I freeze, unsure how to stop the impending affection. He's not going to bite me, is he? It's not that biting is something I'm not into. It's just only when a certain cryptid is the one sinking his teeth in—and *not* drinking my blood.

"And just who might you be?" King Magnus asks, our eyes meeting for only a moment while my hand moves closer to his lips, seemingly in slow motion.

The door swings open, causing the king to freeze mid-action. My cheeks flush pink at the sight of Moth, fully transformed—his strong shoulders pulled back, his dark wings trailing behind him like a cape. I gape as he strides into the room as if there's nothing unusual about his appearance. Like me, every noble struggles to pick their jaws off the floor. I don't blame them. No matter what skin he's in, he is predictably the most appetizing thing at this table.

Though, I'm not sure those from the Butterfly Court would agree as they openly gawk. I tense, fighting the urge to dive right into his firm chest and feel his cool feathers on my skin.

"Mine." Moth snatches my hand, which had been inching dangerously close to the vampire's lips. The low boom of his voice sends tingles down my spine. There's a slight baring of his fangs from beneath his lips when Moth speaks, and *dear god,* I hope this isn't going to start a war or something. It's not an uncommon fantasy for two people to be fighting over someone—but not when there's diplomacy at stake! I have no idea what the Moth Court's standing is with the vampires. In fact, I don't know anything about them at all. But when Moth tenderly raises my hand to his lips, it distracts me from anything else.

"Other than that, I'm Heather. Hi."

"Heather..." King Magnus says. His eyebrow raises as he stares at me, a smile still at the edge of his lips. "An unusual name."

Not really, I want to say, but here among the Oaks, Hollys, and Plumes, I suppose it is.

"And Death, we never had the pleasure of meeting."

"He goes by the name of Moth now," Queen Plume states.

"Oh, my sincerest apologies." The king stands to bow. To his credit, he looks sincere. "Prince Moth, it is good to make your acquaintance."

Moth does not bow back—in his hulking form, I'm not even sure what such a refined gesture would look like. I manage to lightly nudge at his side from my seated position to remind him there's a game to play, but he doesn't oblige.

Great.

"How ... understated." Lady Webworm—a noblewoman with sleek silver hair and grey antennae—stares, her jaw spilled open. Transformation like this isn't in fashion, and no one seems to know where to look, so she gawks shamelessly with a hunger in her eyes I am no stranger to.

"That is the general consensus," Holly mutters with a grimace she doesn't bother to hide.

"And how did you come to meet the prince?" King Magnus asks, straightening his posture. In appearance, he seems a similar age to Moth—mid- to late-twenties, and while not as devastatingly handsome, he's good-looking with violet eyes, and long red hair that he wears pulled away from his face.

"Oh, we just fell into each other's lives," I say, casually eating something that looks kind of like a sliced apple but tastes like the lovechild of a peach and strawberry. I close my eyes, hoping the sweetness of the fruit will distract me from the awkward energy building in this dining room. One of my top tips after all my years of networking events? People like this love talking about themselves.

"And you?" I beam, turning to the rest of the table as an attempt to get the attention off Moth. "I'd love to hear more about the lovely company I'm dining with this evening."

Lady Webworm is excited to tell us about the prosperous gemstone mines this season. She and her friends carry the entire conversation like a group recording a podcast for the first time; as much as I want to piece together what life looks like outside the castle walls, I can't follow anything except that crystal seems to be a really big deal here.

"Real genuine crystal, unlike what the villagers are hawking at the night markets." Lady Webworm scoffs—and god it's hard not to roll my eyes at how pretentious she sounds.

"I have yet to have anything counterfeit reported," Holly responds coolly. "Just because they are crafting cheaper options to adorn themselves with does not mean they are doing anything wrong."

"Totally," I pipe in when I know I shouldn't. "I mean, I love costume jewelry, and the markets are honestly the cutest. Some friends and I went out shopping today, and may I just say, Your Highness, the village is lovely." I hope the compliment will lighten the mood.

"A lady like you deserves the finest jewels." The vampire king—what's his name?—says, and *no thank you*. Oh, absolutely not. I have enough going on without king of the vampires flirting with me. But I smile politely before stealing a glance at Moth.

"I prefer a field of flowers—"

From across the dinner table, he catches my eye for just a moment. That's all it takes for my heart to beat out of my chest; even in this form, I just can't take my eyes off of him. More than that, I can't focus on all the bends and flows of the conversation.

"Even so, you would never catch someone wearing such a thing in these grand halls..." Lady Webworm scoffs, inching closer to Moth. "Don't you agree, my prince?"

"Considering most villagers will be present, you may wish to rethink that statement." Moth's deep voice rumbles through the dining room, causing everyone to glance in his direction.

"They will?" Queen Plume's eyes widen for a moment before her expression goes blank.

Shit. Shit. Shit. No one told the queen.

"Oh yeah, I thought I mentioned that. We kind of invited the entire village," I say, giving Queen Plume an apologetic smile. Except it feels like I might as well be flashing her a cheeky grin and saying "sorry, not sorry" by the worry creasing her brow.

"I would expect nothing less of my son." Queen Plume exhales with the energy of a mother who just discovered their child came home with another snack in their pocket— weary, yet unsurprised. I wonder if this is the radical future king behavior Oak and Ruby were talking about. "We will discuss further arrangements after dinner."

"Uh, the villagers are all very excited."

After that huge conversational flub, I do my best to channel my inner influencer and bullshit my way through the night. But like everyone keeps reminding me, I know so little about this world, and it's hard to keep up. Not only that, but it's also taking all of my power to remember what comes out of my mouth. The conversation is hazy at best, but the smiles and nods from around the table and periodic bursts of laughter are the confirmation I need that I'm keeping up alright, even if I feel more lost than ever.

Just when I'm worried I'm making an absolute fool of myself, Queen Plume gives me a nod of approval, which is exactly what I need to keep my focus.

Two more days, I remind myself. I just need to power through for two more days, then I can take the most epic nap of my life.

Dinner moves at a snail's pace, and when we are excused and away from the guests, Holly's laugh catches me by surprise. "Well, you've certainly given Lady Webworm a blow to the ego."

"*Who?*" I ask, unable to place which name belongs to which noble. The whole conversation feels like a puzzle that's been tossed on the floor.

"A cutting reminder that not all pain comes from a sword."

"Something tells me she'll survive."

"Yes, how very unfortunate for us."

Are we ... vibing right now? Huh, well, Mom always says the best way to make friends is to have a common enemy. Is it toxic? Yes. But if it scores me a few points with Holly, maybe that's okay. A little mean girl behavior is worth a few more points with her.

"To the parlor?" she asks, and without looking back at Moth, I follow her lead.

"It is not that they cannot come. Of course we can accommodate the entire village, but we shall need more food, refreshments..." Queen Plume says. Wow, maybe Moth should have thought before adding hundreds of people to the guest list, for his poor mother's sake. Unbothered, he sits at the piano, and if we weren't still fighting, I'd be taken by how cute he looks hulking over the instrument in his monstrous form—but that's something I'm obviously not paying attention to.

"If we are inviting the village, the servants should also be able to attend," Holly says with unexpected softness toward the people who work here.

"But then how will we manage to keep the party going? Even with the food out on platters, it will have to be replenished." The queen pinches the bridge of her nose in a gesture that reminds me even more of Moth—who, besides the subtle eye contact at dinner and that jealousy-fueled hand kiss, has barely spared me a glance since our fight yesterday. "Again, this is not a 'no,' my darlings. I just cannot see how to manage it."

"Magic?" I suggest with an unsure uptick of my voice.

"That is not how magic works," Holly snorts.

"Well, since no one has really explained it to me, I'm taking my best guess over here!"

"Children, please save your squabbles for after we have a solution," the queen orders. The two of us fall silent, like toddlers fighting over a toy at daycare.

"I mean, you do have a lot of nobility, right? No offense, but if Lord and Lady Webworm are any sort of indication, they seem a little..."

"Unbearable," Holly says with a roll of her eyes that makes her look more like an overdramatic teenager than captain of the guard.

"I was going to say 'out of touch' but, honestly? Yeah, *totally unbearable*."

"I fail to see how they will help the situation," Queen Plume says, her eyes closed tight as she pinches the bridge of her nose.

"Well, hear me out: I think everyone should work in the service industry once in their life. Even I did a summer as a barista in high school, and yeah, it was mostly for the cute barista aesthetic and to do cute little doodles on mugs. And yes, I quit after a customer screamed at me for not making his cappuccino dry enough. Coffee is supposed to be wet, right? You should *not* yell at people for that."

They have *no idea* what I'm talking about—and ugh, I can *feel* Moth's judgy gaze as I ramble.

"Okay! Summing all that up, what I'm trying to say is maybe they could use a little empathy. They could do shifts during the ball," I spit out, the pressure in my head building. Ugh, I might have to finally admit to myself that the choices I've made this week are causing the telltale signs of a flare up.

"Heather, it's a wonderful idea, but how do you suppose we get them to agree?"

"There are plenty of soldiers who signed up, as Heather said, for *aesthetic* purposes. They are of noble birth and do not show up for training. I would be happy to make them a part of the list." Holly beams at the thought of potential vengeance. It's a great idea and a reminder not to get any further on her bad side.

"But I would like everyone to come." Holly frowns, stabbing her needle into her embroidery hoop. "Even my soldiers who are only enrolled to shine their armor."

"Hmm," I pause, trying to think of a solution. My thoughts are like wading through grape jelly, but maybe...

"I once worked a table at an event that had everyone do four-hour shifts, so we could all still enjoy the weekend. Blocking out time like that so that everyone could enjoy the ball would be helpful," I muse, remembering the long weekend filled with makeup samples and florescent lights.

"That is ... very sound." Queen Plume nods. "Yes, yes, I believe that would work."

"The palace kitchens may overwork themselves if they provide food for the entire village," Holly chimes in, stabbing violently into her embroidery.

"Oh, that is a problem." I shrink, unsure if this is how Holly relaxes or if I'm being directly threatened. "What if we brought in some stalls from the night market?" I suggest, thinking about the candy floss and pastries Moth and I shared on our walk. "If they organize a shift schedule, they can enjoy the festivities as well."

"Do you have any suggestions on how to accomplish this?"

"Oh..." I let out an exhale. One more thing on my plate, just what I needed.

"I will draw up some contracts and see if they would be willing." Holly shakes her head as if sorry she asked.

"Moth," I begin, and when he looks up, the air goes still between us. It's the first time I've said his name all day, and with the blank look he's giving me, I'm not sure he wanted to hear it. "Uh, is there anything you think we should add?"

"The three of you seem to have covered it all while I have languished away on these keys," he says in the usual melodic way, giving me no hint at what his true thoughts are. I wouldn't mind just a little of praise.

"Your languishing has been very inspiring!" Queen Plume says with a sharp nod of her head.

"It is good to hear you play again," Holly agrees, the dewy spark of admiration returning to her eyes.

Sprout barks in agreement, not bothering to pick his head up from its place near Moth's feet. He's been camping out there since we sat down.

The conversation picks up before I can chime in, and I'm glad. As much as I would love to swallow my pride and compliment him, seeing those strong fingers glide across the keys has been distracting in the worst kind of way.

"Heather, there is something else Holly brought to my attention that I'd like to discuss with you," Queen Plume begins. The cadence of her voice reminds me of a teacher about to send someone down to the principal's office. I look toward Moth for support, but he's already shown himself out. The base of my shoulders stiffens, and I feel my antennae go rigid. I know we're still mad at each other, but couldn't he have stuck around for a few more minutes?

"That device you carry around... your cellular phone?"

"Yes," I gulp, taking the phone out of my pocket. I've been careful to keep it turned off during the day, but I'm dangerously close to empty on this thing.

"I understand you have been taking portraits using it."

"Oh, is that not ... okay?" I scramble to slide open the gallery so she can take a look. "I haven't taken photos with anyone, but I can delete anything you want me to."

God, I can't believe I didn't ask first. I'm turning into my mother. A flash of guilt sinks through my chest. I remember the feeling of my privacy being invaded when she came to visit and took pictures of Moth and my home. Yeah, she posted them to all her followers, but still...

Maybe Queen Plume doesn't want me to have the memories of this place captured in my pocket.

Skillfully, she copies the swiping motion I had used to open the app. With wide eyes, she flicks through the gallery, studying each photo long enough to make me squirm in my seat. "These are—"

A horrible invasion of privacy.

A silly and frivolous waste of time.

Totally vain and ridiculous.

"Absolutely stunning," she gasps. For the first time, I notice the bright curiosity in her wide, green eyes.

"*Really!?*" Holly and I shout in unison.

"They are so terribly personal; I feel as though I'm getting an actual glimpse into your day," the queen remarks musically. "Would you replicate this for us?"

"Like a photo booth?" I frown. "I love that, but I don't think I'll have enough battery to take pictures all night."

She hums. I know she's capable of getting me a phone charger—or heck, I could go through the portal myself. But that would raise questions with Moth, and I feel bad enough keeping one secret from him. We really do need to talk.

"For just us then—a family *photo*." She nods decidedly. "Our portrait is long overdue for an update—"

"Which I have already commissioned," Holly interrupts.

"Yes, my darling, but I'm curious to see what Heather comes up with." She taps her chin, tilting her head to one side then another, looking not unlike a porcelain doll. "I would like something less ... stiff."

"I'll try my best." That is, if I can get Moth to stand next to me for long enough to take a picture. It's not like we haven't gotten into squabbles this past year, but nothing like this. I keep retracing each of our words, and I can't figure out who even started it. Given our history, it was probably—no, *definitely* me.

We usually talk about it by now.

"Do you want it to be displayed at the ball?" I ask. If so, I'm going to have to figure out how to get a printer...

Queen Plume hums to herself. I think she's about to say yes until Holly stands.

"No, nothing this intimate will be shown to our public."

"Well, you heard the princess." Queen Plume nods. "This will be something special for us after the ball."

"After the ball." I nod.

Will the photo be a memory of our time here or the beginning of a new future?

18.

THE THING ABOUT HAVING CONVER-sational warfare over dinner is that you rarely eat much. My growling stomach has been keeping me awake for hours. Moth hasn't come to bed, and as much as staring at him across the room has unlocked another kind of hunger, he's not the snack I'm looking for.

I need to find actual food in this maze, and considering it's pitch black, and I can't remember if I took a left turn or a right, I'm having a really *fucking* hard time doing that.

The stone floors are cold beneath my bare feet, sending shivers through my body with each step toward the palace kitchens. At least, I think this is the way to the kitchens. The moon is covered by clouds and isn't doing much to pave my way. There's a staircase around here *somewhere*, and I hope my eyes adjust before I find it by accident.

I can see better in the dark than before my transformation. This space is just so large and unfamiliar, and the shadows from the statues cause me to keep looking over my shoulder.

"This world might seem like a paradise," Ruby's words echo through me, *"but it has threats, the same as any—it would be wise to be careful."*

At the time, I thought she meant the rigid social hierarchy, but now, wandering through the castle in the dark, I worry those threats might be more ... *tangible.*

Shadows play against the wall, and my imagination runs wild with monsters and men that could be lurking behind the pillars—and you know what? Who needs snacks? Not me! No, this was an awful idea. I will suffer 'til morning, if I can figure out my way back to the bedroom, that is. I pivot and slam into the nearest thing—which happens to be breathing.

Awesome.

Light laughter tickles my ears, along with a gentle and familiar heartbeat. When I raise my head, I'm greeted by Moth's toothy grin, amusement dancing in his ruby eyes. He's shifted back to his human form, and despite the harsh shadows that play across his face, he looks so much softer than the hulking creature who had been playing the piano.

"Just who I was hoping to find," he whispers. He holds a candelabra in one hand and a plate of sandwiches in the other.

"It looks like we had the same idea."

He holds out his hand, and the flickering candles dance between us, igniting sparks deep in my stomach. Why are we fighting again? The flames cast yellow light across his strong cheekbones and make his eyes look like burning embers. This man is a painting come to life—moody and misplaced in this world of cream and pastels, and yet just as beautiful.

"You're so pretty. Have I told you that lately?" I ask, reaching up to stroke just under his chin. He leans into my palm, like a cat who has been waiting all day to be stroked.

"I could stand to hear it again." And there's the smile again—that coy look with just a hint of pointed teeth.

I love him. I love him so much that my whole body aches to have him close.

"You." I kiss him, a quick peck on the lips that catches him off guard.

"Are." Another kiss, and he smiles against my lips.

"So, so, *so* pretty." I flutter up to him, so we're face to face and rest my forehead against his. "And I'm so sorry."

"As am I," he whispers, his hot breath on my skin. "It has been torture keeping myself from you."

"Shame your hands are full," I tease, running my finger up the middle of his chest where his shirt billows open, revealing just enough of his chest to make me ache. It's not lost on me that he's still holding a plate of sandwiches in one hand, and the other holds a candelabra he's carefully holding away from our flush bodies.

"Do not think I would not cast these things aside and carry you through fire and glass to our bed."

I swallow hard, imaging flames licking my skin and the crash of shattering glass. But louder than any desire is the sound of my stomach growling.

"Real talk though, I would actually really like some of those snacks... and more than that, we should probably talk, right?"

"That can be arranged."

We flop onto the bed, a platter of sandwiches and fruit between us. We exchange apologies and kisses, both as life-giving as oxygen. I don't know how everything got so thrown off—but I'm glad we're here now.

"You said you wanted to talk." Moth stiffens in his seated position, his wings tense.

"Honestly, I just want to apologize. I can't imagine what you are going through, and I was pushy and defensive, and … I'm sorry." I shake my head until my hair is a curtain in front of my face.

"I was also not at my best. I apologize." He shifts in his seat, pulling back my makeshift hiding place so we're looking into each other's eyes. "I would like to tell you more … about what happened."

"Oh, Moth, no. I *so* did not mean to make you feel rushed. If you're not ready—" I stop when his firm hand strokes up the middle of my back until it reaches the base of my wings.

"I am ready."

"Okay, okay, if you're sure."

"It is an unsavory tale."

I nod, placing my hand on his thigh. We cuddle together while he breaths out a long sigh.

"Take your time," I whisper, guiding his body to rest against mine. He's the largest little spoon I've ever held, but it's nice all the same. His head falls onto my chest, and for a moment, he breathes deeply, getting up the courage to speak.

"My father was not as he is in the stories."

When his voice finally rumbles against my chest, I startle. "But that doesn't make sense," I blurt, then bite my lip. This is Moth's moment to tell me what's been going on. I will not ruin this with my rambling. "Sorry—ugh, *sorry.*

It's just that your mom told me she loved him, and she seemed so sincere about it."

"I'm certain she did, my flame." His fingers comb through the tangles in my hair. "That does not mean he deserved it."

"No, no, I guess not." People fall in love with assholes all the time. "And he did kidnap her, which isn't a great look."

"*What?*"

"Yeah, there are apparently some interesting customs here for us to unpack later." I make note of the WTF look on Moth's face. This is a surprise to him as well. I throw my hands up in the air. "I know we have our 'no secrets' rule, and it's not like I've been trying to keep things from you, but babe, there is *so* much going on here. I really need to get you up to speed." I groan, cutting myself short as he draws in another heavy breath.

"One thing at a time." It's less of a request than a plea.

"Yes!" My discoveries can wait, especially when he's already obviously overwhelmed. "Anyways! Okay! I'm done taking over the conversation. Please keep going."

"You are obviously aware of my power to heal?"

Pretty intimately.

I nod, forcing myself to stay silent and listen.

"It is a gift only some members of the Moth Court can perform. When I was young, I had a hard time mastering it. I would come into the dining room filled with cuts and scratches from whatever the day's adventure had been. It made my father furious. I can still recall the furrow of his brow when I walked in the doorway."

He swallows, glancing at the humble plate of food in front of us. "I was not permitted to dine with the family with so much as a scratch on my skin."

"So, you snuck down to the kitchens at night?" I ask, my heart breaking for tiny Moth. We all learn skills at different times, and that's so unfair.

"I did." His head tips toward the ceiling. "My mother would turn a blind eye to the plates with crumbs left in my chambers come morning."

That's why he was so comfortable when we were there together.

"But she didn't stop him?" I ask, a little in shock. The queen seems like the picture of a doting mother.

"I do not believe she approved, but I cannot pretend to know of what conversations happened behind closed doors." He presses his palms to his eyes, letting out a gigantic sigh—right, too many questions.

"Sorry, I'll stop. I said I'd just let you talk."

"No, my flame, it is not you." He untangles himself from my arms, lying flat on his back with his wings pressed against the soft mattress. He stares at the ceiling. "It is ... the feeling of old wounds ripped open."

I tentatively place my hand on his thigh, patiently waiting for him to continue.

"It went on for a long time, and I still could not manage to heal myself. I believe it was why I couldn't heal when you found me. At that time, this was my home, and though my father was certainly not a source of comfort, I felt safe here."

We lay next to each other for a long time. It takes everything I have in me not to prompt him with a, "Then what happened?" and wait 'til he's ready. Finally, he lets out a sigh.

"Did you know that the fae used to hunt animals like Sprout?"

"*What?*" I shoot up in my seat. "No, no way. He's basically a giant puppy. That's terrible."

"My father thought that ... if I could not heal myself, perhaps something I loved..."

The dots connect in an instant. I gasp, covering my mouth with both hands. No, no one could be that cruel—especially not a parent. My head spins at the gravity of what it all means. "*No.*"

"He used a crossbow while I watched. They said Sprout got mixed in with the wild herd, but you have seen the sweet creature. He needs to be coaxed to simply leave bed in the morning."

"No, he would not have wandered out on his own." Moth squints, as if still trying to make sense of it all. "It was *no* accident."

"Moth..."

"It was the first time I tried to use my powers on anyone else. I encased him in a cocoon. Unlike with you, my body was left half-exposed, attached to a giant egg that held his body. I did not know if he would survive. I could not bear to be seen or consoled, so I hid in the one place I thought no one would find me."

The Crystal Caves.

"Oh my god. Moth, I am so sorry." As if on cue, Sprout launches his giant body onto the bed, and for the first time, I realize his little antennae are not a part of his species, but a mark of his new life—just like mine.

"It is no wonder he's taken to you," Moth says, ruffling his fur. Sprout huffs, laying his head across my legs. If the creature I have the most in common with in this world is a dog, so be it.

"My mother found me before Sprout emerged from the cocoon. She was horrified. At the time, I thought it was of what I had done. But she held me and quietly whispered through her tears that it would all be alright. I understand it was my father's actions that made her look down at me with such disgust. Her face twisted in a way that made her look unrecognizable to my child eyes."

"Moth..." For the first time, I'm speechless. "You know none of it was your fault, right?"

"Perhaps—"

"No, babe, you were a child." I reach down, weaving my fingers between his. "What he did wasn't your fault at all."

"It did work," he says bitterly, giving my attempt at comfort no acknowledgement. "I could heal after that day because this realm no longer felt like home. Shortly after was the start of Father's illness. I put all my focus into becoming a better king than he was, and until his body weakened, he put even more pressure on me to learn. That is why I was so ... *prickly* about the idea of staying here."

I bite down on my bottom lip. Trying to process all of that in one afternoon? God, no wonder he was angry journaling in the middle of the night.

"You are literally reliving terrible trauma." Reaching over, I brush a dark curl from his face. "I give you full permission to be prickly—and honestly? I was no picnic either. I'm so sorry."

"It has been a long week." He shakes his head, a deep bitter laugh rising from his lips. "My flame, you could make this place your own, yet I feel like a guest in this world. I don't recall my grand plans, the changes I wanted to make, the person I wanted to be. *Death* is truly gone, and only your Moth remains. I do not believe this man who delights in quiet and pastries and books is the same who wanted to rule a kingdom."

"Don't be so hard on yourself—whatever you decide." I sit up, sliding my arm around Sprout. "You have the two of us in your corner."

"Whom I have forever changed..."

"Hey, I'm okay. Sprout's okay. As evidenced by this cuddle puddle, we both very much love you."

Moth has enough happening without worrying about me—which is good because besides the newfound ache in my joints and the fuzzy feeling I've been having at the base of my forehead, I am totally fine.

"Whatever you need, I got you, okay?"

"Mmm," he hums, weary and unconvinced. "Now, what is it that's bothering you?"

I gulp. Considering he's still carrying around some baggage about me being *forever changed*, I can't exactly tell him that the base of my wings aches like a muscle after a long workout, that Chris is back in town and maybe, just maybe, I'm not as okay as I've been pretending to be.

And it doesn't help that I'm fighting what feels like my biggest flare up in years. I just need a good night's sleep— then everything will be better in the morning.

"Just worrying about you. Honestly, my thyroid stuff is getting a little wonky. No more gluten for the rest of the trip, and I'm sure I'll be fine," I say, letting my head fall back on the pillows. It's the biggest understatement in the world, but for now, it will have to be enough.

"I will speak to the chef tomorrow."

"No, please don't."

"Why?" he asks. "I am disappointed that I neglected to do so when we first arrived."

"But now they're so busy with the ball. I don't want them to hate me."

"No one will hate you." He catches my hand, placing a kiss on my wrist. "I will speak to someone in the morning."

I have a feeling there's no talking him out of this one.

"Fine," I begrudgingly agree. "Let's try to get some rest, huh? Tomorrow is going to be a big day, and hey ... thank you for talking to me. That couldn't have been easy."

"It is a memory I would have liked to stay lost in time, but I thank you for listening." Moth sighs. "There is much I want to say, but you are right, we must rest. At the right time, I will tell you everything."

Tell me everything? It seems like I'm not the only one keeping secrets. But why does that sound so ... *cryptic*? Pushing my anxiety down, I snuggle up next to Moth.

Tomorrow is the start of the ball. After that, we'll have plenty of time to talk about everything. He's right—now is just not the right time.

19.

"WHAT'S ON THE AGENDA today? If you're feeling up to it, I was hoping we could see more of the castle together before the big night."

"I have promised Holly that I would be her sparring partner." A nervous breath shakes through him. Moth looks down at me with a fond glimmer in his eye. "After my recollections, I am not eager to hold a weapon."

"You don't have to go."

"It is just one more day," he says, resting his chin on top of my head. I twitch my antennae, the sensation tickling more than expected.

"Really?"

"I want to be home with you." He pulls away, reaching down to stroke the length of my jaw. This time, I believe him. Despite Holly's ideas for the future, Moth has no desire to be king. After this, we're going back to our cozy life in the woods—we'll be as happy as ever.

"Well, in that case, you looked super gallant with a sword. Plus, you'll do better than I did." I pick myself up on my tiptoes, kissing the closest thing I can reach, which happens to be his jaw. He pulls me up by my waist to close the distance. The kiss is sweet but way too short.

"I am sure Holly would not mind you in attendance," he says, pulling at my waist.

Yeah, no. Two training sessions with that drill sergeant was enough. Even with the small moments where we've vibed, I still don't think she's my biggest fan. Honestly, if I tag along, I'm just going to ruin it.

"I think your mom probably needs some help with all the final details. We did throw a few hundred extra people at her." I ignore the way my muscles ache for rest. "Just be easy on yourself and watch out for that horde of tiny hooligans."

"Vicious to be sure." He grins, the sun glows off his silhouette like a dark angel; a year together and I'm still in awe of every inch of him.

"Then ... 'til tonight?" I ask, unable to keep the frown off my face. After the heavy conversations last night, I was hoping for more of a slow start to the day. His large hands squeeze my waist before he releases me, and I fight the urge to drag him back to bed for the rest of the day. I lean up, letting my wings flutter until I can softly kiss the tip of his nose

"Until tonight." There's a weary quake to Moth's quiet voice. When I step back to look at him, I notice the slight bags under his eyes. Ironic that we finally have a bed big enough for us both to fit in, and neither of us will probably get a good night's sleep until we're back at home.

"Have fun, okay?"

He nods his head slightly before disappearing through the doorway. I feel worse than yesterday, but before I head back to bed, I decide I should check in with the queen about any last-minute details. After Moth's confessions last night, answers would be nice too.

Like, where was she during all of this? In all our conversations, why didn't she mention that the former king was a terrible father? On my way, I *definitely* don't go to the library, and I *absolutely* do not look in every single desk drawer. I trust Moth, and I don't need to see what he wrote—especially since the book is nowhere to be found.

I don't find Queen Plume in her chambers or the parlor; it's not until I peek out the windows that I see her attendants waiting outside a large greenhouse. I hurry down to the grounds, eager to explore a new part of the castle I haven't seen yet. It's been almost a whole week here, and I've visited the same rooms over and over. The gardens are lovely, but something cozy like a greenhouse has my interest piqued. The windows are small and tinted green, and the roof juts up in arches just as grand as the castle itself. Her attendants bow as I pass them, and I can't help but walk just a little taller at the sign of acceptance.

I may not be a part of this world, but I am becoming a part of this family.

"Welcome to my little slice of calm *away* from the palace," she says, setting a small tin watering can on the ground. "It may seem silly, but I like to have a moment to escape before the festivities begin."

"It's beautiful."

"Isn't it just?" she says, walking to meet me at the center of the greenhouse. "It was a marriage present from the late king. He knew how much I loved flowers..."

"About him." I gulp, unsure if this is even something I should talk about or not.

The queen straightens, her eyes growing wild and wide before settling back into the demure expression she always wears.

"Moth... he told me what he remembered, about the day you found him in the crystal caves."

"I thought he might."

"The old king—your husband," I begin, but she holds up her hand as if ordering me to stop speaking.

"He threw fits. I threw parties, making sure any visiting dignitaries thought the food and drink were more memorable than the most recent tantrum of a fickle king."

"So, why does Holly seem to idolize him? No offense, but he seems awful," I say, not caring how plainly I'm speaking. King or no king, he doesn't deserve respect, especially after what he did to Moth.

"Awful people can have such wonderful moments, but Holly did not know her father, not really," she says. "She was so very young and blissfully unaware of his outbursts. Without the expectation to rule, he favored her with dresses, dolls, and daggers—even before she was old enough to wield them. I dare say the sickness that befell him softened his temper in later years. I know she has been ... disappointed in my ruling since Atlas disappeared. She thinks Eclipsica needs a firm hand. She does not know the power of a well-timed smile and a warm cup of tea. But you do, don't you?"

I nod, the air suddenly thick with pollen and secrets. I understand more than I'd like to.

My whole brand was built on unending positivity. Never let the haters win, never let them see you sweat, and disarm them with kindness. It worked fine for 22 years until I yeeted myself off the internet. But there's one other thing that doesn't make sense. If the Moth Court prides themselves on their healing powers, how did Moth's father get sick in the first place?

"You said fae don't suffer from the same sort of illnesses humans do, right?"

"No, I can't say they do." She shifts under my gaze, the soft smile never leaving her face, even for a moment. "My husband's case was unique..." Queen Plume moves through the greenhouse, away from her attendant's listening ears. I follow her, watching her elegant fingers pluck a pair of gleaming garden shears from a nearby potting table.

"We should have a bouquet at the head table, shouldn't we?" she asks, carefully trimming flowers and gathering them in her arms. A spare set of shears rests on the potting bench in the corner. I gather them in my hands, helping her select roses and baby's breath for this impromptu bouquet. We work in silence, the memories she shared of the past settling inside my head.

Poor Queen Plume...

Her relationship seems like it was complicated at best. Could she really grow to love someone like that? I'm glad Moth doesn't want this life. Obviously, I know he's different. He's as kind and gentle as he is fearsome. A life of well-timed smiles is not the kind I'm after—not anymore.

"It's gross that he was such a dick about Moth not learning to heal while he couldn't even heal himself of whatever sickness he had." I think—no, say out loud. My lips clamp shut. I don't know if it's the lack of sleep or the growing brain fog, but I did not mean to say that.

Instead of getting upset, Queen Plume lets out an unexpected laugh—before something unrecognizable plays across her face. All the warmth she radiates shifts to something cold and flat.

"The illness took years to claim him. It was a secret to most of the kingdom and a mystery to all in the castle." She violently snips a flower.

"The plants here are truly magnificent, don't you think?" Her fingers trail across the petals. "There are all sorts of properties that come out in recipes and teas. I may not look it, but once, I was quite fond of putting afternoon tea together for the late king. It was my little ritual. My husband always appreciated the way I took the time to make something just for him."

"You, you—" I begin but can't get the thought out. Moth's mother has been nothing but warm, kind, and welcoming. There's no way—absolutely no way—she's a murderer.

Puzzle pieces click together, creating a full picture of the events in my mind. Queen Plume finding her terrified son in the caves and plotting her husband's slow demise. I wonder how much pain King Death inflicted before she decided murder was the best course of action. My stomach twists at the grim reality that her life in this castle is not the fairy tale it has seemed.

"And you did this for—"

"Until the king was no longer with us."

"No one thought it was odd that you'd take the time to ... care for him like that?"

"And question my devotion to the king? No dear, of course not."

"But you were so heartbroken. When we spoke you said—"

"It is true I loved my husband." She snips and the head of a red rose rolls to my feet. "But I love my children more."

I swallow a shallow breath, steeling my nerves before Queen Plume turns to face me. As she rises to her full height armed with nothing more than a winning smile and a pair of garden shears, she's suddenly the most terrifying person in Eclipsica.

"It is getting late," she says, glancing up at the sun. "Would you be a dear and see that everything is going according to plan?"

"Totally, yes. I will do that now." I rush back the way we came, the flowing skirt of my dress catching on thorns and leaves as I trip and stumble over the potted plants.

As if in a trance, I walk back to the bedroom. The mental checklist weighs heavily on my mind, but not as heavy as the information I just learned. Queen Plume killed Moth's father, and I'm not even sure I'm upset at her for it after what he did. Honestly, I'm just totally and completely stunned.

Queen Plume killed her husband and confessed to it as casually as some gossip you'd overhear at a hair salon.

Sprout trots over to me, plopping his head on my lap.

I want—need—to lay down.

But I can't move, can't think. I melt into the chair by the window. Fading into the darkness, I rest my eyes for just a moment.

20.

"HEATHER, MY FLAME, MY flower." Moth's claw strokes my cheek, and ugh, the pressure in my head has gotten worse in the few minutes I've been asleep.

When I crack my eyes open, Moth is fully dressed. There are extra gold sparkles around his eyes, and a dark kohl liner beneath them. His suit coat has feathers on the lapel that match the ones on his wings. Damn, he looks incredible.

"Why are you ready so early?" I groan, rolling over and taking the blankets with me. My mom was like this back when I was still living at home. If we had a shoot scheduled, she'd be in a full face of makeup at the crack of dawn—and it's like ... why? You're just going to have to touch it up later! Pulling a pillow over my head, I close my eyes tight. Sleep tingles at the edge of my body, ready to pull me back under.

"I had Holly take on your last-minute tasks," Moth continues in a low voice.

"What?"

"I tried to wake you hours ago, but it appeared your body required more rest."

That is enough for me to sit up, running my fingers through my rat's nest of a hairstyle. I tilt my head toward the windows. The sky is dark and spotted with stars, and music flows through the air, paired with laughter.

I was sleeping through the grand ball.

"No, *no*—oh my gosh, are we missing everything?" I hop out of bed, stumbling as I head to the vanity.

My hair—my face! God, everything is a puffy mess.

"Heather—"

"How much time do I have?"

"An hour before the main festivities."

An hour?! Okay, okay. I suck in a deep breath, steeling myself. I've gotten ready in less time. I can totally do this. Rushing around the room, I begin the process of doing my makeup, and for my hair—ugh, my *hair*—a whimsical yet slightly messy half-up seems like the only thing I can manage. So much for Ruby's suggestion of soft waves and flowers.

"Allow me," Moth offers, and before I can protest, he brushes through the tangles, skillfully twisting the strands into two braids he weaves around my antenna to create the perfect crown for my head. Instead of flowers, he takes gold sparkle pins and places them throughout. "No need to rush, my flame."

"But you're the prince. We should be there when—"

"Whenever we please," he cuts me off. "Your hair is lovely."

Once he's finished, I can't help but agree. I should ask him to do this every single day—but *ugh*. Even with his help, the more I try to snap myself awake, the worse the haze around my brain feels. It's like my entire head has been submerged in quicksand. I powder my face, applying mascara, blush, and the gold sparkles I bought at the market to my cheeks. The girl in the mirror doesn't look fatigued or sick, but that doesn't change the ache in my bones, or the way I feel more buried in the sand by the second. If I hadn't felt this countless times, I'd think maybe Queen Plume was poisoning me too. But no, I don't need some wildly sneaky murder plot to bring me down. All I need is an inconsistent dose of T4 and some gluten and dairy. Nothing can kick my ass like my own body.

Thanks, Hashimoto's.

Still, I head to the closet to retrieve one of the ballgowns from Miss Widow's shop when Moth catches my wrist, gently pulling my body toward him. "You do not have to pretend to be alright just for everyone else's sake."

"I'm fine. It's no big. It's not like this is the first time this has happened."

"No big..." He lets the words roll over his tongue. "I have heard you say that often and find that it is seldom true."

"I just want this all to be perfect. Your mom has been working so hard, and your sister just adores you, and Moth, you..."

Should be treated like the precious gem you are.

"I?"

I squeeze my eyes shut. What was I talking about?

"You ... should have everything you deserve."

"And what do I deserve, my flame?"

For that whole ballroom to see him for the wonderful person he is. To never be sent away from his family because his power or person doesn't measure up. To be loved and wanted forever and always.

"Anything you want." It's a simple statement that doesn't even begin to cover what he *deserves.*

In one fell swoop, Moth throws me over his shoulder. In a few giant steps, we're on way back to the bed.

"This is so not what I meant!" I shout, giggling despite myself with every step.

Within seconds, we're enveloped by pillows—together, my heels kicked off as my legs slide under the silky sheets.

"Fine," I concede. "Just five minutes."

Of course, it's not five minutes. It's *never* five minutes.

I'm glued to the bed like a pancake stuck on an ungreased skillet, and Moth is putting in little effort to be my spatula. This would happen to me. I've been transported to a literal fairytale land, and I am having the worst flare up of my life.

The guilt is making me feel even sicker—I've been burning the candle at both ends since we arrived, ignoring the fog in my brain, the ache in my joints, skipping pills, and eating whatever the heck I've wanted. This is my own damn fault! I helped plan half the ball, and I won't even be there.

Moth should be dressed to the nines, meeting other royals and spinning me around the dance floor.

Instead, he's reading from one of the books he snatched from the library. The deep rumble of his voice soothes my racing mind. I just wish it could soothe my aching joints, too.

Flare ups were bad enough in my human form, but now, instead of my arms and legs feeling like rusted tin in need of oil, my wings ache, making it impossible to get comfortable.

I lie on my stomach with pillows tucked under my legs and supporting the crook of my arms while Moth strokes my forearms with blunted claws.

It would feel nice if it wasn't *so awful.*

"You should be at the party," I whine, pushing against his chest.

He ignores me—no, that's not true. He lets out a deep breath before continuing to read, and I sink closer to him.

"You're the whole reason they're having this ball. You can't miss it because of me."

"I am where I am required."

Required… Like he's here out of obligation, not because he wants to be.

"Moth, please just go. I'll summon some energy and join you later tonight."

Don't let me ruin this for you. That's what I want to say. He was born for this life, and I've kept him snuggled away in a cabin for a whole year. He can't want to be here, not when there's a giant celebration for him just outside the door.

"Do not act like it is a punishment for me to be lying next to you."

"Wouldn't you rather be having fun?" I ask, my eyes getting heavier by the second.

He holds up the book he is reading. "Yes. May I continue?"

A night of taking care of me can't be what he wants. Why won't he just be honest?

"You really won't go without me?"

"As you said, the celebrations will continue all night. If you are still feeling unwell by then... I suppose, for your sake, I will make an appearance."

"Please." I stretch, trying and failing to find a spot that's comfortable. My head feels like there's TV static at the base of my forehead, and my thoughts ping around, becoming harder and harder to grab onto. Despite everything he's said, the guilt of him being here to take care of me is all-consuming.

I close my eyes, trying to tune out the sound of music echoing from somewhere in the castle.

"I'll take a little nap, and we'll go together, okay?" I say, snuggling in until I finally find a spot that's comfortable. "Honestly, I don't really want to be alone." I yawn. The mental fog I'm wading through makes the words slip past my lips.

"And you will not be for a second."

Well, that was an overstatement. Because when I wake, Moth is nowhere to be found.

I told him I didn't want to be alone. Technically, I'm not. Sprout is still here, but the giant marshmallow has completely melted into the pillows and isn't giving me much feeling of safety.

Still, I try to cuddle back into the bed, taking comfort in his furry presence, but with the sweat from my nightmare clinging to me like a second skin, it's no use.

I'm frozen under the covers, as if the moment I move, something terrible will happen. It's a nice calm, normal moment ... just like the one last year when I walked across my cabin for a glass of water and ended up tied up in the back of a truck.

Every time I've had a nightmare like this, Moth's arms are always right there for me to roll into. Falling back asleep is easy when I know he's next to me—we've proven time and time again that no matter what, we'll always protect each other. But that's when I'm not alone ... well mostly alone.

"Bud, you'd bark if there was anything scary in here with us, right?" I whisper to Sprout, whose snoring doesn't give me much confidence. Sure, the giant ball of fluff might surprise me, but I'm pretty sure he's more pillow than guard dog.

It's silly. I told Moth to go; I wanted him to, but now that he's gone, it feels pathetic to be lying here with terror gripping my chest while I can still hear music echoing off the walls.

Given the excitement of the ball, I doubt he's hidden away in the library. His clothes are gone. That's a good sign that he actually joined the party and isn't just traipsing around the gardens naked, not that it would be an unwelcome sight if he were.

Moving to the mirror, I touch up my tousled braid crown and makeup. For my first grand ball, I had hoped I would have looked less *thrown together*, but it's good enough. I turn to fetch my dress from the closet when I see *it*.

Pale green fabric pops against the blush-colored fainting couch near the window. The little pink flowers look like they've been plucked straight from the garden, shrunk down, and placed across the billowing fabric.

My heart swells at the sight of the dress—*my dress*—from Widow's window display.

Someone bought it indeed. I grin and, with greedy hands, clutch the impossibly soft gown to my chest, hugging it as if it could hug back.

Moth is really something.

It's a little tricky to lace the corset on my own, but I manage. Then I work on the strings of my dancing slippers, tying them into little bows at my ankle. These must have been from Widow's shop too. The green leaves embroidered on the toe match the gown perfectly.

Okay, maybe this is a little more than good enough. I squeal, spinning around the room, watching the shining fabric bell out around my body.

Do I feel better? No. But in this dress, no one will be the wiser.

Heaving a deep breath, I stand. I have a ball to attend and a prince to kiss.

21.

INSTEAD OF MAKING MY WAY DOWN the grand staircase, I opt to use one of the many side doors to the ballroom. As much as I love a dramatic entrance, tripping in front of everyone doesn't seem like my idea of fun. The décor Queen Plume and I worked tirelessly on is no less beautiful from below. The ballroom gleams. Crystals and ivy hang from the ceiling, and for a moment, I wonder whether I took a wrong turn and stepped into the garden.

Beautiful faeries in every shape and form crowd the ballroom. In the corner, refreshments are served on golden platters, including towers of tiny cakes and coupe glasses filled with amber liquid and topped with candy floss. A band plays a lively tune at the bottom of the staircase. Nobles and villagers mingle, the crowd spilling into the hallways. Though I notice a few sharp glances, everyone seems to be having a good time—and they all look incredible. Pride builds in my chest: *We did this.* All of Queen Plume's and my efforts were worth it.

I just wish I could find someone I know in this dense crowd; a flash of dark hair catches my attention, and with the grace of one of Rosie and Clara's baby goats, I trip over my own feet. The sharp end of a stinger is inches from my waist as I topple headfirst into a member of the Bumble Court talking with their peers. The collision upends a goblet, and they're soaked with their own drink.

"Oh my god, I am like ... so, *so* sorry." I try to find something to clean the mess—a cloth, paper towel, pile of cocktail napkins, but nothing catches my eye except for the growing scorn on their bug-like faces. Dozens of tiny, very angry eyes stare at me.

"You think your apology is enough for this offense?" The first puffs up–literally. The sharp stinger gleams under the lights.

I am so dead.

I let out a small squeak, glancing around the room for an ally. What are they going to do—challenge me to a duel?

I have way too much brain fog to figure out how to navigate this.

"I'm going to be real with you," I say, shaking my head. "I'm like ... the worst at sword fighting. Do you want to settle this with like a dance off or...?"

At this, the group roars with laughter, and a large bee-like hand pats me on the back with the stinger safely pointed away.

"Let no one say the Moth Court is without humor." The bumble-fae chuckles, giving me a turned-up expression I hope is the equivalent of a smile. "Be off with you, little moth." I get the feeling he's much older than anyone else I've encountered—the grandfather of all bumblebees.

I leave with a polite curtsy and go back to my search for Moth.

Instead, a trio of redheads catch my eye. The butterfly sisters who have been mean-girling me this whole week flank King Magnus. The vampire king nods politely along with whatever conversation they've dragged him into, his shoulders stiff. He looks up, his light eyes catching mine from across the ballroom, and with a pleading glance, he mouths the words, "Help me."

Moth would hate it, but those girls *are* awful...

"There you are!" I charge forward, causing the butterfly sisters to spin on their heels, gaping at me. I assume they're thinking, *Not her again.*

King Magnus—with his bright red hair and pearly fangs—retreats behind me. Considering he's about a foot taller than me and a literal vampire, it's kind of hilarious.

"Oh, I'm sorry," I say, as if I've only just realized they're standing there. "King Magnus's presence has been requested by the queen. You will excuse us, won't you?" And they do, with bows and apologizes befitting royalty.

"You will save a dance for us, won't you King Magnus?" Vanessa shouts as we inch away.

"Of course, my ladies." He lightly bows before allowing me to lead us to safety. "Shall we?"

"So nice to meet you!" I call back, watching their sweet faces turn sour. It's good to be the drama sometimes.

"I thank you, my lady." He sighs. "Those two are..."

"A lot, I know." I nod. "No big, okay?" I scan the ballroom for any sign of Moth.

"No big..." His lips part in a grin. Oh my god. I just helped a literal vampire king out of an awkward social situation. *What is my life right now?* I gulp at the memory of Holly mentioning that he could "bleed me dry" and take a cautious step back. At dinner, things felt different, but in a room this crowded, no one is paying attention to me.

"Heather," he begins, snapping me out of my hazy thoughts.

"Yup!"

"It has only been a short while, but I would like to ask for your hand."

Like a favor? I mean, I did kind of just do one for him, but ugh ... sure. Yeah, I could do that. His sharp canines flash at the edge of his smile, reminding me of exactly who I'm talking to.

"Uh, right now?" I ask. Trading a dance with one stranger for the next isn't exactly the kind of help I needed.

"I will find you when the time is right."

I raise my eyebrow. God, is this one of those "help make my exes jealous" things?

"Is this you asking to drink my blood because that's a no."

"Your blood is not necessary," he says with a deep inhale. "But thank you for considering it, however briefly."

You know what? I take the gratitude back; the vampire is worse than an angry court of bumblebees—at least they seemed straightforward.

"Okay, yeah ... sure." I nod. "But nothing weird, okay? I have a boyfri—"

And he's already gone.

Great.

Whatever. I'm sure this won't have consequences later.

As I continue to weave through the crowd, I catch sight of Ruby wearing a shining gold ballgown that pops against her dark skin. Her hair is up in a large bouffant decorated with faux crystal bees and honeycomb shaped gems.

"Oh, I'm so glad to see you!" she says, flashing an enormous grin. "When Moth mentioned you were unwell, I was bit worried."

"Just exhausted." As if trying to really get my point across, a yawn escapes me. "I would sell my soul for a cup of coffee."

A few fae spin their heads in my direction, a chilling reminder I need to watch what I say in the middle of this crowd.

"Oh, my god, it's a figure of speech. *Calm down!*" I groan as Ruby bursts into laughter as the gawkers disperse.

"There is some strong tea at the refreshment stand." Ruby loops her arm in mine. "Why don't we grab ourselves some cups while we watch the festivities?"

"Don't you want to dance with Pepper?" I ask. I'm sure with six kids they don't get a ton of chances to be alone.

"They are currently helping in the kitchen, per Holly's schedule, though they should return to me soon." I swear there are literal hearts in her eyes.

"Multi-talented." I nod, giving her a thumbs up.

"They really are." She nods. "Now come. I too could use a caffeine boost—my two youngest have decided naps are no longer in fashion. Neither is sleeping in."

"To the tea cart!" I exclaim. As much as I want to find Moth, caffeine comes first, especially since Ruby needs a boost just as much as I do. The more I'm here, the more I realize the faeries are immortal but not invincible. They may not get a common cold, but they certainly can become tired, weary, and heartbroken. My eyes find Queen Plume across the dance floor for just a moment. She regards me with a small nod, then smiles when her eyes fall on the way Ruby's and my arms are looped together.

Of all the things I thought I'd find here, friendship wasn't one of them. I wish I could tell her who I really am and why I keep talking about things she's never heard of, but I appreciate Ruby's support, nonetheless. Considering at least three of her children are still in the babbling phase, nodding politely and pretending to understand is undoubtedly a skill she's gained with practice.

Still, I can't help but wonder what her reaction to a cute little coffee shop would be. I bet she'd order a floral latte and look out the windows at all the cars passing by. She and Moth would share inside jokes—but without accessible portal travel, that's never really going to happen, is it?

Moth and I can be guests in this world, but his friends and family will never really be guests in ours—not with ease, at least. That would require Queen Plume to share her secret portal, and if that was something she wanted, I'm sure it already would have happened.

No. Tonight will be our last night here.

Maybe we'll be able to visit from time to time, but it'll be worse than having friends who live in a different time zone. No FaceTime or group chats—just radio silence.

"Did you hear me?" Ruby asks. We're standing at the tea cart, stacks of decorative cups on one side, large teapots on the other. The smell of rich black tea, hints of jasmine, and rose hangs in the air around us. Delicate flowing script on pretty labels indicates each of the flavors. We both opt for a breakfast tea, and I hope the caffeine will do something to make me feel human again.

"What? No, sorry." I shake my head. "The music is loud!"

"Cream or sugar?"

"Both!" I nod, watching her plop two sugar cubes in each of our cups. She adds in a dribble of cream before placing it in my hands.

We clink glasses, taking large sips before letting out contented sighs. It's not coffee, but it's definitely hitting the spot.

"How do people typically stay in touch when the season is over?"

"The usual—letter writing and weekend visits. We do not live far—a little outside of the palace walls in a big open house with lots of space for the children." She nods. "You will have to visit soon."

"I would love that but—"

Her face falls. "You're not staying?"

I shake my head.

"And you're not going back to the Butterfly Court either, are you?" She raises her dark brows and... oh, she knows. She absolutely knows.

I sigh, shaking my head. I'm too tired to hide anymore but will not admit anything while we're in earshot of other people.

"Am I that obvious?" I whisper.

"A little. Oak figured it out first." She shrugs.

I knew it.

She opens her mouth to say more just as Pepper sneaks up behind her, wrapping their arms around Ruby's waist. She catches herself before any tea is spilled—literally and figuratively. The elegant fae shoots back her tea in one gulp before Pepper whisks her away to the dance floor.

I'm left alone once again.

My wings fold tight against my back, and with each step, I feel smaller in this grand space filled with kings and lords—and what *am* I doing here?

Ruby and Oak have been able to tell I'm just a human this whole time. Sure, I helped pick out flowers and tasted cakes samples, but it's a joke to think I belonged here.

Wandering to the far corner of the ballroom, a tall shadowy figure catches my eye on the opposite end of the dance floor.

Moth.

The black suit perfectly contrasts with the room of pastels. His wings drag behind him like a cape, but it's his human form he's wearing. His makeup is a little smudged under the eyes, and the gold freckles across his skin look even brighter under the shining crystals hanging above him.

The eclipse of moth-creatures circle the ballroom in front of where he stands. They seem unguarded and free, as if everyone is on their third glass of wine.

Even Moth appears to be more relaxed with his cravat loose around his neck and amusement in his eyes.

And then our eyes meet, and that lighthearted gaze turns to something molten. As he stares, I am shaken to my core by the power he holds over my heart with just a simple look. He is completely still, apart from a hard swallow that makes his Adam's apple bob.

The song changes, and so does he. With long strides, he moves without breaking my gaze. The crowd parts for their prince. It is as if we're drawn together by an invisible force—my moth, his flame. The spectators don't fall away like they do in movies; they watch as their prince's clawed hand encompasses mine and all of my anxieties fade away.

"You are here." His whisper is warm and hypnotic. The faerie prince pulls me to his body just as the music swells.

"And you..." *Are so fucking gorgeous,* I want to say. Instead, I silently gape at the man I love. With skillful hands, he guides me in what I think is a waltz—it's hard to think about the steps when I can't tear myself away from his eyes.

"If I must dance, let it be in your arms only, my flame."

Moth leads us around the dance floor with ease, where the intimate waltz becomes more of a performance. I blink, trying to process the choreographed dance I'm witnessing. It's one of those old timey things where you circle around each other, only instead of hands touching, it's the tip of each dancer's wings.

"You know how to do this?" I ask, trying to commit the steps to memory. Twirl—step—circle while wing to wing, sidestep, switch sides, repeat. We can totally do this, right?

"It will be like riding a bicycle."

"Babe..." I try to look up at his smiling face without tripping. "Have you ever ridden a bicycle?"

"I have not."

A giggle escapes me as I take his hand. If we're going to look like fools, we might as well do it together.

I look down to make sure I don't step on his feet.

"My flame..." he whispers, gently guiding my eyes from the floor.

"My Moth." I smile, feeling my anxiety fall away with the swell of the stringed instruments. After that, it's like I've fallen under a spell. My dress swishes with every turn. The feeling of his hands on mine has me weak in the knees. When the tips of our wings graze, I fall deeper and deeper under his spell.

This man is pure magic. With his patience, poise, and grace, he really was meant to be king. And all of that aside—he's kind. With the way he glows brighter than any crystal, it's clear. He really is happy here. Maybe Holly was right: our tiny little cabin was just an interlude for something bigger. This could be the life we are destined for—a life of smiling at strangers, influencing the Court rather than followers on Instagram.

But with Moth next to me and people like Ruby and Pepper, we could make a real life for ourselves here—with me throwing parties and smiling at just the right moment. But is it one where Moth will be sneaking out of bed every night? That's not the future I want, no matter how covered in glitter it may be. I'm not sure it could ever make me as happy as our little cabin in the middle of nowhere.

No. I swallow hard, dizzied by each thought building as the spell of the music breaks. Suddenly, the room is too loud, too crowded, and far too overwhelming. I close my eyes, focusing on the feeling of Moth's powerful arms around my waist, guiding me from the dance floor and toward the balcony.

"Let us get some fresh air."

"You are a natural." His fingers skate up my shoulders; the feeling leaves shivers up my spine and, for once, not in a good way. Considering I almost slept through the entire ball, he can't mean that.

"Yeah?" I ask, shaking out of his grasp, forcing the most convincing smile I can muster. Overall, I guess I have been handling the Court with ease. At the night market, I suggested we should stay here, but since then, I've had second thoughts. A lifetime of tea parties, balls, and high society feels too much like a never-ending influencer networking event. Or wait—does he mean on the dance floor? I bite my bottom lip, trying to quiet the loop of thoughts fighting for attention in my head.

Even when this flare up has passed, I don't know that I'd want to deal with this sort of thing all the time. Heck, in my heyday, I was really more of a content-creating hermit.

Sure, my calendar was full of events, but I'd always been happiest at home.

And right now, I miss the home I created with Moth. The one he *said* he wants to return to.

"Why don't you head back in?" I say, sensing his restlessness next to me.

"I am worried about you," he admits, tucking me close to his chest.

"Aw, don't be." I pull away just enough to hold tight to his arms. "Your mom wanted to throw this ball in your honor. I'm sure she's already looking for you."

He laughs, craning his head to look back at the overcrowded ballroom. Sure enough, she stands in the center of the crowd surrounded by beautiful, masked creatures. With an elegant flick of her hand, she waves him over. He's hesitant until I give him a small squeeze on the arm.

"I'll be right behind you." I sigh, rolling my shoulders and taking a few more breaths of the cool air.

"The night is young," he assures me, leaving only after a kiss on the hand—ever the gentlemen.

He's right.

Tonight is just about enjoying a night of fun after a week of hard work and preparation.

The ball has just begun, and there will be plenty of time for overthinking and deep conversation tomorrow.

I breathe in the thick night air, leaning off the balcony to watch the gold fireflies swarm; it's like they're having a ball of their own.

Moth loves me, and I love him. As long as that's true, we can get through anything. Besides, being *stuck* as royalty wouldn't be so bad, especially if he's the one my throne is next to.

"He's right, you know," a voice calls from the shadows. I jump, whirling around to face...

Holly?

What is she doing out here?

"Relax." Holly puts her hands in the air as if to show me that she means no harm. Her cat-like smile has another story to tell. "It's just me."

I study her—she looks stunning as always. Her gown is white and blue brocade sweeping all the way down to her feet, and there's a crown of baby's breath pinned to her short hair.

"Sorry. Last time someone snuck up on me from out of nowhere, I kind of got kidnapped." I laugh, nerves bubbling up from my chest. "Also, I almost died *sooo*..."

"Yes, Mother mentioned your harrowing past," she hums, sounding uncannily like Queen Plume. "My brother saved your life, gave you powers, brought you to this world where you could rule beside him, and yet..."

"And yet?" I echo, waiting for her to make her point.

"You are clearly unhappy."

"I'm not..." I cross my arms, biting my bottom lip. "I'm not, *not* happy."

"But he was right. You could be so very good at this." She circles around me. "You have charmed a lot of people in that ballroom. That isn't a simple task."

"Are you kidding? I thought I was going to get into a duel with the Bumble Court," I say, glad that they thought my awkward rambling was funny enough to excuse the matter.

"What is a party without a little duel?" She glances back toward the crowded ballroom. "Your smile and biting words may be sharper than my sword. You could be an excellent addition to the Court. You could do well here," she repeats. I understand why she wants to convince me to stay—she misses her brother—but I cannot do this again.

"Moth and I are going home tomorrow after the ball."

"Tomorrow?" She laughs "Balls in Eclipsica last days. Even if you were going home, it would not be for at least another—"

"Days?"

"Clearly, you have never been to a Faerie ball." She shrugs. "There will be rests, costume changes, small events—but the dancefloor will remain full 'til the moon begins to wane."

"No! No, that is not what we talked about. You said we could leave in one week."

"This again?" Holly slides behind me, turning my shoulders so that I'm looking at the center of the ballroom. Moth is ... *wow*.

"Of course, he wants to stay."

Moth gleams like onyx in a sea of pastel gemstones. He is art. Even here, he towers above the crowd. When his red eyes set on mine, he smiles, fangs on full display as he tips his head back. He beckons for me as the music swells, and another dance begins to spin around him. He politely declines when someone else tries to take his arm.

He really *does* look happy here...

"You would take that smile off of his face to go back to a crowded cabin in the middle of nowhere? Force him to hide for the rest of his life?" Holly's whispers are becoming more frantic, the aggressive tone taking hold and driving tension into my shoulders.

"No, I–"

"Heather." She clasps my hands. "For years, I looked for my brother, and he's home. He's finally home and he's *happy*. You will not last here. It's written all over your face, and he will follow wherever you go."

"I don't understand what you're saying." I shake my head. She can't be telling me to leave, can she?

"I believe the expression is 'rip off the bandage.'"

"If you don't like me, whatever, but like—"

"That is just the problem." She grimaces as if whatever she's about to say causes her physical pain. "I *do* like you. This ball would be nothing without your efforts."

"Okay..." I pause, waiting for the inevitable "but" that will surely follow.

"However..."

There it is.

"No." I hold up my hand. The dizzy feeling that kept me in bed all day is seeping back the longer I allow this conversation to keep going. We talk in circles, and as soon as a word leaves my mouth, I have a hard time remembering what I said.

Oh god, this level of brain fog is *bad*. I really should have just stayed in bed. Last time I felt this bad in public, I had to BS my way through a panel and a meet and greet. If not for pictures, I'd think the whole event was a dream.

"You are *so* not trying to tell me to leave your brother in the middle of a grand ball," I say for what I think might be the second time.

"I will tell him you took to bed. You have been feeling unwell, then you can—"

"Can what? There isn't a way home, remember?" I may know the secret about her mother's portal, but she doesn't.

"I will come for you once I have an opening." She grimaces. "I believe I can send you back with the materials gathered."

Well, that's reassuring. If it was up to Holly, who knows what bizarre new world I'd end up in.

"Uh, hello? What part of 'I'm not going anywhere' do you not understand?"

"The part where my brother has been trapped in another realm for decades, and he is finally back where he belongs." She's shouting now, her butterfly wings sprawled out behind her like the tail of an angry cat. Can't she see how selfish she's being? I understand Holly has missed her brother, but we have a life together—not a dalliance or an interlude, a real life that he *wants* to return to.

"He gets to decide where he belongs. You're being ridiculous." I cross my arms.

She visibly calms herself, pinching the bridge of her nose—a family trait that's beginning to make me cringe.

"Heather, please," she begins, and the tone shift is ... alarming. Instead of anger, her eyes have grown wide and pleading as she reaches toward me. "You will tear him away from this place, along with any shred of happiness."

"He's happy with me!" I half-shout before reminding myself I'd rather not be the one to make a scene during this lavish party. The feeling at the base of my forehead swells, and the ache in my joints multiplies.

It was because of *me* that he missed opening ceremonies and the feast. I could see how distracted he was; he's usually always stoic, but Moth was *antsy.* Something has been bothering him, and in the deepest pits of my stomach, I've been worried it's me. But I'm not going to let Holly twist this. This place is a reminder of both terrible and wonderful things. There's pain etched into each of the hallways, and the anguish is clear from the way he's been spending his nights alone in the library.

Moth doesn't want this, and tomorrow, he'll be free of it all.

"He is loyal. I've watched how dedicated my brother is to you." She shakes her head. "He will stay at your side so long as you want him there."

"Is it so hard for you to believe we're in love?" I'm so over this. I push past her, ready to return to the ballroom. "Nothing you say is going to change my mind."

She lurches forward, pulling a crumpled piece of paper from her pocket.

"Are you certain his love is true?" Her voice is not cruel or taunting, no—there's a sadness there that's unexpected. She flattens the piece of paper to reveal Moth's hand-writing. *What is this?* The cursive script is almost impossible to read with all its flourishes, but I could recognize it any-where. I've seen it a dozen times on scribbles he leaves around the house and on the extremely formal-looking grocery lists he writes for me. But this isn't a request for more sweets to line our cupboards or a different tea.

This is a breakup note.

"We met as but a human and a monster. You offered me kindness, a life, a home, the warmth of a flame I will always be drawn to. Now, how can I exchange a golden crown with a simple band of flowers?"

My eyes flick across the page over and over, scanning for a missing line.

"This is a misunderstanding." I suck in a shallow breath. "You faked his handwriting."

"I wish I could say that was true."

"When did you find this..."

"The night before last when the moon was full. He left his notebook on my desk. I admit, curiosity got the better of me..."

My stomach twists. This is what he was writing? Brainstorming ways to break up with me? I think of all the times back home he sat up in bed, and I'd listen to the sound of his pen scratching against paper...

How long has he been wanting this?

"You have helped him pass the time. He has given you the gift of flight. Do not make him stay out of obligation—let him go."

"You're full of shi–" I have every intention of cursing her out, but I can't, not when I watch Moth get pulled into a dance. He tries to resist at first, but the crowd has him; within moments, he's smiling, dancing with a woman the same way he danced with me. Oak joins in the mix, then Pepper, followed by Ruby. The four of them spin and bow, lightly touching their wings before throwing their heads back in laughter.

"He deserves a conversation," I say, unable to stop watching the growing happiness on his face. *Home.* He has my friends—but here? Here he has an entire community—people who admire him. This whole time I thought that, among all of them, I was his biggest fan—and that's still true, but looking down at the letter, it's clear he's not mine.

How can I exchange a golden crown with a simple band of flowers? he wrote.

He can't. Who would?

"He deserves freedom," Holly counters. "Only you can give that to him."

Freedom...

As if the home we've shared has been a cage.

"You keep him like a bug with its wings pinned to a frame. Do you really think he's worth so little?"

"Of course not!"

Holly places her hands in mine. I twist my head up at the warm gesture.

"He turned you into one of us." Her eyes are wide and sympathetic; she's just the messenger here. Moth is the one who's unhappy. "It makes sense that he would not want to leave you alone in your world."

"So, I'm supposed to leave him alone in his?"

Her hands move to my shoulders, so I'm forced to look at him standing in the middle of the lively ballroom—the centerpiece of the perfect painting.

"See, that's where you've got it wrong. He's not alone, not anymore."

The terrible thing is she's right, and I know it.

It's easy to slip away unnoticed—well, almost.

With every step toward Queen Plume's quarters, Sprout follows. Apparently, nothing gets past the world's largest sentient pillow.

Every once in a while, he grabs the hem of my gown and tries to pull me backward, but after I press on, he has given up and opted to trail at my heels. Sprout hesitates when I reach Queen Plume's tower but follows after me regardless until I'm up the stairs to the tower. Walking through the museum of broken clocks, I stand in front of the mirror.

Can I really do this?

I cringe, reaching out a hand; the glass-like surface ripples like the water of a pool in the middle of summer just begging me to jump in.

No, this is awful. We should at least try to talk things out. Right?

But, I mean, if Holly is right, then Moth will follow me no matter what he wants, out of obligation...

What is it he said when we were cuddled in bed? *I am where I am required.* The knife in my chest twists deeper. I don't want to be a requirement. I want to be a desire, a want, a need. I thought that's the kind of love we had. But that note...

I guess I was wrong.

"Look after Moth for me, okay?" Blinking tears from my eyes, I pat Sprout on top of his fuzzy head. He lowers his head with a whine, his big puppy eyes widening as if begging me to stay.

"He doesn't want me here, Sprout," I explain, holding back tears. I stroke one of his long fluffy ears as they fall flat against the back of his head. I wish there was some way to help him understand me. "But he'll have you and his family, and I'm sure he'll be way happier," I ramble, wishing anything that came out of my mouth felt true. But his feelings are written as plain as day, and Holly is right.

Holding my breath, I step through the rippling mirror.

The best thing I can do is set him free.

Now Moth can have the future he really wants—without me.

22.

PORTAL TRAVEL FEELS JUST LIKE stepping through a doorway—a doorway that should have Moth back on the other side of it. But no, he's back in his real home, I'm faced with a place I thought we'd return to together. The crumbled letter is a weight in my pocket that keeps me pinned on the forest floor. Getting up means walking into the next chapter of a story I thought would have a happy ending with the man I loved.

So, I stay until my tears dry, and the sun has shifted. I stay until the swirling golden portal in the center of the old oak closes.

Sucking my wings back into my body, the pressure in my shoulder blades sends a shooting pain up my spine. God I forgot how much this hurts, but hey, might as well get used to pretending to be a *normal human*—especially since I've lost the one person who could understand.

I trudge through the woods back to the cabin, regret filling my lungs with every heaving breath. Nothing could make this worse—*oh fucking hell.*

A man with strawberry blonde hair scrolls through his phone on my porch, wearing the sorriest smile I've never seen. Two coffees sit beside him.

Chris—the man who has become my nightmare—is smaller than I remember but still towers over me as he jumps to a standing position.

"Nope! Absolutely not!" I shout, stomping up the porch steps. My monster-hunting kidnapper is the last person I want to see right now.

"Heather, listen—I am so sorry."

Not as sorry as he's going to be. With a kick of my foot, I knock over the lattes I'm sure are meant to be a peace offering. What once would have been a welcome gift makes me sick to my stomach. I can't believe I used to be so naïve, thinking he was harmless.

"You can't be here," I shout, not caring that my fancy fae-made shoes are now stained with coffee. It's not lost on me that I'm dressed in a literal ballgown while staring him down—but thankfully, he doesn't say a word about my attire. He probably thinks I was off doing a photoshoot or something.

"When you didn't respond to my letter, I thought... it's my last day in town. I just had to see you. Rosie told me not to come."

"Rosie's a good friend," I mutter, crossing my arms. Is he really just going to keep standing here?

"She almost didn't meet with me at all."

Maybe she shouldn't have.

"What I did was terrible. I should have listened to you. I am so sorry—I was obsessed."

"So, you want me to forgive you so you can feel better about yourself?" I huff, shaking my head which makes the world around me feel light and dizzy. I utter words I should have said to him a long time ago. "*Leave*. You need to leave."

"That's not it! I know, I know, if you never want to see me again after this, I understand. I'll go." He tries to reach for me—a gentle touch to the hand. But I dodge, my heart racing in my chest. "I had to tell you how wrong I know I was ... face to face."

"Go! Now!" I can't bring myself to say anything else. All the well-crafted arguments I had imagined, the things I've longed to scream at him—they all fall out of my head. I'm not ready for this today.

"More than that, I just had to see that you're okay," he continues, the same speech he's been trying to give since laying eyes on me. "Everything happened so fast."

Fast.

The memories of that night flick across my skin like hot coals: the gun in his hands, the fire in Moth's eyes, the feeling of my whole life slipping away. That night, everything went dark, and I didn't think I'd ever wake up again.

"I'm glad that ... after everything, you're still in one piece," he says with a slight upturn of his lips. Bile rises in my stomach. Does he realize I'm whole after being split into a million pieces? If Moth hadn't glued me back together, I wouldn't be standing here at all.

"When I woke up, there was a bloodstain on the floor, and you were just gone." His gaze is unfocused before it snaps back to me. "I was worried I killed you, and I—"

"You did." I cut him off. My voice is dark and unfamiliar. A bright and visceral rage rises up inside me—hot with the taste of moss and dead leaves at the tip of my tongue. If he comes any closer, I'm going to snap—and part of me desperately wants to see how far I can toss him with my bare hands.

Tension releases from my body, and in one fell swoop, my wings spread wide. My antennae pokes through my hair in two angry points, and my vision blurs as though there's a burst of bright red confetti over my eyes.

"T-this... No—no, there's no way."

"Get off my porch now!" My nails twist into claws at the extension of my hand, and *God,* I didn't know I could do that.

For a half-second, he is slack-jawed and wide-eyed. It's one second too long.

"Now!" I repeat and I swear I feel the force of all the wind from the forest at my back, ready to throw him off the porch.

He's scrambling back to his car before I have the chance to utter another word, and it's just as well. These claws are new, and I don't want slime under them.

He's left another letter of empty apologies. Written words to ease his guilt but will never heal my pain. I shred it into pieces but even that doesn't change the hurt that radiates through me.

He came back.

Inside, I move carefully wondering if he's left a trap for me. Chris knows what I am now. What if he comes back, and I'm unprepared? This form has changed into something powerful and strange, but I don't know if I could actually do anything with it. Despite Holly's best efforts, I'm no good with weapons.

I already know a lock won't keep Chris out, and fear was enough to drive his actions last time. Hell, I just scared the shit out of him, but is that enough to really keep him from coming back?

Maybe I should have stayed in the other realm. At least I would have been safe—unwanted, but safe.

There's one place I know I'll always be welcome, so I spread my wings and burst into the sky, racing toward the last place I called home.

ORLANDO: **HOME OF GREAT COFFEE** shops, a million bakeries, and most importantly, my mom's house. I stand in front of my childhood home with my backpack—just small enough to fly with clutched to my chest. I can explain how I got here later. I needed to leave, and the idea of being confined in a car for hours was suffocating.

I'm grateful to still have a key, although I didn't expect to be sneaking through the backdoor at 2 a.m. like a teenager breaking curfew.

"Hey, kiddo," a familiar mellow voice calls from the kitchen. It's not my mom seated at the kitchen table, but a welcome surprise, nonetheless. My mom's older brother—and my favorite uncle—Doug sits at the pristine white marble table, an antique clock laid out like a science project in front of him. While my mom has always shined bright in the spotlight, her brother is quintessential quirky artist, always tinkering with antiques or paintings of oddities and creatures, demons and creepiest of all in his sad clown era. But seeing the clock laid out takes me right back to Queen Plume's tower, and a chill cuts through the air.

Moth will never even know the portal existed. Holly probably won't even finish her transportation spell. The reality that I'm never going to see him hits me again like a ton of bricks. *What have I done?*

"Kiddo?"

"Oh." I look up, meeting his worried eyes. Even when I'm not in a crisis, he always looks so chronically worried.

"Very nice greeting for your favorite uncle," he manages, setting down his tiny toolkit.

"Sorry, no... hi. It's just ... I was expecting to see my mom," I explain, running my hands through my windswept hair.

"She's out of the county doing... well, honestly, I don't really know. Something about designer ... Tupperware? She sounded very excited, flew to Italy last week. She asked me to come up and watch Peanut."

The overfed chihuahua growls from the other side of the house. I'm pretty sure Peanut can take care of himself, but god, am I glad Uncle Doug is here.

"I don't think they have designer Tupperware in Italy."

"If not there, then where?" He shrugs.

"I—I'm sorry, I'm way too tired for this." I shake my head, heading to the fridge to retrieve a can of sparkling water that I promptly place on my forehead to ease the building pressure.

"Well, it was something food container related and sounded very fancy. Sweetpea, what happened?"

"I uh—" I open my mouth, and nonsense pours out. The unopened can falls from my grasp, and before I can catch myself, I am sobbing in the center of the kitchen. Uncle Doug sweeps me up into a hug. The wool of his sweater is a familiar soft kind of scratchy; it's nostalgic and comforting the way I'd imagine the stubble of a father's beard feels when you're a kid. Only instead of coming home with a scraped knee, I have a scraped heart.

"Shhh. It's okay, kiddo. You can let it out," he says in a tone that would match my mom's if she were here, only softer—he was always the quieter one.

"I think I messed up, like ... really, really bad." I sob, replaying every word of the conversation I had on the balcony with Holly. "Have you ever let someone just push you into a corner? Everything is spinning, and you feel so terrible and lonely, and nothing makes sense, so you do what you think is right, but then you think you might have made the biggest mistake of your life?" I say, at least, *I try* to say. Every other word is a muffled sob. Uncle Doug, bless his heart, tries so hard to comfort me with a series of *uh huhs* and *mmms*.

By the time the tears run dry, he's picked up that this is all about a breakup and we're eating giant slices of gluten-free coffee cake with his signature hot cocoa. The mouthful of coconut whipped cream should taste like nostalgic heaven. Instead, the lump in my stomach twists even tighter. Still, the coffee cake disappears from my plate the longer we sit at the kitchen table.

I take my time recapping the story, editing all the parts about traveling to a literal fae realm and murdery family members, although I'm positive he'd be obsessed with Queen Plume's clock collection.

"So, let me get this straight. You went off your medicine for three days, binged every piece of bread in sight, overworked yourself without asking for help, and ... left your boyfriend without talking to him." He lets out a large exhale. To his credit, he doesn't sound judgy—confused, but not judgy, *never* judgy.

"There was a letter... he wanted to break up with me."

"But Heather—"

"I know, I know! I don't know... it just it felt like I didn't have a choice. Everything was just screaming at me like, of course it was all too good to be true, right? How could *he* love *me*?"

"From what your mom says, he's crazy about you."

"Mom has actively planned a wedding for every person I've ever dated." I sigh, taking a large gulp of cocoa, wishing the chocolate and cinnamon could act as a balm for the scratches on my heart.

"This was your first time meeting his family, and it was a big reunion, right?" His fingers fiddle across the table.

"Something like that." It's as close to the truth as we're going to get.

"Did you feel a lot of pressure to impress them?"

"Well, yeah, if they don't like me, he's not going to stay with me."

"You know the best way to get them to like you?" He leans across the table, his light eyebrows raised high on his forehead.

"How?" I ask, genuinely curious to hear a scrap of whatever wisdom he's going to throw at me.

"By being yourself."

Suddenly, I'm not a 23-year-old running home after a breakup—I feel 17, overwhelmed with life, my mother, my following, facetiming my favorite uncle only to have him say...

Just be yourself.

Ugh, leave it to him to make this a wholesome life lesson. The trouble is, I am being myself. The overthinking, the self-doubt, the people pleasing—that's all classic Heather.

"It makes sense. I mean, in a giant room full of people, why wouldn't he want someone with more followers—"

That's not what I meant to say. More important, more beautiful, yes, but the old anxiety slips out before I can catch it.

"I thought Moth didn't do the whole internet thing?" He leans back in his seat, eyeing me suspiciously.

I cringe. This week has muddled old anxieties with new ones, creating a cocktail of worries I'm still trying to digest. Moth has never cared about what the public thinks of him, online or offline.

"Oh my god, he doesn't." I groan. "What is wrong with me?"

"Do you think I'm a people pleaser?" I ask from across the kitchen table.

"You've spent most of your life trying to make other people happy."

"So that's a yeah?" I frown. Worrying that my favorite uncle is disappointed in this less than desirable personality trait only confirms the sad truth that I'm still obsessed with likes.

"It's a yeah, kid."

"Ughhh," I groan, resting my forehead on the kitchen table. "This is the worst. I'm the worst."

"You are not the worst."

"I am! Like, what have I been *doing* this past year? I thought I made progress on myself. I thought..."

I thought that my cryptid boyfriend was madly in love with me—not planning on breaking up with me via a beautiful cursive letter.

"One year of your life versus the last twenty-two. Give yourself a little more credit, kiddo." He gives me a gentle smile. "You need another slice?"

"I need a distraction."

"Well, I am taking my wares to a big festival this weekend. It's going to be a long drive, but if you want to be my helper..."

"I'll go!" I shout, not even hesitating to hear more. Anywhere is better than here, and honestly, the more I think about seeing Mom, the more I regret coming here. After spending the holidays together, I think she likes Moth more than she likes me, and leaving before her flight home is in my best interest.

"West Virginia, here we come."

24.

OKAY, SO WHEN UNCLE DOUG SAID "West Virginia," I was worried there would be small reminders of Moth in whatever town we ended up in. I just didn't realize that there would be a whole damn festival. I really need to work on being less impulsive. At least I managed to get a decent nap on the long drive here. Honestly, I feel a little bad for Uncle Doug. He invited me along for company, and I've been either sleeping or buried in my phone during drive. Rosie has sent me a million messages. My eyes heavy, I struggle to reply:

[ROSIE: So, uh, you okay?]

[HEATHER: Not really??]

[ROSIE: I'm so so so sorry about my brother. I really had no idea he was going to do that.]

[HEATHER: ...What did he tell you?]

[ROSIE *is typing*]

[...and deleting...and typing and typing...]

[HEATHER: That I fully hulked out on him?]

[ROSIE: Basically?? Honestly, well done. I am so so sorry Heather. I told him to leave you alone. Are you alright?]

[HEATHER: LOL nope! Cliff Notes version? Moth and I are done. Driving up to WV to help my uncle vend at what I just found out is the Mothman Festival sooo hahaha FML.]

[ROSIE: Oh boy...]

[HEATHER: Water the plants for a few more days?]

[ROSIE: Of course!!]

The phone slips from my hands as I pass out for the rest of the drive. When I wake up, my back is sore from how long I've been hiding my wings, and we're surrounded by cars and people walking around in a mix of regular clothes and costumes.

So, this is the fabled Mothman Festival.

The town is cute and, though crowded with people, has a small cozy feeling underneath. I do my best to help my uncle set up his booth but can't help but be drawn to the sights around us. When Moth was sent through the portal, this was the first place in the mortal realm he stumbled into. It makes me want to explore every corner.

As we walk through Point Pleasant, I'm in shock at just how many people are obsessed with Moth. I knew there was a fascination with Mothman, but I didn't realize there was this much love. Not to mention a whole museum, giftshop, and over a dozen enthusiastic cosplayers—and a surprising number of Ghostbusters.

A crowd gathers around the infamous statue to take pictures. Moth is way better looking in his monster-form—taller too—but it doesn't stop me from staring at his likeness.

"Ah, the shiny hiney," Uncle Doug says with a laugh, pointing to the statue's exposed butt. Oh, wow, there's actually a line of people waiting to touch it. If only they knew the real thing was even more glorious.

And it used to be mine.

Uncle Doug's wares are a mix of steampunk clock sculptures and edgy goth paintings of skulls and classic monsters. The clocks stand out in the lineup of adorable cryptid crafts and nerdy merchandise. I cringe at the sight of a few *Mothman is My Boyfriend* t-shirts, though let's be real, a few weeks ago I would have absolutely bought one just to embarrass Moth. I can't imagine the look on his face...

"Was your ex into this sort of thing?" Uncle Doug asks. "With the nickname 'Moth,' I always assumed."

"Uh, no." I bite my bottom lip. "I don't think he would have been a fan of this at all." Uncle Doug places a reassuring hand on my shoulder. Judging by his downward smile, I can tell he's sorry he brought it up. He slides me a five-dollar bill.

"Why don't you pick us up some coffees?" he says. "Take your time, see the sights—you could even sit in and listen to one of the speakers."

Somehow, I don't think that's going to be the distraction I need; still, the more time I stand in the crowd, the more I feel myself being drawn in. Coffee? Right! I can do that. Forcing a smile—something I've been doing a lot lately—I walk away from his booth and into the crowd in search of caffeine. A noble quest no matter what realm I'm in.

Pulling up the map on my phone, I navigate past the vendors, music, and attractions until I reach an impressive line for a small coffee shop on the main street. There are even more reminders of Moth here, including a specialty cold brew, coffee blends, and a Mothman-shaped cookie— which I order for Uncle Doug *obviously*. I'm too jittery to want something for myself.

A group press their faces through a cardboard cutout of Mothman drinking a cup of coffee, smiling for the camera. I wonder if they'd be surprised at just how sweet he takes it.

I wish he was right here in this café next to me. I bet he'd get the sugariest thing on the menu—and the cinnamon bread behind the glass case.

If only he missed me the way I miss him.

I make a quick stop back at the booth to drop off the coffee and cookie before my uncle shoos me away again. Maybe all my gloom is scaring off customers. I send Rosie a few pictures and lament that the Mothman Festival is post-breakup hell. At the same time, I'm fascinated by all the joy everyone has celebrating Moth's legend. To say it's surreal would be an understatement. After popping into the museum, gift shop, and spending a few dollars on an adorable chibi Mothman keychain that, despite everything, I just can't resist, I wander back toward that silvery statue of the man I love.

With the way the sun is beating down, I don't know how anyone is dressed in polyester. Pulling my glasses down, I suddenly wish I had ordered an ice latte or packed a sunhat or vintage parasol. The sight of so many antennae headbands makes my scalp itch. There are a lot of costumes; would anyone even notice if I let my real antennae spring free? I wait in line for one of the few public restrooms and let out a whimper as my wings and antenna go free.

In Eclipsica, I got used to seeing this version of myself in the mirror. If I'm being totally honest, I'm not sure that I am used to her yet, but I do like her all the same. Drawing in a deep breath, I decide that if there's anywhere I can get away with being my true self in the mortal realm, it's this festival.

I nod and smile whenever anyone compliments my wings and "headband." Maybe I should move back to a big city. In LA, everyone would think I was dressed up for a photoshoot, and in New York, I don't think anyone would bat an eye. I might have trouble getting onto the subway though, and really, that's not the life I want.

A few clouds shift in front of the sun, casting me in darkness for a moment. A few gasps and shouts make me think that it's a storm cloud or—

Oh dear god.

A dark, hulking body hangs in the sky, his glowing red eyes and his fangs on full display. His wings span out wide, and even in his rage, this creature is beautiful—and absolutely terrifying.

And coming right for me.

25.

OTH LANDS WITH A THUD, towering over both me and the silver statue made in his honor. Side by side, I really can confirm that he's much more attractive. Now shouldn't be the time for that.

He's here—it's impossible, and wrong, and so horribly wanted. But what about the life he deserves on the other side of the portal?

"You left me..." he growls, stalking toward me. There's hurt and anger in those glossy orb eyes, though right now I'm not sure which emotion has a hold of him. Moth's beak twists downward in what appears to be a grimace and—why should he be upset when he's finally free of me?

"I had to—"

"No, my flame, you did not." Another step toward me. I feel like I should back away, but my feet stay firmly planted on the ground. "You are the bane of my existence, the love of my life, and I am taking you home."

Home.

He's talking about the castle, of course—he came here with a way back. Why? So that he can break up with me in Eclipsica instead of the mortal realm? No, no—that doesn't make sense. If he really didn't love me, why would he be standing here of all places? But the fact remains...

"I can't make you hide in the shadows here forever," I say in a low voice. The life he deserves is a world away—the Crown Prince of Eclipsica should have nothing less.

He growls, his wings spanning wide across the gathering crowd. Warmth pools in my stomach, contrasting a chill at the back of my neck. He's here. He came for me—why? Why would he do that if he didn't still love me?

"Do I appear to be hiding?" he growls. God, I've never seen him this angry; there's something about this newness that makes me want to jump him right here and now—what is *wrong* with me? The sorrow on his bird-like face snaps me back to reality. My giant, wounded birdman is baring his heart to me, and I'm thinking about wanting to pull him into a kiss.

The surrounding crowd grows, intently watching us—okay, *mostly him.*

"Do you think any part of me wanted to be in that ballroom without you?"

"Uh, Moth..."

"What, my flame, has given you the impression that I enjoy being surrounded by people?"

"Moth!"

Finally, he blinks, following my gaze. Wow, there are a lot of cameras and dropped jaws; realization dawns over him. It's like this entire time he was only half-aware of the situation, as if everyone else besides me was simply part of the scenery.

The crowd swarms around us, and his wings shield us both. He seems to be bracing for impact, but instead, a series of voices break through his feathered barricade.

"We love your costume!"

"Mothman is my favorite."

"Can we take a selfie?"

"The budget for this year must be wild! That was amazing!"

"I think that's *really* him."

"I want a picture too."

Slowly, Moth tucks his wings back. He turns, revealing himself to the excited locals and tourists. It's different from the fanfare back at the palace; the royals love the prince while this crowd loves the monster.

I'm *lucky* enough to love both. All of that stuff Holly told me—the letter—it has to be a misunderstanding, right?

I loop my arm in his. He bends down so I can whisper in his ear.

"Come on. Let's get you out of here." I pull him forward. Surprisingly, he doesn't budge—his beak dips into something I've come to recognize as a smile. The crowd around him has only grown. A group of kids who can't be more than ten years old stand off to the side with their cameras ready. Their grins are wide as they bounce on their heels, gathering the courage to approach.

"We could perhaps stay a little while," he whispers back. To my surprise, he beckons the group forward.

For the next hour, we're doing a full-on meet and greet with an entire queue of fans. I don't even want to peek at the festival hashtags to see what's trending after all of that.

When the crowd thins, Moth gathers me in his arms—literally flying us off the beaten path. We land in a wooded area a few miles away, and I relax under the cover of the forest.

"That was ...unique," Moth says under his breath as he places me down in front of him.

"What are you doing here?"

He grins, toying with the new keychain on my purse.

"I could ask you the same."

My face burns. I look down, trying to obscure my expression. What was I thinking buying that silly—yet adorable—thing?

"My uncle has a table here. He needed help, so ... what about you?"

"I certainly did not come for the festivities." His tone is grim, but he can't hide the amusement in his eyes. "Rosie told me where I could find you."

Ah, in hindsight maybe texting her was not my smartest move, but with Moth here in front of me, I can't exactly regret it.

"She and Clara are watching Sprout," he continues, cocking an eyebrow.

"Sprout's here?"

"Who do you think led me to the portal?"

Oh my god. I can just picture him bursting into the ballroom and pulling Moth out by the hem of his suitcoat.

"And you flew straight here after that?"

"I did."

"What about the ball?"

"As if my mother's silly party means more to me than you, my flame—"

I put my hand up, shaking my head. I don't want him to see my cry; if he feels sorry for me, it might add to whatever obligation he feels to stay here by my side.

"I read the letter," I choke out, brushing tears away from my eyes before they can fall.

"The letter?" He tilts his head. I huff, crossing my arms protectively. How dare he act like he doesn't know what I'm talking about?

"'How can I exchange a golden crown with a simple band of flowers?'"

"'With ease. I will let the crown fall to another while I warm the side of my flame in the place I truly belong. For the love I have found here shines brighter than gemstones, and blooms wilder than a garden filled with neat rows of flowers.' I am sorry you had to see it unfinished."

"You wrote that for me?" I gasp, unable to fathom that the breakup letter of my nightmares was actually the most romantic poem I've ever heard.

He nods, the barest hint of a smile on his lips.

"I'm an idiot."

"You are an unfathomable dream—"

"—who acted like an idiot."

"Heather..."

"I can't—I shouldn't be selfish. You belong to your kingdom. You're supposed to be king."

"I belong to you and no one else."

"I've been rude, and irresponsible, and weird, and—"

"Mine," he fondly strokes my cheek, "and I would like to marry the rude, irresponsible, weird woman who stands before me."

"You know you could do like, so much better, right?" I shrink a little under his gaze. "There's a whole realm of suitors just waiting for you..."

"I could say the same for you."

Ugh, Moth clearly never saw my online dating matches—it's slim pickings out there. "*Please.* Everyone at that festival wants to bang you."

"But would they love me?"

"Probably? Yes?"

"Would they dance with me in a cramped kitchen and wipe sweat off my brow when I am ill? Would they stay by my side on dark lonely nights and be the light that shines through the window in the morning? Would they smell of lavender and fresh-baked cookies and scrunch their nose when they smile? Only you, my flame, can set my soul ablaze. It is you I want, forever and always."

"I love you," I say, unsure if it's enough but hoping it will be.

"Then, be my bride, Heather. Be my partner in all things from here on out."

"Yes, obviously yes." I wrap my arms around him and feel the slip of something cold on my finger. When I look down, there's a golden band, designed to look like a small wildflower tied in a knot around my finger. A stone gleams in the center, and each petal twinkles with cut amber gemstones.

"It is why you found me in the ballroom instead of next to you in bed," he explains. "I procured it from a jeweler at the market, but it was delivered to the palace the evening of the ball. I was spotted in the hallway and dragged into the festivities before I could protest."

"You were going to propose to me in bed?"

"It would have been on the saucer of your teacup, waiting to be noticed."

"I like this too." I plant a kiss on his cheek. "Though, we could have probably done without you chasing me back to the human realm, huh?"

"Perhaps." His forehead presses against mine. "But like a moth to a flame, I will come to you so long as embers in your heart burn for me."

"I never stopped caring," I say, stroking his cheek down to the tip of his jaw. "I just thought you did. I'm sorry."

"You did say you wanted a dramatic proposal," he teases. Though he's not wrong, I didn't think I'd be the reason for the drama.

"Should I circle back to see if there's a *Mothman is My Fiancé* T-shirt? Or maybe *I'm married to Mothman* for our honeymoon?"

He grimaces and shakes his head. Leave it to me to ruin a sentimental moment like this, but then he guides me by the chin to a kiss that's deep and tender. Oh my god, I'm going to marry this man. A glow radiates deep inside me as the kiss builds and builds until we are gasping for breath. Wordlessly, we hold each other with only the sound of the woods between us.

"I suppose we cannot allow your uncle to think you've disappeared." He sighs. "Together?"

"Always," I say, tugging on his hand. This time I'm not going to let anyone—*myself included*—get in the way.

Our lips meet soft at first, the hardness of his mouth shifting as the monster dissolves into man. As we kiss, he scoops me up into his arms, launching the two of us into the air. We fly until we're just on the outskirts of town.

"Perhaps we should walk the rest of the way," he says, a slight blush covering his pale cheeks. His chest is bare and glorious and, when we get closer, gives the festival-goers something else to stare at.

"Moth?"

"Yes, my flame?"

"We are so getting you one of those t-shirts."

Moth and I left the festival by nightfall after grabbing dinner from a few food trucks with my uncle. He was all too happy to offer his congratulations and send us on our way, confirming my suspicion that his invitation was never actually about me being his assistant or whatever.

Forever a fan of cheesy romance movies, my uncle is happy to wish us well on our next adventure. I hope one day he'll find someone too.

After what feels like a million years, Moth and I are sitting in the living room of our cabin together. I can't believe I let Holly and an out-of-context letter get into my head so badly. As much as I'd love to blame the gluten-brain fog, I should have known better than to question the admiration Moth has for his flame. But there is still one thing that's been bothering me...

"So, all those hours in the library. You were working on my proposal?" It's a question I've been holding onto since the first time I woke up alone. Looking back, I wish I hadn't pushed down my feelings and confronted him as soon as the anxiety started to build.

"Not exactly." He sighs. "You are not the only one who has keep keeping secrets." Hunching his shoulders as though he's about to reveal a midnight candy stash, he moves across the house to pull a notebook from our bookshelf. He flips it open to reveal pages upon pages of familiar flowing cursive script.

"What is this?"

"A novel, " he groans. "Or at least the start of one. I fear the other half is in the castle."

"Wait, you're writing a book?! Babe, that's amazing."

"If you read it, you would not say that."

"Why didn't you tell me?"

"Because it is horrendous."

"*Babe!*"

And I..." He sighs, running a clawed hand through his perfectly messy curls. "I wanted to keep it to myself a little longer. Besides your presence, escaping into that story was my only way to ... cope with the events of last week. It doesn't all make sense. I put all the questions I had for what my life was like down on paper—the half-thoughts, the nightmares, and daydreams. I scribbled versions of Ruby, Oak, and Pepper on parchment. What is fiction and what is memory? I couldn't tell you."

"But it helped?"

"It did."

"That's honestly amazing." I squeeze his arm; if I hadn't been so wrapped up in planning a ball and my own problems, maybe I would have noticed. "Thank you for telling me."

He nods stiffly but says nothing. I know how it is to show your art to someone—his heart has bled onto those pages, and he can keep them a secret for as long as he needs to.

"I can't wait to read it."

"You will be waiting a long time."

"Can I at least hear what kind of story it is?" I press, letting my curiosity get the best of me.

"A romance." A pink flush rises to his cheeks. "The prince happens to fall in love with a faerie he meets at the ball..."

"Oh, does he?" My lips curl into a devious smile.

Moth's arm curves around my back, pulling me into a dance; our bodies flow in time to the memory of the music we heard in Eclipsica.

"Yes."

"Okay now I need to read it!" I squeal, breaking away from our dance. Patience be damned, I playfully reach for the notebook with the sudden and very urgent need to see what's written on those pages. He stands at his full height, holding it high.

"Okay okay, I'll wait! We have forever, right?" I tease. "In the meantime, maybe I can figure out how to make up for being such a jerk to you."

"My flame..."

"No—I know, sorry. I don't know why I even started thinking about it again. Maybe it's thinking about how worried I was in the castle, and... ugh I can't believe I made such a ridiculous mistake. Like I literally said I wouldn't run away from my problems! I didn't even *talk* to you. I didn't even *notice* you were working on this! I should have been paying attention."

"We have been through this..."

"I know! I know! Sorry, I'll get over it."

"Or perhaps you need a reminder that no matter how far you run, I will always be drawn back to you."

"Well, I think we've proven that." I laugh, picturing the way he looked crashing into the literal Mothman Festival. Those fans got a show they'll never forget—and honestly, so did I. I hate to admit it, but *he's kinda hot when he's angry.*

As if reading my thoughts, Moth raises an eyebrow.

"Hmmm." His claw is suddenly at the tip of my chin, raising my face to meet his. "I believe there was a discussion in the gardens about a different ... *scenario.*"

At his words, I feel my face tingle. Is he talking about what I think he's talking about?

"If it still holds your interest," he says flippantly. "Our bed is just as appealing."

I swallow hard, nodding.

"I, yes, very... very much still want ... that."

"Remind me what it was you wanted. *That* is so unspecific."

The command has me blushing from head to toe. "For you to chase me through the woods..." I swallow hard.

"And have any of your boundaries around this changed?" His hand delicately traces the curves of my body. "I cannot have my prey in any discomfort." His fangs peek out in a not-quite-smile "*Unwanted* discomfort, that is."

"They haven't, and I know we can stop anytime."

"Yes, my flame."

We're quiet for a moment. He rests his hands on my waist as I try to wipe the silly grin off my face. The anticipation builds in my chest.

"Heather—"

The familiar sound of bones cracking echoes off the cabin walls. His claws lengthen, and his grip tightens around me as his face shifts from man to monster.

"*Run.*"

26.

WITH HEAVY FOOTSTEPS, I CLUNK down the steps of our cabin, landing roughly on the ground. No time for shoes—not when a ferocious and *very sexy* monster is hot on my heels. He's giving me a head start, I think. Not daring to look back, I forge deeper into the woods toward our favorite field of wildflowers.

The sun slips behind a cloud, leaving me in shadow. Blades of grass stick to the bare skin of my legs. Moth's laugh echoes above me before he lets out a shriek that turns my bones to jelly. A cloud wasn't creating the shadows at all—it was the large body of the monster chasing me. I yelp, swerving into a thicket of trees and quickening my pace, darting backward and forward in an attempt to throw him off, but the only thing I accomplish is making myself dizzy. When he swoops down, my instincts take over, and my wings sprawl forth, launching me into the air. But it's too late. He's bigger, faster, and looking at me like I'm something to be devoured.

He lands in front of me with the grace of a hawk. His body seems bigger out here, hulking and feathered. I back away, trying to hide the smile that pulls on my face.

"What do we have here?" Moth circles me, appraising every inch of my body. I'm dressed in a short chiffon nightgown in a babydoll cut. The billowing, transparent fabric does little to hide my shape. He tugs lightly at the base of my wings. "A faerie in the monster's den..."

"I didn't mean to—"

He tugs again, as if he means to rip them off my back. I groan, letting myself struggle against the barbaric fantasy.

"Have you any idea what happens to those who trespass here?"

"Let me go!" I shout, but I can't get rid of the shrill laughter in my voice. He catches me by the waist and pins me to the trunk of a tree.

"Do you think it will be that easy to escape me?" he whispers, sending a chill down my back. "That, now that I have you, all it will take is a little begging for me to release you into the night?"

His hand curls around my neck, squeezing just lightly enough to provide the delicious pressure I've been craving.

"I'll run as far as I can. You'll never see me again," I promise, swallowing the smile at the edge of my lips. I don't want the game to be over yet, not when it feels like it just started.

"Hmmm," he appraises me, glancing up and down with a flick of his bulging eyes. "And why, my little lost faerie, would I want that?"

He trails a claw down the length of my jaw.

Fuck, he's good at this.

"You are my prey. I will let no one else have you."

To further admire me, he loosens his grip, drinking in the sight of me. That's his first mistake.

The game of cat and mouse is still on, and I haven't given up. Launching into flight, I soar through the trees, feeling him right behind me with the way the breeze shifts around us. We chase each other through the branches of the tallest pine trees, diving and soaring until—

Uh!

A branch comes out of literally nowhere, hitting me square in the stomach and causing me to tumble. I scramble upward, pulling myself up by my arms rather than using my wings. The branch is thick enough to stand on though the width is less than a balance beam, and despite my recent gift of flight, the world tips when I look down. It doesn't matter though. As soon as breath returns to my lungs, Moth's shadow is upon me. His weight shifts the branch downward as he settles onto it.

A large monstrous hand grips my chin, forcing my gaze up; with the popping and cracking of bones, his monster form melts away until I'm staring at the face of a faerie prince.

With all the play-acting and struggling, the sight of this softer version of him is a surprise—but right now, he's not my lover, and the hunt is still on.

I swerve on the branch, trying to knock him off balance—it works, for the most part. It wasn't in my plan to tumble out of the tree too.

But here I am—falling from the sky. Before I can get my wings to cooperate, Moth swoops up, throwing me over his shoulder. The top half of my body hangs down his back, leaving my pantie clad ass almost entirely exposed on his shoulder, giving his palm the perfect position to land two sharp slaps.

Moth pauses mid-flight, as if wondering if he's crossed an unsaid boundary. Breaking character, I fumble for his hand, giving it a little squeeze.

"I didn't say stop."

A laugh rumbles from his chest—the sweet sound making it easier for me to be caught off-guard when three more slaps to my ass follow. I groan, grinding against his strong shoulder muscles as he brings us to the ground, laying me down in a bed of leaves.

There's a force to his touch that's even better than it was in my imagination. His firm lips capture mine in a possessive kiss that leaves me gasping for breath—a reminder of a love that spans two realms and is all ours. My claws grow as they drag across his newly shifted flesh.

"*Harder,*" he demands, arching his wings so I have access to his bare shoulders. I rake my claws over his broad shoulders until deep pink marks are left across his skin. His soft mouth captures my earlobe, biting down just slightly before he whispers, "I said *harder.*"

An order this time. I scratch the surface of his skin, digging in at the last second.

"Show me how much you want me, little faerie—" He kisses my collarbone. "Show me how glad you are to have ended up in the wrong part of the forest."

"Oh fuck—" My legs hitch around his thighs, but he stays as still as stone.

"Mmm, that is an idea," he rumbles. "But this is not how you wanted me, is it?"

Again, the sound of him shifting fills my ears until it's his bug-red eyes staring down at my writhing form. I reach down to touch him—try to at least until I find my wrists captured between his hands and hoisted above my head. The desire I feel for him is so strong I can't stand it. With a claw extended, he trails the length of my body, tearing down the flimsy fabric of my nightgown.

"Please—" I beg, and his dark chuckle fills my ears. In response, he trails his cock up and down, teasing my opening.

"What is it you desire, my little lost faerie?"

"You."

In one swift movement, he thrusts inside me so hard the only sounds I can make are muffled groans against his shoulder.

This is exactly what I've been wanting, the monster unleashed and in full control of the moment. My body shakes with every deep thrust as he drives his body into mine.

"Oh my god, yes—" I scream, holding tight to his shoulders. My nails dig in the way he instructed, and despite not being able to break the skin while he's in this form, the moan he lets out sends ripples of satisfaction through me. I can feel myself getting close when he suddenly stops. I'm a ragdoll in his arms as he bends and moves me to his whims, throwing my legs up over his shoulder and somehow driving even deeper into me.

I fist handfuls of his feathers as I scream into his shoulder. The thread of control I had over my body runs out. Sounds pour from my lips I've never heard myself make as I writhe and, finally, melt into him. Just when I think we've peaked, pleasure builds again and again and again until—*fuck*.

He pulls away, leaving me unbearably empty for just a moment as he tosses my legs to the side.

"On your knees." He orders, and even with my limbs in this blissful jelly state, I'm happy to obey and roll to my hands and knees, waiting for him to plow me into the forest floor. His fingers tease before he thrusts, deeper and deeper until I'm pressed into the leaves below me screaming his name. He twists the length of my hair around his hands and—oh my god that's it.

I'm shuddering uncontrollably when I feel Moth begin to quake, finally allowing himself to fall off the cliff and join me in an ocean of pleasure.

The monster of the forest, prince of Eclipsica, and love of my life collapses on top of me in absolute bliss.

"Wow" is all either of us can say as he rolls the weight of his body off of mine, and I curl to his side, and it's per-fect—absolutely perfect. We lay together in the leaves in comfortable silence for a long time.

"You are ... really, really good at that."

"I will gladly chase you through the woods whenever you desire."

A boom in the distance causes me to jolt from my place next to him. Followed by another. Sparks light across the night sky. And—oh my god—a firework. Of course, obviously.

We're safe.

We're safe.

I draw in another deep breath.

So, why won't my body stop shaking?

"Heather, Heather, darling Heather." He holds my shaking body close to his. "Have I hurt you? Oh, my flame. I am—"

"No, no god. It was perfect—you're perfect. It's just... you heard that, right? Can we move this inside?"

With the doors locked.

"Of course, my flame."

We stand, and my legs are, as expected, jelly.

"May I?" he asks before scooping me up in his arms. I nod, leaning into his chest—my nightgown is in shreds, and blades of grass tickle across my skin. Another firework sparks, glittering in the sky, but instead of marveling at the sight, I tuck in tighter to his chest.

"The hunter is gone. These woods are safe."

"He came back."

"*What?*" he seethes. His face begins to shift back and forth from monster to human as if he's a hologram glitching. I place a hand on his cheek, bringing him back to the moment.

"Let's get home, okay? Then I'll tell you everything."

27.

WITHIN THE HOUR, MOTH AND I sit on the porch, a cable knit blanket wrapped around my shoulders and home-made matcha, courtesy of Moth, in my hands. Biting down on my bottom lip, I steel my nerves. I guess there's no use hiding anything anymore.

"So, Chris—the hunter—he was right here when I came through the portal." I stand in the same spot on the steps. "I scared him off—it was awful, actually. I didn't feel like I was in my body. I didn't transform, not like you, but my nails got long, and my vision was all red and spotty. I *wanted* to hurt him."

"No one would blame you if you had. In fact, I will be happy to finish him off..." he begins, heading toward the door.

"Wait—no!" God, this is exactly why I haven't talked about any of this with him. "Right now," I say, grabbing his hand, "I just need you to listen."

He nods stiffly, allowing himself to be guided farther into the house with me.

"It happened right here," I say, standing in the kitchen—the same place I stood when Chris broke in. "I heard footsteps. I thought it was you, and I was so happy, but then—"

I shake my head. I so do not want to cry about this right now or honestly ever. That asshole doesn't deserve any more tears.

"He tied me up and threw me in the back of his truck. He was so focused on catching you, and I was just ... nothing. Bait on a hook to lure you out."

"Heather—"

"I didn't think he'd actually hurt me. God, how stupid can someone be?"

"You are *not* stupid."

"If I wasn't so focused on making sure everyone likes me, I would have never let it go so far... and now I'm like *this*. Do you feel like you're stuck with me now?" I ask, bringing my hands together in front of my chest. Anxiously, I turn the engagement ring on my finger, the words *Obligation* and *Requirement* playing through my mind.

"Do you need me to propose again, my flame? I have never been stuck—you are a fire, a life force, a need, not a want. If you had remained human, I would feel the same."

His fingers trail down the base of my wings, and I shiver.

"Does it hurt?" he asks. I stop myself from shaking my head and telling him it's "no big deal" and nod.

"Honestly, it can be ... uncomfortable. Like, when I'm not fully shifted, it feels *tense*, like they could burst out of my skin at any second—and my antennae too."

"They cause you discomfort as well?" he asks, tenderly stroking my hair.

"No, I just can never figure out how to style my hair around them!" I burst out, causing Moth to laugh.

"I apologize. I just did not expect you to say that." He lightly rakes his fingers through my hair. "You always look lovely."

"It's just..."

"Different?" he offers. I nod, settling into my spot next to him. The weight of his body crammed against mine on our small loveseat is a comfort I didn't know I missed so badly.

"Why have you not mentioned this before?" he asks softly, his fingers combing through the tangles of my hair.

"I was worried it would make you feel like I was ungrateful to you for saving my life," I say. "And honestly, I do like everything, you know? Flying with you is incredible, and I wouldn't trade this for the way I was before, but... it's different." I settle on the word he offered. Even that small truth has been hard to get out.

"Heather, I have never once asked for your gratitude," he says, tucking the top of my head under his chin. "The choice to save you was not done with your blessing."

"I think I thought maybe Eclipsica would be good for us, but that's not the life I want either."

"Thank goodness for that," he scoffs, causing both of us to chuckle.

"The thing is, I liked all the planning. It's not the place or the parties that made me flare up—"

"You were not taking care of yourself."

"Exactly, and that wasn't Eclipsica's fault." I sigh. "Like, if that was the life we wanted? Cool, it would be amazing. But damn, was I ignoring every sign of burnout, and being mean to my body was not my best choice, especially when I should have been focusing on you."

"I should have taken notice."

"You were kinda busy."

"Still."

"Nope. Next time I play party planner with your mother, we are enlisting more help, and we are starting way further in advance than a week."

"*Next time?*"

"I don't know. I know it's not easy to go back and forth, but like, there were parts of it that were fun, right?"

"I suppose I did not mind twirling you around the dance floor," he muses, flashing the toothy grin that I love.

"Yeah," I say. "We do fit together pretty well, don't we?"

"Especially here ... together."

"Sure you don't want to run off and rule a kingdom?"

"Truly, I do not think it was ever my want—only the only path I was given." He backs away, turning so we're facing each other. "You have given me so much more to explore."

"More to explore..." I muse, looking at the space around us. The good memories here outweigh the bad, but maybe now that we're both winged fae, something with higher ceilings might be worth exploring in the future. Somewhere where monster hunters, summoning spells, and portals are a thing of the past.

Just not today.

Suddenly, I catch a wisp of blue hair outside the window.

"Holly..." I groan, letting my head fall into my hands.

"I will tell her to take her leave," Moth grumbles. "After the way she deceived you, she is hardly a welcome guest."

"I'm not sure she knew. I mean, she found the note and was warning me, right?"

"Heather." Moth raises an eyebrow. "You are still too forgiving."

"I know! Ugh!" I exclaim, kicking over a decorative basket holding extra blankets to watch them tumble to the floor. "You know what? I'm going to give her a piece of my mind." He moves to allow me through, and I puff up like the angriest cupcake at the bakery.

"Do you seriously think you can just show up here?" I say, barreling through the door. I glance back, and Moth gives me an uncharacteristic thumbs up in approval.

"No, I doubt I am welcome. I apologize."

"You *what?*"

"Apologize," she says through gritted teeth.

"Yeah, I don't think I heard you right." Isn't she here to beg Moth to come back? I freeze, and everything I wanted to say leaves me as if it's been carried away with a gust of wind.

"I am sorry," she says, shoving her hands in the pockets of her gown, looking sullen rather than apologetic.

"Well, you'll have to say it a little louder because I'm not sure your brother wants to come out here and see you—"

"I am seeking an audience with you."

"Okay, now I *know* I'm hallucinating." I blink, taking a seat on the porch. "Why exactly are you here?"

"I believe I just said."

"Um, maybe try me one more time."

"I am sorry, Heather." She tightly crosses her arms. "I thought once you had left, things would finally go back to normal."

"Yeah, I got that impression," I grumble, copying her stiff posture. "So, didn't go how you expected?"

"No, Sprout made sure of that. I had to clean the paw-prints that led all the way up the tower before I left."

In response, Sprout happily thumps his tail on the wooden floor. Holly's plan may not have worked out, but his did.

"I would have found her regardless!" Moth shouts from inside the house.

"I am speaking with Heather!"

Oh my god, the sibling energy is off the charts. Holly turns back to me, letting her stiff shoulders drop.

"He is right though. He would have torn through the whole kingdom to find you," she huffs. "I hate to admit it, but you are his home."

"I tried to tell you," I say, surprised at the gentleness of my own voice.

"Yes, well—I am not always the best listener."

Tell me about it.

"Mother was not the only one who lost themselves on the day Father died and Moth disappeared," she begins. "While she sat in the garden in silence, I dedicated myself to finding my brother. Nothing else mattered—not suitors, not old hobbies. Finding him was my whole purpose."

I nod, trying to understand. I'm the wrench in her life-long mission; of course, she'd do anything she could to get rid of me.

"You may have already guessed, but I did not really kill Uncle Atlas..." She gulps, shaking her head. "He could be hiding anywhere on the outskirts of the winged courts or here in the mortal realm."

Lord, let's hope not.

"Why did you let me think you murdered him?" I gasp, fighting the urge to throw a pillow at her.

"Fun... mostly." She shrugs, her mouth quirking into a sideways grin. "The look on your face was priceless."

"Right. So, I think you were supposed to be apologizing," I remind her with a sigh. Well, at least one person in Moth's family isn't a murderer.

"Uncle Atlas... he had taken the place of my father and brother in one night. He should have never been king, especially if he was going to be so ... fickle."

"So, why didn't you take the throne for yourself? Why spend so much time looking for your brother?"

"Me?" She blinks as if the thought never occurred to her.

"Uh yeah, you don't think your mom is the best choice. You've made that clear, and you're probably old enough to rule by now, right?"

"I have never been meant for the throne. Father taught Death—*Moth*, I apologize." She shakes the old name away before continuing. "He taught him how to lead, to be ruthless and fearsome, but fair. All I know is how to stitch a sampler and swing a sword."

"You are underselling yourself so much." I cross my arms. "Who figured out the logistics of inviting everyone in the kingdom? Who planned out all the schedules and took on my whole to-do list?"

"I suppose I had a good deal to do with it."

"Holly, you did *everything*."

"It was you and my brother's idea—"

"You're the one who made it happen! That takes serious leadership skills—and you're the one who wanted to add everyone who works at the castle to the list. We would have left out an entire group if you hadn't spoken up."

"I let my soft heart show." She heaves a sigh. "*Look at me. I would not strike fear into the heart of an enemy.*"

Is she kidding?

"You have been scaring the shit out of me since the day we met."

"Truly?" This seems to perk her up a bit. Her eyes sparkle like I just told her she was the most beautiful fae in the ballroom.

"Um, yes, you're terrifying."

"You are just saying that..." she deflects, batting her long lashes, tilting her head away from me.

"Holly, I barely wanted to be in the same room as you," I explain. "I'm just going to say it one more time because even though I'm complimenting you, I feel super rude. You are one of the scariest people I've ever met."

"And you too kind." She shakes her head. "I take back what I said. You forgive too easily to be at court."

"I'm sorry. When exactly did I say I forgive you?"

"Technically, once just now." A childish glint plays in her eyes. "It isn't fair. I thought I would hate you forever for the way you are stealing my brother from his place of honor. But unfortunately, I think I would like to be friends."

I flash my ring finger in her direction. "How about sisters-in-law?"

"If we must."

"Pfffft, whatever. You basically want to be my BFF."

"I do not know what that means."

"Moth!" I call. "Your sister wants to be my BFF!"

"By your laughter, I assume this confession has your approval," he shouts back.

"Brother, I do not understand what your betrothed is saying."

"Yes." He smiles fondly in my direction. "You get used to that."

A zap drags our attention from each other to a form tumbling through the portal and inelegantly landing onto the front porch. Queen Plume dusts herself off, standing to her full height. I can't help but notice the way her fabric draped wings sort of *crunch* behind her for a moment before bouncing back into place. She's dressed in a beautiful yet different ballgown than the one she wore on the day the festivities started. Holly did say there would be costume changes, but are they seriously still partying in the other realm?

"Now, just what do you think you are doing hiding in the mortal realm?" she scolds, zeroing in on her children.

"Mother," Moth speaks first. "I do not wish to take the throne."

Her face twists into an expression I can't figure out at first. Her eyebrows pinch in the center, and her mouth straightens; I brace myself for some full-on mom rage, recalling the way my mom reacted the first time I told her I didn't want to be an influencer anymore. "Well, of course not."

"What?" Holly gasps.

"I have no intention to pass the crown to someone who doesn't want it." Queen Plume regards her son with a small smile. "It is clear Moth's heart is somewhere else."

"Was this ball not to mark his re-entrance into society?" Holly asks.

"Society? Yes. A welcome *home?* Yes. Not..." She looks between the three of us. "What did you children think was going on? Can a mother not throw a welcome home party?"

"During the height of the social season?" Holly's mouth hangs open. "Mother, even you must know the implications of such an act."

"A party is a party, my love."

"Not in Eclipsica."

"Moth, darling, this ball is in your honor. I have never expected you to return to the throne, but everyone, and I mean everyone, is asking where their long-lost prince has run off to. Holly, darling, I cannot manage to figure out how your schedule is meant to rotate as the days go on, and the more wine is consumed, the more people cannot seem to figure out where they are supposed to be. Heather, the small talk is suffocating. If you could just take a few of these nobles off my hands... and why are you all just standing there?"

"What do you think?" I ask.

"I suppose we could do with one more dance," Moth says, a hint of mischief in his eyes.

"And I believe there was a family photo to take." Queen Plume nods.

"Let's do it here—really quick!" I jump to my feet. Setting my phone on self-timer, I balance it on one of the potted plants in the garden. "Everyone gather together."

We sit together on the porch, my legs dangling off the side; Queen Plume and Moth sit beside me while Holly is aloof, hovering near the stairs. Sprout leaps into frame at the last second, shoving us all together.

It's a chaotic, dysfunctional composition and filled with love—the picture isn't too bad either.

I'm sure we'll take something more organized later, but for now, this is perfect. We stand, shaking ourselves off, and I slip my phone back into my pocket. The portal both Queen Plume and Holly tumbled through still gleams, ready to transport us back to Eclipsica for one more song.

"Ready?" I ask, turning to Moth.

"Almost." He sighs with a shake of his head. "I will not suffocate under another stiff suit." He shifts, growing taller and feathered and as gorgeous as always.

Holly blinks a few times—still not used to seeing him this way while Queen Plume is unfazed and happy.

We step through the portal hand in hand, racing down to the still-raging party. A low laugh escapes Moth as a few high-fae gasp, seeing him like this on the dance floor. We make quite the pair—him, a giant winged creature, and me wearing a casual linen dress that in this crowd might as well be a pair of jeans and a t-shirt.

I take a deep breath, focusing on the way Moth's arms feel around my waist—and catch Oak, Ruby, and Pepper off to the side, waving and shouting their congratulations. Either news travels faster in the fae realm than expected, or they can see this ring sparkle across the ballroom. Either way, they're a reminder that in this room full of judgmental gossipers, the people whose options matter most are the ones who are cheering in your corner.

I think living most of my life online might have made me forget that.

Moth twirls me with ease. With the full span of his wings, he's cleared the dance floor, but I don't think he's paying attention to anyone else in the room. His round bug eyes are focused on me and me alone.

"I suppose we have a wedding to plan."

Excitement swells in my chest as white lace and puffed sleeves dance through my mind, but most importantly, I'll have the best groom at my side. With him, it could rain all day and still be perfect.

"Don't laugh, but I've been daydreaming about this kind of thing my whole life."

"No elopement then, I suppose?"

I laugh as he dips me low, and I plant a kiss at the tip of his beak.

"Not a chance."

Want to get a peek into Moth's thoughts? The pair will return for the final installment of the series, I'm Getting Married to Mothman in 2024—a duel POV countdown to Moth and Heather's big day.

ACKNOWLEDGMENTS

OW! FIRST OFF, I WANT TO SAY thank you to everyone who read and enjoyed *I'm In Love With Mothman!* I truly didn't know what to expect when book one of this series was published. The excitement, support, reviews, and kind messages have sincerely made my dreams come true. This is the first time I've written a series, and knowing you were waiting for the next book not only motivated me but was also intimidating! I hope you enjoyed learning more about Moth's history—and I cannot wait to share his POV in the next installment *I'm Getting Married to Mothman.* We are going to have so much fun!

Thank you to 4 Horsemen Publications for being a dream team to work with! You've believed in this Mothman romance every step of the way and have been a joy, and I feel so lucky to have gotten to work with Beau Lake as my editor for two books in a row!!

A shoutout to the Monster Romance writing community. Everywhere from TikTok to Discord has been the most fun and supportive group of writers. I love the support we share for each other and can't wait to continue to get to know you all in years to come!

Thank you to my beta-readers Taylor, Kim, Nathan, Nicolette, Selena, Erin, Meaghan and Kim. Y'all gave such timely and insightful feedback and helped me with my final round of edits so much!

Thank you to Liyadraws for once again knocking the character art for the book cover out of the park! They are everything I dreamed of and more!

I need to say a giant thank you to my husband Matt for always being my biggest fan. Thank you for listening to me pace around the house chatting plot points, helping me brainstorm, and generally just being an awesome swoon-worthy partner. If I have to dance, let it be in your arms only—and preferably in our kitchen.

BOOK CLUB QUESTIONS

1. Do you think Moth has any secret desires to be king?

2. What surprised you most about Moth's world?

3. Why do you think Heather wasn't being honest with Moth about her problems?

4. Which of the Winged Courts would you want to be a part of?

5. Which of the supporting characters did you relate to the most?

6. Did anything about the characters surprise you?

7. Do you think Moth will ever show Heather the book he's writing?

8. Which of the Winged Courts would you like to visit?

9. What kind of favor do you think King Magnus was asking Heather for at the ball?

ABOUT THE AUTHOR

PAIGE LAVOIE IS A HALLOWEEN-loving cinnamon roll who writes stories about misfits, monsters, and falling in love. Her affection for cozy autumn moments, charming protagonists, and all things cute and creepy reflects in the worlds she creates. When Paige isn't writing, she can be found hunting for treasures at the local antique mall and sipping oat milk lattes under a lacey parasol as she hides from the sun in her home state of FL.

Fantasy, SciFi, & Paranormal Romance

AMANDA FASCIANO
Waking Up Dead
Dead Vessel
The Dead Show
Dead Revelations

BEAU LAKE
The Beast Beside Me
The Beast Within Me
Taming the Beast: Novella
The Beast After Me
Charming the Beast
The Beast Like Me
An Eye for Emeralds
Swimming in Sapphires
Pining for Pearls

CHELSEA BURTON DUNN
By Moonlight
Moonbound
Bloodthirsty

D. LAMBERT
Rydan
Celebrant
Northlander
Esparan
King
Traitor
His Last Name

DANIELLE ORSINO
Locked Out of Heaven
Thine Eyes of Mercy
From the Ashes
Kingdom Come
Fire, Ice, Acid, & Heart
A Fae is Done

J.M. PAQUETTE
Klauden's Ring
Solyn's Body
The Inbetween
Hannah's Heart
Call Me Forth
Invite Me In
Keep Me Close
Heart of Stone

KAIT DISNEY-LEUGERS
Antique Magic
Blood Magic

KYLE SORRELL
Munderworld
Potarium

LYRA R. SAENZ
Prelude
Falsetto in the Woods: Novella
Ragtime Swing
Sonata
Song of the Sea
The Devil's Trill
Bercuese
To Heal a Songbird
Ghost March
Nocturne

PAIGE LAVOIE
I'm in Love with Mothman
I'm Engaged to Mothman
Dear Galaxy

ROBERT J. LEWIS
Shadow Guardian and the
Three Bears
Shadow Guardian and the
Big Bad Wolf

T.S. SIMONS
Project Hemisphere
The Space Between
Infinity
Circle of Protections
Sessrúmnir
The 45th Parallel

VALERIE WILLIS
Cedric: The Demonic Knight
Romasanta: Father of Werewolves
The Oracle: Keeper of the
Gaea's Gate
Artemis: Eye of Gaea
King Incubus: A New Reign
Queen Succubus: Holder
of the Crown
Val's House of Musings: A Mixed
Genre Short Story Collection

V.C. WILLIS
The Prince's Priest
The Priest's Assassin
The Assassin's Saint
The Champion's Lord

DISCOVER MORE AT
4HorsemenPublications.com